CHESAPEAKE CRIMES
STORM WARNING

IN THE SAME SERIES

CHESAPEAKE CRIMES
STORM WARNING

Fifteen Tales of Wicked Weather

**Edited by Donna Andrews,
Barb Goffman, and Marcia Talley**

Introduction by Hank Phillippi Ryan

WILDSIDE PRESS

Chesapeake Crimes: Storm Warning

Coordinating Editors
Donna Andrews
Barb Goffman
Marcia Talley

Editorial Panel
David Dean
Sujata Massey
B.K. Stevens

This edition is published in 2016 by Wildside Press, LLC.
www.wildsidebooks.com

Contents

INTRODUCTION
by Hank Phillippi Ryan

A good short story is like a wallopingly successful joke. Get in quick, set it up, make the reader care, give it a twist, leave 'em satisfied: smiling or crying or surprised. Or all three.

But there's a skill to it, a talent. It's not like writing a novel, but shorter. Ask any savvy author. It's tough to snag the reader's imagination in an instant, hang onto it, and then go for the unexpected.

So now the diabolical sisters of the Chesapeake Chapter of Sisters in Crime have raised the stakes: not only asking their astute members to offer up a gem of a short story, but to add a degree of difficulty. It has to be about the weather.

You know the admonition about the weather, delivered from on high by the illustrious Elmore Leonard in his Ten Rules of Writing. "Never open a book with weather" is number one! It is such a trope, such a pitfall, such a looming mire of authorly disaster that "It was a dark and stormy night" is now the stuff of Snoopy comics and international contests for bad writing.

But yes, the Chessie sisters (and brothers) have accepted the challenge. Applauded it. Rain, snowstorms, hurricanes. The glare of the sun. The shrouding fog. Clouds, mist, hail, and icy roads. The Chessies have used their writerly talent to embrace the weather, to relish it, and to provide us with a raft of meteorological (and deadly) delights.

The weather can be an ally or an enemy. An inspiration or an obstacle. Or even a weapon. Take that, Sir Elmore. Rules are meant to be broken—especially when they are broken with such skill.

So whatever the weather, wherever you are, if it's a sunny morning by your garden window, a stolen moment on a rainy afternoon, or you're snowbound in front of a cozy fire, dip into *Storm Warning*. Open the pages and see what lures you. It's always reading weather, right?

Hank Phillippi Ryan is an on-air investigative reporter for Boston's NBC affiliate, winning thirty-three Emmys and dozens more journalism honors. Bestselling author of eight mysteries, Ryan's won five Agathas, two Anthonys, two Macavitys, two Daphnes, and the Mary Higgins Clark Award. Reviewers call Ryan "a superb and gifted storyteller." Her *Truth Be Told* is a *Library Journal* Best of 2014 and won the Agatha for Best Contemporary Mystery. Her newest book is *What You See*, named a *Library Journal* Best of 2015. A founder of MWA University, Hank was 2013 president of national Sisters in Crime.

CABIN FEVER

by Timothy Bentler-Jungr

"The National Weather Service has issued a severe winter storm warning for central and northern Minnesota."

Well, crap. Chelsea Warden's gaze flicked from the television with its dire predictions, to the streaked, grubby window of the double-wide, where the first flakes of snow were already swirling, to the stained, smelly recliner where her stained, smelly boyfriend sprawled in stained, smelly sweats. *Crap, crap, crap.*

"...are advised to stay off of the roads and to stay indoors whenever possible. Temperatures are expected to reach lows of zero to six below, with a windchill factor of minus thirty."

"Shut that damn Weather Channel off," Larry snarled from the recliner. "There's gotta be a game or something on. Anything's better than this bullshit."

"I want to hear the forecast."

"Hell, you don't need the TV for that. It's January in Minnesota. Look out the damn window. There's your effing forecast."

"Here." Chelsea passed him the remote and went to look out the window, just as a blast of north wind roared across the lake and slammed into the broad side of the old trailer, shaking it like a tambourine. She shivered and zipped up her hooded Arizona State sweatshirt. *God, what I would give to be back in Arizona now. Or California. Hell, even Alabama. Anywhere but this frozen wasteland.*

"Grab me a beer while you're up," Larry said.

She turned to look at him. Unshaven and slovenly, he didn't look anything like the laughing, suntanned, sunbleached Viking hunk who had swept her off her feet back in July. Even the shitty trailer house had looked better then, perched on the shore of a sparkling blue lake with summer sunlight streaming through the windows and red geraniums blooming in clay pots on the steps. Any man who planted geraniums had to be a decent guy, right? So she'd moved into his little trailer by the lake, and it had been fun playing house for a while. Then the days got shorter and darker and colder, and Larry's temper got shorter and darker and colder, too. The sunshine in his hair faded to dirty blond and the tan gave way to pasty white. The geraniums died in their pots, and whatever affection Chelsea felt for him died along with them.

If only she'd left then. If only. Then the worst winter in living memory hit, in a place that remembered a lot of bad winters, and now she was stuck. Stuck here, and stuck with him, with nowhere to go until the snow melted and she could rescue her old Toyota from under the drifts behind the trailer. She'd been saving her tips from the diner, as much as she could squirrel away without Larry getting suspicious. Come April she'd get a new battery and some new tires, then she'd point that thing south and never look back.

If she could last that long.

"Hey! Earth to Chelsea!" Larry's voice cut through her thoughts. "Beer?"

"Hang on just a freaking minute. Jeez." She crossed to the corner that Larry called the kitchen—only three steps from the "living room"—and opened the fridge. *Well, crap again.* They only had four—no, five—beers left, and it was too late to drive into town for more. The roads would already be drifting over with visibility down to the length of her nose. You never knew when they'd get around to plowing way out here at the edge of nowhere. They could be snowed in for days. There was about two thirds of a bottle of bourbon in the cupboard. That would keep him happy for a while, until it turned him mean. *Crap, crap, crap.*

She cracked open a can of Coors and handed it to him.

"Thanks, babe. Come over here. Give us some sugar." Larry grabbed her hand and pulled her down onto his lap, pinning her tight. Though he had grown a little pudgy and soft over a few months of too much beer and not enough exercise, he was still strong. "Only three things you can do when you're snowed in. Drink beer, watch TV, and get busy under the covers." His hand snaked its way under her layers of sweatshirts and squeezed her left breast. "What say we take this into the other room? I don't think this old chair will hold up under the strain."

Chelsea shivered again, this time not from the cold. *I'm not sure I'll hold up.* Then she remembered the four cans of beer left in the fridge and sighed. She was going to have to do something to keep him occupied. *Crap, crap, crap.*

* * * *

"Ooh, baby, am I the man or am I the man!" Larry flopped back and aimed a self-satisfied grin up at the water stain on the ceiling.

"You are the man." Chelsea sat up, feeling sore and soiled. Where the hell had men gotten the idea that long lasting was the same thing as being a good lover? From what sports magazine or locker-room bull session or online porn site did they learn that stamina equaled skill? Larry could go all night, as he would proudly brag to just about anyone, including the mailman and his own grandmother, but it took all of *her* stamina to keep from screaming, "Just hurry the fuck up and get it over with."

"If there's one thing I know, it's how to take care of my woman. Right, baby?" Larry opened the drawer on the nightstand and pulled out a pack of cigarettes. "Damn. Baby, I left my lighter in the other room. Be a sweetheart and go get it for me."

"Oh, come on, Larry. You promised not to smoke inside. It's bad enough being cooped up in here without that." The trailer was so small, one cigarette could fill the whole place with smoke. There was no escape.

His eyes narrowed. "What's the world coming to when a man can't even smoke a damn cigarette in his own house? If you think I'm going outside in this weather, you're crazy."

"You really should quit, sweetie." If badgering him wouldn't work, maybe sweet-talking would. "Those things are going to kill you."

Not soon enough.

"That's a bunch of bull. My grandpa smoked his whole life, and he lived to be eighty-seven. Hell, I just screwed you for over an hour, and I'm not even short of breath. Now get me my lighter, and maybe we can go another round in a few minutes."

Ooh, great. Something to live for. Wrapping the sheet around her torso, she padded into the living room and retrieved the lighter. "Here," she called, tossing it through the bedroom door. "Just one, though, okay? The smoke really does give me a headache."

"Yeah, yeah, sure. Whatever."

She watched him through the bedroom door, lighting up and blowing clouds into the stale air. When she'd first moved in, he'd been so considerate. Always taking his cigarettes out onto the cement slab he called the patio. She didn't even have to ask. But that had been summer, before the lake froze over and their hearts froze with it. Now it was a battle every damn time, and she was getting sick of it.

"I really worked up an appetite," he said, grinning at her through the smoke. "Why don't you go rustle something up? They say this storm is going to last for a couple days. I'm gonna need to keep my strength up." He wiggled his eyebrows in what he probably thought was a suggestive way. "If you get what I'm saying."

"Yeah, Larry. I get what you're saying." *Crap, crap, crap.*

* * * *

"My God," Chelsea moaned. "How long can this last? It hasn't stopped snowing in twenty-four hours." She didn't bother going to the window. The last time she'd looked it had been nothing but a wall of white, as if the whole world had been erased around them. Now, the white had turned to black, but the snow still flew, and the wind still shrieked and clawed at the trailer like a predator trying to get inside.

Larry laughed. A mean-sounding laugh, no real humor in it. A half-bottle-of-bourbon laugh. "This is nothing. I remember once when I was in elementary school it snowed for a whole week solid. Couldn't even open the front door when it was over. Had to go out the upstairs window."

"Uh-huh." Chelsea was pretty sure that wasn't true. Minnesotans, she'd noticed, were prone to telling tall tales about the weather, probably intended to make it sound like living up here was heroic and adventurous instead of just plain stupid. But then, she never would have believed a storm like this was possible, so who knew?

"You don't believe me?"

"No, I believe you. I'll believe just about anything at this point."

I believe you are a jerk.

I believe I am losing my mind.

"Supper's ready," she said, putting two plates onto the tiny table.

Larry poked at the congealed orange mass. "What is this crap?"

"Macaroni and cheese. You know, from the box."

"Tastes like shit. What did you do to it?"

"I did what I could. What do you expect? We're out of milk. We're out of butter."

"We're out of beer," Larry grumbled.

"We're out of effing everything until it clears up and we can get to the store."

"I can't eat this. You got anything else?"

She felt tears burning her eyes and blinked them back. She could barely stand to look at him right now. Why should she care if he didn't like her cooking? Hell, she didn't even like it.

"I think there's some crackers. Maybe a can of tuna."

"Gimme that. I can't eat this mess."

Chelsea pushed back from the table and opened the cupboard. "Here." She slammed the can of tuna onto the table, then pulled the can opener from the drawer and slammed that down next to it. "Knock yourself out."

Larry surged up from his chair, toppling it over, and grabbed her by the shoulders. "I'll knock you out if you're not careful."

"Ooh, big man, beating up a girl half his size. There's something you can brag about to your friends."

He shoved her away, and she stumbled backward, her hip smacking painfully against the counter. "Watch your mouth, and get me the damn crackers." He sank back into his chair, his face still a frightening scowl.

Chelsea fought to keep her hands from shaking as she dumped Ritz crackers onto a plate. She'd seen him get mean before, especially when he was drinking, but there was a glint in his eye today that had never been there before.

That was stupid. Don't poke the bear. Especially when you're trapped in his cave.

Trapped. She turned to the sink and began running water into the macaroni pot. At least with her back to him she could pretend for a moment that he wasn't there. That was the closest she could get to privacy. If she focused on the wind, it almost drowned out the sound of crackers crunching.

Just fifteen minutes by herself and she'd be a new woman. Ten, even. Maybe if she went to bed early, left him to stay up with the TV and what was left of the bourbon, he'd pass out in the chair, and she could have the bed to herself. That would be heaven.

God, how had her life come to this?

Behind her, the crunching stopped, and a belch signaled he was finished eating. She turned to retrieve his plate and found him shaking a cigarette from the pack.

"God damn it, Larry. I ask you for one small thing and you can't even do that." Without really thinking what she was doing, she snatched the pack from his hand. "Take these damn things outside."

He lunged for her, but she was quicker on her feet. In just a few steps, she was at the door. Flinging it open, she tossed the cigarettes as far as she could. Wind-driven snow blew into the trailer, pelting her face like tiny nails.

"You crazy bitch!" Larry stared out into the icy blackness. "That was my last pack. Go out there and get 'em, right now."

"You want them, get them yourself." With all the fury and frustration built up in her over the past few days—over the past few months, really—she threw her weight against his back, pushing him through the door. As he tumbled down the steps, she pulled the door closed and turned the lock.

Ten minutes. Just ten minutes by myself.

"Chelsea! Damn it, Chelsea, open the door."

"Not until you calm down."

"Open!" *Bang.* "This!" *Bang.* "Fucking!" *Bang.* "Door!" His fist pounded like a wrecking ball against the door, shaking the trailer all the way down to its floorboards. "Now!"

What the hell have I done? Chelsea stared at the rattling door as the full significance of her impulsive action hit her. *He's going to kill me. If I open that door, he's going to kill me. Crap.*

Crap, crap, crap.

Larry rattled the door again. "Come on, babe. I'm sorry," he said, switching from rage to sweetness. "It's freezing out here. Open the door. Let me in."

She reached a shaky hand toward the door, then stopped. Mister Nice Guy was an act. A ploy to get her to let him in. And then…

I can't. I can't trust him.

"Chelsea!" Another crashing blow to the door confirmed her suspicions. "If you don't open this fucking door right now, you're going to be sorry."

"I am sorry," she whispered. "I can't."

Larry continued hammering on the door, screaming obscenities. Could he break it down? If he got inside, there'd be no place to hide. The only other lock in the place was on the bathroom door, and even she could probably kick that down.

Backing into the kitchen area, keeping her eye on the door the whole time, Chelsea groped in the drawer until she found a knife. If Larry made it through the door, she'd be ready. Seeing the bourbon bottle on the table, she grabbed that as well and took a swig for strength. She pulled a kitchen chair up, facing the door, and sat with the knife in one hand and the bottle in the other. *I'm ready for you. As ready as I'm going to be.*

After about twenty minutes of alternately swearing, pleading, coaxing, and threatening, Larry grew quiet. Chelsea tensed, straining to hear over the sound of the wind. Was he still out there? He didn't have his pickup keys, so he'd have to walk. It was more than a mile by road to the nearest house. Maybe half a mile if you crossed the field and went through the woods, but the snow was deep there and the darkness deeper. He'd never make it that way. If he went by road, someone might pick him up. If anyone was out driving in this blizzard. How long would he last without a coat? With only slippers on his feet? She had no idea.

Did she dare check? What if it was a ruse, to trick her into opening the door? She couldn't risk it. She took another gulp of bourbon and kept her eyes on the door.

* * * *

Chelsea woke with a start, sunlight stabbing her eyes. Morning. How long had she slept? Still slumped in the chair, she felt stiff and cold. Her head ached and her mind was groggy from bourbon. On the floor, the brilliant sunlight glinted off the sharp steel of the knife. *Oh, crap. It really did happen.*

Crap, crap, crap.

Her joints creaked and popped as she stood and tried to stretch out her throbbing back and limbs. The storm had passed, she realized, taking in the brightness and the eerie, almost palpable silence. *Thank God it's over.*

Except, she realized, it wasn't over. The real shitstorm was about to hit.

She stared at the door, afraid to open it, afraid of what she would find.

What choice do you have? You have to look. Squaring her shoulders, steadying her shaking hand, Chelsea turned the lock and opened the door.

At first, all she could make out was a sea of dazzling, sparkling white, as if the whole world had been washed clean. Then she saw the lumpy drift of snow at the bottom of the steps. Larry's hand protruded from under the glittering shroud, still clutching the pack of Camels.

* * * *

After throwing up, the bourbon and revulsion burning her insides like acid, Chelsea placed an appropriately hysterical 9-1-1 call, reporting Larry's terrible accident. It had taken the sheriff and the ambulance, following a snow plow in an emergency services miniparade, another two hours to get through the drift-clogged roads from town.

Time enough for her to get her story straight. It had been self-defense, of course. He would have killed her if he'd gotten inside. She truly believed that. Hell, he was killing her already with the secondhand smoke. But she'd never sell that, not to a jury of Larry's friends and neighbors. She'd have to make sure it never got to a jury.

"I was in the bedroom, asleep," she told the sheriff, wiping her eyes with a wilted tissue. "I didn't even know he was gone. He must have tiptoed out so he wouldn't wake me. He was always considerate like that. If I had been awake I would have told him not to go out in this weather." She sobbed, burying her face in her hands. "It's my fault."

"Now, now." Sheriff Roland Lindstrom shook his splotchy bald head, setting his jowls swinging. "No need to go blaming yourself, Miss Warden."

Chelsea looked up into the sheriff's pale blue eyes, producing a weak, quivering smile for his benefit. "You're so kind, Sheriff."

The sheriff looked shaken, his skin pale beneath the spiderweb of tiny red veins that rouged his cheeks. Despite decades in law enforcement, he apparently hadn't dealt with a lot of bodies. Most people around here had the good sense to die conveniently in their beds or at least their hospital beds. The sight of Larry, once they'd excavated him, had turned the old sheriff a little green.

She'd read somewhere, years ago, that freezing to death was peaceful and painless, like falling asleep. At the time she'd wondered, how do they know? Larry sure didn't look like he'd fallen into peaceful sleep. The rage, and the fear he must have felt at the end, were frozen in place, a grotesque, angry mask.

"Let me warm up your coffee, Sheriff." Chelsea turned and reached the pot on the counter without having to get up from her chair. She hadn't lived in Minnesota long, but she'd been here long enough to know you had to offer people coffee. Weak, tasteless coffee, preferably. God, she could really use a mocha cappuccino right now. "Deputy?"

"No, thank you." Deputy Craig Norquist stood by the door, his oddly pale, bulgy eyes studying her like she was a bug under a magnifying glass. "Funny."

"Funny?" The sheriff gave the tall, lanky deputy a perplexed look. "What exactly in this tragedy do you find funny?"

"Well, not, you know, funny as in 'ha-ha.' Funny like strange. Peculiar."

"Get to your point, Norquist," the sheriff grumbled. Chelsea got the impression the two were a poor match, rubbing along in a constant state of low-key annoyance. Or maybe it was just the weather taking its toll on them as well.

"I just think it's strange Miss Warden didn't hear anything." His gaze flicked from Chelsea to the door and back again. "Looks like he banged pretty hard on this door here. Must have hollered, too, you'd think."

"Oh," Chelsea said. She'd prepared for this. "I was totally zonked. Exhausted," she said, turning back to the sheriff, just in case *zonked* was an unfamiliar expression to the old man. "You see, we'd just... I'm sorry, this is kind of embarrassing."

"It's all right, little lady." He gave her hand a grandfatherly pat. "We're professionals."

"Okay, well, we'd just... made love. Larry"—she sniffed dramatically and blinked a few times, as if holding back tears—"he said there were only three things to do when you're snowed in. Drink, watch TV, and make love."

That brought a little color back to Sheriff Lindstrom's cheeks.

"Had you and the deceased been drinking?" the deputy asked. He, she noticed, did not blush. He also liked to use words like *the deceased* instead of *Larry* or "*the Bergen boy*," as the sheriff referred to him.

"Yes. We'd had quite a bit of bourbon." She pointed to the empty bottle on the counter. "And then we went into the bedroom to... well, you know."

He didn't blink. In fact, she wasn't sure he'd blinked in the whole time they'd been there. "And then?"

"And then I fell asleep. Passed out, really."

"So you didn't hear a thing?" He was really starting to get on her nerves.

"Well, you know, the wind was howling so bad, I'm not even sure I would have heard him even if I was awake. Oh, Sheriff," she gripped his hand in both of hers. Time to put this interview back in the hands of the sympathetic old man. "What am I going to tell his poor mother?"

The old witch.

"Don't you worry about that. I'll speak to Mrs. Bergen. In fact, Norquist, we should head out there now. Wouldn't want the poor woman to hear about this through unofficial channels." With a wheeze and a grunt, he hauled himself out of the chair. "This is a terrible tragedy, Miss Warden. Are you sure you'll be all right out here by yourself?"

"Thank you, Sheriff, but I'll be fine." She squeezed two fat tears out and wiped her eyes with the tissue. "Makes me feel closer to Larry, you know?"

The sheriff shook her hand. "You're a brave girl. Let's go, Norquist, and get this over with."

* * * *

For two days she worried, wondering whether she was going to get away with it. Larry's family regarded her with suspicion, or at least blame, and the whole community followed their lead. Then, on the third day, her luck changed. The newspaper came out—at least, what passed for a newspaper around here.

The *Lakeland County Weekly* was usually nothing but a mishmash of obituaries, high-school sports scores, senior-citizen activities, coupons, yard-sale ads, and hotdish recipes. Calves for sale and kittens for free. This week it carried actual news. Larry's death made the front page, the biggest story in years, probably, with a handsome color photo that looked like it dated from high school. The reporter quoted Sheriff Lindstrom, who called it "a terrible, tragic accident" and reminded everyone to be careful. "Cold can kill," he warned, in case anyone in the *Weekly*'s readership might be unaware of that.

And just like that, people no longer gave her sideways looks at the diner or whispered behind her back in the grocery store. A tragic accident. The newspaper had printed it, so it must be true. Chelsea was magically transformed from "that out-of-state girl shacked up with Larry" to "that poor, brave young lady," again according to the words of Sheriff Lindstrom. Even Larry's mother hugged her and insisted Chelsea accompany her to the funeral home to, as she put it, "make Larry's final arrangements."

I thought I'd already made his final arrangements, she thought, but of course she didn't say so.

As much as she dreaded it, there was no escaping the funeral. If she failed to show up, or didn't mourn enthusiastically enough, the clouds of suspicion blown away by the *Weekly* article would loom over her again. *Just a little bit longer. Make a good showing at the funeral, and then you can put Larry and Minnesota and this whole miserable experience in the rearview mirror.*

The only funeral she'd ever attended had been an elegant, decorous gathering. A pretty urn, white calla lilies, and a few short words and discreet tears. Compared to that, small-town mourning seemed grotesque and macabre. The night before the funeral she was forced to endure the "visitation," a bizarre cross between a town hall meeting, a prayer service, and a party. Larry featured as the centerpiece, surrounded by gaudy flowers and friends and family in various states of grief and intoxication.

The undertaker had done an amazing job, transforming Larry's frostbitten corpse into a reasonable approximation of the handsome summertime Larry she'd fallen in lust with seven months before. *That's some powerful makeup. I wonder if I could get some of that.*

Looking at him laid out in his coffin—the Wilmington Regency, in golden oak with bronze hardware and a blue satin lining that matched his eyes—Chelsea felt a twinge of… something. Not grief, exactly, but some kind of sadness. Maybe a little regret. She didn't have to fake the tears she brushed away as she placed her little pot of geraniums with the other arrangements.

"Why did this happen to you?" wailed Bill Goff, one of Larry's high school friends. Chelsea remembered him from keg parties by the lake in the summer, though he hadn't been around much since then. Driven indoors by the harsh winter, no doubt, like everyone else. "I told him those cigarettes were going to kill him. But would he listen?"

He hugged Chelsea, a little tighter than necessary, telling her to "be strong," then rejoined his friends. Red-eyed and obviously drunk, they clustered at the back of the room, avoiding the coffin, their whole world apparently tipped upside down and shaken by the idea that one of their own could be dead so soon.

"Only the good die young," one of them slurred.

"Then you should live forever," another said. They laughed, the sound ricocheting around the room, and then abruptly fell silent, glancing sheepishly like schoolboys up to some playground mischief.

Chelsea stuck close to Larry's mother, like a good almost-daughter-in-law, thanking guests and acknowledging their condolences. People were watching, and she needed to play the part. At one point she thought she saw Deputy Norquist's buggy eyes following her across the crowded Slumber Room II, but when she looked for him later, she couldn't spot him. Had she imagined it? Was her conscience playing tricks on her?

Just keep it together. One more day and he'll be in the ground, and this nightmare will be over.

* * * *

The morning of the funeral dawned clear and bright and bone-shatteringly cold. The only coat Chelsea could find warm enough for the day was Larry's puffy orange hunting parka. It was pretty hard to maintain any sense of funereal dignity when she looked like a giant cheese curl, but it would have to do.

The Reverend Carl Norquist, pastor of Good Shepherd Lutheran and father of Deputy Craig—God, she was getting sick of this inbred little town—droned endlessly about a promising young life cut short and God's purpose in such a seemingly senseless tragedy, but at least he had the sense to keep the graveside service brief.

Afterward, the mourners gathered in the church hall for what Larry's mother called "a little lunch."

An ancient-looking lady—one of Larry's great aunts or maybe his kindergarten teacher, Chelsea couldn't remember—handed her a cup of coffee. "Wasn't that a lovely service?" she said. "You know, when I was a little girl, we couldn't bury 'em in the wintertime."

"Uh... what?" Surely she hadn't heard that right.

"Nope. Ground was too froze. Had to keep 'em in a shed behind the church until spring when the gravediggers could get to work."

"You don't say." Chelsea tried to disengage, but the woman wouldn't take the hint.

"They'd keep real good until about April, just like a beef roast in your deepfreeze. Some winters we'd have six or seven of 'em stacked up there, 'specially if there was a flu going around or something. Now they got them fancy backhoes and you can stick 'em straight into the ground any time of the year."

My God, I'm talking about gravedigging with a woman who thinks a backhoe is fancy. "I'm sorry. This is really fascinating, but there's someone I need to talk to." Scanning the room for a friendly face, she spotted

Sheriff Lindstrom tucking into a plate of ham sandwiches, coleslaw, and pasta.

"Sheriff. It's so good of you to come. No, don't get up."

"How you holding up, little lady?" he asked, maybe the fiftieth person to ask her that question. *How you holding up?*

"Fine. I mean, you know, as good as can be expected," she said, repeating her stock answer for the fiftieth time. It seemed to be what people wanted to hear.

"This here's my wife, Arlene." The sheriff indicated a plump, sixty-something woman with round glasses and an unnatural apricot-colored hairdo. "Arlene, this is Miss Warden that I told you about."

"I'm so sorry for your loss, dear." Mrs. Lindstrom's handshake was clammy and soft. "Have you eaten yet? We lucked out because it's Group B's turn to do the lunch."

"Group B?"

"Oh, sorry, dear. You see, Pastor Norquist has all the church ladies divided into groups, A, B, C, and D, and we take turns doing the funerals."

"I see." *Maybe I was better off with the backhoe lady.*

"I'm in Group C myself. We do a nice enough spread, but Betty Rudnicki's in Group B, and her hotdish is about the best thing you'll get at a funeral this side of Minneapolis. It's that one at the end with the shell macaroni. She says you can use any kind of noodles you want. Says she just likes the shells because it looks nicer. But for Jessie Christianson's funeral back about three years ago she had to use those wagon-wheel noodles—you know the ones I mean?—because Schmidt's Grocery had run out of the shells, and I swear it didn't taste as good. Isn't that so, Roland?"

The sheriff shook his jowls. "I can't recall that they tasted any different."

Mrs. Lindstrom rolled her eyes behind her owlish glasses. "Men. Am I right? Anyhoo, you make sure you get some before it's all gone. I tell you, folks almost look forward to someone dying so they can get some of that hotdish."

"You sit here." The sheriff patted the empty seat beside him. "No need for you to be standing in line for food on a day like this." He glanced around the room. "Norquist!"

Deputy Norquist emerged from the crowd, casting his long, thin shadow over the table. Chelsea shivered. "Yes, sir?"

"Get a plate of food for Miss Warden here," the sheriff instructed. "Make sure she gets plenty of Betty's hotdish."

"And some of Merle Olson's Jell-O salad," the sheriff's wife added. "Wouldn't want her to miss out on that."

"No, ma'am." The deputy addressed Mrs. Lindstrom, but his eyes never left Chelsea. "I'll see to it she gets everything she should."

Chelsea didn't like the sound of that.

Crap.

* * * *

As soon as she got back to the trailer, Chelsea started packing. Two hours of scrutiny from Deputy Norquist had her seriously creeped out. Screw the Toyota. No way was she waiting around here until spring thaw, if that ever came. Whoever found it after the snow melted could keep it. She considered driving off with Larry's pickup, but that was the surest way to make sure she was followed. No. She would take the money she'd saved and get on the first Greyhound pointed south.

She was in the bathroom cramming toiletries into a plastic bag when she felt a cold draft blow through the trailer. She turned to find Deputy Norquist standing at the open door.

"Oh, Deputy! You... you startled me. I didn't hear you drive up."

He just stood there, not saying a word.

Chelsea swallowed. "What are you... I mean, is there something I can do for you?"

He scanned the room, taking in the suitcase on the table and the plastic bag in her hand. "Leaving town?"

"Oh, well, you know. Too many memories here, right?" Her skin began to pucker from the cold air pouring in. "Um, it's getting a bit chilly. Would you mind shutting the door on your way out?"

He stepped inside and pulled the door closed. Not exactly what she had in mind.

"I would offer you some coffee," she said, forcing a smile. "But as you can see, I'm kind of busy right now. So, if you don't mind, I really need to get back to it."

"You're in no hurry." He twisted the knob on the door, locking it. "You're not going anywhere anytime soon."

Chelsea's heartbeat kicked up a notch, like a warning drumbeat. "What are you doing?"

"I'm a modern kind of lawman." The deputy stepped closer. "Sheriff Lindstrom, now, he's kind of old fashioned. What's the word... chivalrous. Yeah, that's it. Chivalrous. Sees a damsel in distress, and automatically he goes into knight-in-shining-armor mode."

"He's... he's very kind."

"Sure, he's kind. But he's not always very observant. Sometimes he can't see things that are right in front of him, especially if there's a pretty young lady looking at him with those sad puppy-dog eyes. But me, I see everything."

"And what is it that you think you see?" Chelsea asked, though she had a pretty good idea.

"All kinds of things. That door, for example." Chelsea couldn't help noticing he was blocking the way between her and the exit. "Funny thing about that door."

"Funny?"

"Not funny as in 'ha-ha,' of course." He took off his coat and threw it over her suitcase. "Funny as in strange. You know?"

"No, I'm sorry, I don't know what you mean."

"Oh, we both know that's not true." One stride closed the distance between them, backing her against the wall. Long, bony fingers slid up her arms and fiddled with the top button of her blouse. "Because, what the sheriff didn't notice, but I picked up with my keen powers of observation, is that that door locks from the inside."

Chelsea tried to pull away, but his grip tightened, and he pressed against her, holding her in place. His breath felt hot on her face but didn't relieve the goose bumps that studded her arms.

"You can't actually lock yourself out," he continued.

"Yes, you can. Larry—"

"Nope. Not possible. Someone had to have locked it from the inside."

Crap. Her knees felt weak, and the tiny trailer seemed to be closing in around her. "What do you want? If you were going to arrest me, you could have done it already."

"Oh, I think we can come up with a mutually agreeable arrangement." He twined a strand of her hair in his fingers, twisting it until it hurt. "Don't you think?"

* * * *

Deputy Norquist grunted and rolled off her. At least, Chelsea thought, he was quick, unlike Larry. More of a sprinter than a marathon man, thank God. He hadn't even taken all his clothes off. She barely had time to throw in a few fake moans before he collapsed on top of her, crushing her into the mattress.

Now he sat up and reached for his pants. Digging in the pocket, he pulled out a pack of cigarettes and lit one, then held the pack out, silently offering one to Chelsea.

She shook her head. *Oh, crap.*

"Well," he said, blowing a stream of acrid smoke in her face. "I think this might be... how does it go? Oh, yeah. The beginning of a beautiful friendship."

Chelsea fell back on the bed and stared up at the gray-blue clouds hovering near the water-stained ceiling. *Crap, crap, crap.*

Growing up in the woods of northern Minnesota, Timothy Bentler-Jungr always had the voices telling stories in his head to keep him company. After twenty-three dark, bone-chilling winters, the voices suggested that it was time for a change of scenery, and he has been wandering the globe ever since. Luckily, the voices travel light and make excellent companions on the journey. An international man of mystery, his exact whereabouts at press time were unknown.

THE KNITTER

by Robin Templeton

Click, clack. Click, clack.
   Whoosh. Screech, slap. Screech, slap.
   Click, clack. Click, clack.
   Jess MacKenzie thought she was going to lose her mind. Or commit murder. Or both. Surely no jury would convict her if she stabbed her seatmate with those damned knitting needles or beat the bus driver to death with his bent and scraping windshield wipers.

   The rain had begun in Cambridge just before eleven a.m., becoming more torrential as they drove away from the ocean she loved, toward the DC suburbs. Lightning lit the sky, and thunder boomed around the bus, but the annoying click, clacking continued.

   Icy pellets mixed with the rain as the bus rolled over the Chesapeake Bay on the William Preston Lane, Jr. Memorial Bridge. Everyone else just called it the Bay Bridge, but Jess remembered how excited she'd been when she'd crossed the newly opened bridge with her parents in 1952. Back then it meant freedom to go to the beach every school holiday. But now the bridge had come to represent a passage to bondage. It took her from her peaceful house in Ocean Pines, Maryland—just five miles from Ocean City and the seashore—to her son's home in Silver Spring, where Jess had become the unpaid, unappreciated housekeeper and babysitter for her son's new wife and children. And she resented the hell out of it.

   Jess pressed her nose to the freezing, sleet-spattered window and began to fantasize about the bus breaking through the guardrails and plummeting into the bay. She was a strong swimmer—even in these terrible conditions, she could survive. But she'd pretend to be dead so her son and his awful wife and stepchildren would never find her. The Piney Plotters Mystery Book Club would give her a nice memorial service, and Jess could change her name and escape to Hatteras or Charleston. She'd give up retirement and work as a maid or a waitress—anything to avoid taking The Bus Trip to Hell ever again.

Jess sighed and looked out over the churning waves of the Chesapeake Bay. Of course she'd never have the nerve to give up her only family or her wonderful little house in the Pines.

Hail pounded against the bus windows, and Jess's neighbor continued to knit and purl with flying, outstretched elbows. The yarn was a strange, glittery peacock blue. Jess wondered if the lavender-haired lady was knitting a boa for her strip act in a retirement home. But as the huge needles clacked and spun, with the woman's flapping arms making her look like a wounded pelican trying to get off the ground, Jess realized that her seat companion was trembling with terror. The 4.3-mile suspension bridge frightened a lot of people, so in spite of her annoyance with the flying needles, Jess tried to reassure her. "Don't worry. We'll be over the bridge soon. The bus stops just outside Annapolis, and you can get a cup of coffee or tea there."

The woman nodded her head, and a large tear rolled down her cheek. But she didn't look up, and she didn't stop knitting.

By the time they pulled into the combination gas station and diner, the winds had picked up, bowing pine trees and stripping the remaining late-November foliage from the deciduous trees. Jess didn't have an umbrella, so she raced to the restroom, hunched inside her coat. She was quick enough to get a stall. As she washed her hands a couple of minutes later, a line formed outside the ladies' room. *Good.* The bus driver would have to wait until all of the women got back on board.

She wandered into the gift shop, selected a small bag of peanut M&M's, a new mystery paperback, and a carryout coffee with real cream. The rain had started to lighten, and folks were getting back on the bus. Everyone seemed to choose their same seats. Except one. The only thing next to Jess was a canvas bag full of yarn. The driver jumped on and said, "Is everyone back?"

Jess surveyed the bus from her seat near the front. "No, the lady who was sitting next to me isn't here. She, uh, had sort of lavender/silver hair and was about my age—seventy or so. And she was knitting a turquoise scarf."

The passengers started buzzing, some making concerned noises, others bitching because they were being held up. The driver counted heads and seemed to compare his results to a sheet of paper clipped to a board. He swore under his breath and stomped down the steps.

After several minutes he climbed back into his seat and started the engine. Jess rushed up to him. "You can't just leave her!"

"The hell I can't, lady. I'm already fifteen minutes behind schedule. It's the passenger's responsibility to get back to the bus. Maybe she decided to stay in Annapolis. It's not my problem."

"But she left her yarn on the seat. Why wouldn't she have taken it with her?"

The driver released the brake. "Like I said, it's not my problem. Sit down so I can get going."

Jess begged the driver to wait. When he ordered her back to her seat for the second time, she grabbed her overnight bag and the woman's knitting satchel. Then she pounded on the door until he let her off the bus.

Even though she was freezing and terrified, another part of her felt triumphant. Jess was tired of being treated like a second-class citizen just because she had gray hair and a few wrinkles. Maybe she'd dye her hair purple, too. But first she had to find the missing woman. Jess searched every stall in the ladies' room twice and even sneaked into the men's room to see if the knitter might be in there. Nothing.

Nobody in the gas station had seen the knitter either. Or in the gift shop. Jess was running out of options when her cell phone rang. It was her son. *Oh, hell.* What was she going to say? Instead of answering, she let the call go to voicemail while she dialed one of her friends from the Piney Plotters.

"Marian? This is Jess. I have a problem I need help with."

She explained what had happened.

"No, I don't know her name," Jess said as Marian pumped her for details. "She never spoke to me, so I don't know if she had an accent. No, I haven't looked in her bag. Wait a second."

Jess pushed aside the balls of glittery peacock and fuchsia yarn. In the bottom of the bag was a bus ticket with the name C. Keller printed on it. "Marian, her ticket was for Baltimore, so she did get off the bus early. At least now I have something to report to the authorities. Thanks. I'll talk to you later."

Jess called her son to let him know she wouldn't be coming that weekend. It was a clarifying conversation. Unlike Marian, who had been helpful and concerned for Jess's safety, her son was angry she wasn't showing up to babysit. After hearing him say three times how selfish *she* was, Jess clicked off her phone and called the police.

* * * *

She spoke to four different people at the station before being told there was an officer nearby who would come to take her statement. He would determine whether the knitter qualified as a missing person and, no, Anne Arundel County didn't have a waiting period before a missing-person report could be filed. Someone was paying attention to her at last!

Jess sat on a stool in the diner reading her mystery novel while she waited. And waited. The clock read 2:34 and two people in her book had already been murdered by the time the police showed up to take her statement.

Not one but two officers introduced themselves and listened to her story. They seemed kind, but she caught the older policeman rolling his eyes toward the younger one. Even they weren't taking the woman's disappearance seriously. Maybe everyone over the age of seventy should go jump in the bay.

The eye-rolling officer took charge of the knitting bag and asked Jess how she planned to get to her son's house. But she didn't want to go to her son's. She wanted to go home. As if he'd read her mind, the handsome, younger officer said he was just coming off duty and was on the way to the beach. He offered to drive her to her door, and Jess accepted.

Officer Tom Kaminsky said his parents lived in Ocean Pines, not far from her house. He visited them every other weekend.

Jess fastened her seatbelt and asked, "Do you have any children, Officer Kaminsky?"

"Call me Tom, ma'am. No, not yet. My wife and I were married last year."

"And please call me Jess. May I ask, do you love your parents?"

He laughed. "Of course I do. They're the best."

Jess took that in, wondering if she still loved her son. There were four new text messages from him—each one more insulting. She pressed the phone's power button, and the screen went blank. That was easy.

"What do you think happened to the lady on the bus, Tom?"

The rain had started again, so he turned on his windshield wipers. "I don't know, ma'am… I mean, Jess. People go missing and sometimes they're hard to track. We get a lot of swimming and boating accidents around here. Seniors who wander off once they get dementia. It's hard to find them if we don't have an ID or if they aren't reported missing."

"If I give you my phone number, will you let me know if you hear anything?"

"Sure. We have your information. And is it okay if I tell my folks to give you a call to introduce themselves? I think you'd really like them, and you're practically neighbors."

Did he think she was lonely and wanted attention? Is that what they all thought?

When Tom dropped her off, it was past five o'clock. Jess was exhausted, but she hadn't had anything to eat since her lunchtime M&M's. After turning on the little TV in her kitchen, she scavenged for food.

At first Jess had loved everything about her retired life. She loved the pine cupboards in her kitchen and the nautically themed dishware. She loved how her screened porch connected her to Manklin Creek, which in its own way connected her to the ocean that was only a few miles away. She loved the egrets and the ospreys that nested in the nearby marshland. But then her son had started pressing her to bus to Silver Spring to babysit his wife's kids. After Jess's husband died, she'd been afraid to be alone, so she visited her son almost every weekend. But once he got married, he didn't know or care who she was—except as a free cook and babysitter for his bratty stepchildren.

Life was too short to be afraid to say no to people—even your own son. The disappearing knitter had shown her that. Jess munched on a tuna-salad sandwich while she watched the local news. The morning storm had come up quickly and had covered the entire Chesapeake area. Jess was about to change the channel when a photograph with a name appeared on the screen: Larry Keller. He'd been found by a couple of crab fishermen in Assawoman Bay near Ocean City, and two hours later, the Coast Guard had recovered his boat, adrift by Northside Park. Jess sat up straight, her sandwich forgotten, as the next image filled her television screen. Keller's wife, Cindy. According to the newswoman, a neighbor of the Kellers saw them both heading out in their boat at dawn. But Mrs. Keller's body hadn't yet been found.

Cindy Keller looked younger and had light brown hair in the picture, but there was no doubt in Jess's mind—Cindy was the missing knitter.

Jess picked up the phone to call Officer Kaminsky. But then she remembered the tear on Cindy Keller's cheek and put the phone down. She didn't know what had happened, after all. Maybe the boat had capsized accidentally and Cindy escaped, her mind numbed by shock. Or maybe Cindy had orchestrated the accident herself in order to escape to a new life.

Jess couldn't take that away from the woman. Maybe the authorities would put it all together. But maybe they wouldn't—Anne Arundel was a very different jurisdiction from Ocean Pines and Ocean City, and the officers hadn't seemed to take Jess's missing-person report all that seriously.

Jess walked out to the porch to finish her sandwich. The sky had cleared, and a graceful white egret extended her wings and took flight over Manklin Creek. *Beautiful.*

One by one, Jess deleted her son's texts and voicemail messages. Then she turned off her phone, tucked it into her pocket, and smiled.

Perhaps she'd visit the yarn shop in the morning and see if they had glittery peacock blue yarn. Winter was coming. It was time to knit a new scarf.

Robin Templeton is a Virginia-based writer. Her long-time career as a professional photographer and experience as a private investigator formed the basis of her work-in-progress, *Double Exposure*. She was awarded the William F. Deeck-Malice Domestic Grant for Unpublished Writers, and an early version of *Double Exposure* was a finalist in the Minotaur Books/Malice Domestic Best First Traditional Mystery Novel Competition. Although she's provided cover photos for some of the Chesapeake Crimes anthologies, "The Knitter" is her first short story submission. She's thrilled to be included with so many terrific writers. You can contact Robin at www.robintempleton.com.

WHITEOUT

by Maddi Davidson

The snowmobile driver leaned forward, willing his machine up the precipitous, powdery slope. As for me, I didn't bother to shift my weight, certain my petite 110-pound frame provided little drag. I was no more than a package to be delivered by Jack, who was instinctively feeling his way up the mountain through the gray cocoon of an early-winter blizzard. A member of Sun Valley's ski patrol for a dozen years, he knew the slopes and trails like the back of his Gore-Tex gloves.

The vehicle bucked forward and veered sharply toward a dark curtain of looming conifers. Jack guided us into a narrow gap and onto a cat track. Another snowmobile ferrying the coroner followed. We sped along the twisty trail until flickering flares emerged from the gloom and Jack brought us to a halt.

I wiped the snow off my goggles, swung my legs over the side, slipped into my snowshoes—essential footgear in the deep bed of newly fallen snow—and trudged to where two other members of the ski patrol were waiting next to snowmobiles.

"Detective Whistle from the sheriff's office." I expected one of the usual wisecracks about my last name, but perhaps it was too darn cold to make jokes. "This is the coroner, David Stele," I added as he arrived.

The ski patrolmen nodded. The slightly taller one perfunctorily introduced himself as Cody and his companion as Dustin before leading us to the edge of the trail where a rope tied to a tree led steeply down into an infinity of white.

"He's about twelve yards down," Cody said. "Right where we found him."

"Good," Stele said. He always told our officers that no one could move a body until he arrived, even if the head had been cut off and was rolling down a hill. The ski patrol had apparently received the same lecture.

Despite the guide rope and snowshoes, we slipped and slid our way down to where the body lay at the foot of a large tree. With his arms and legs twisted at unnatural angles, the dead man resembled a puppet entangled by his own strings.

"Know who it is?" I asked.

"Erik Rotter, the resort's pretty-boy spokesman," Cody replied.

I'd never met Rotter but knew who he was.

"Surprised you spotted him in this stuff," I said.

"We was looking for him," Cody responded.

Stele went to work while I observed. I would liked to have known more, but standing on the side of a mountain freezing one's well-insulated ass off wasn't the time for a detailed interview, even in Ketchum, Idaho, where locals have been spotted in shorts and sandals in below-freezing temperatures. "Freezing" being, apparently, a relative term.

"Rigor mortis?" I asked.

"Can't say yet," Stele responded. "Maybe just frozen."

"Gonna be fun gettin' him outta here and down the mountain," Cody said. "Can't fit him in a body bag without breaking some of his limbs. Or thawing them, and I left my blowtorch back at River Run. Hate it when that happens." He bent over to spit—downwind, fortunately.

Stele, shaking his head at Cody's remark, brushed the fresh snow off Rotter's canary-yellow ski jacket and examined the bullet holes: one, two, three, all near the heart.

"Nice grouping." It was all I could think of to say.

Cody seemed to consider that for a moment. "Doesn't mean the killer was a good shot, you know. In this shit, you've got to be right up in someone's face to see 'em."

"Did you find any bullet casings?"

Cody snorted and, with a few interspersed expletives, ranted that his job was to search for skiers in trouble, not to inspect crime scenes. I was free to look, but several inches of snow had fallen since they found the body. I'd have better luck in April, or whenever the last of the snow melted.

When Stele said he'd seen enough, I instructed Cody and Dustin to mark where they'd found the body and close off the trail. I didn't envy them the task of moving Rotter out of the trees, up onto the trail, and down the mountain. Stele had arranged for an ambulance to meet them at the River Run Lodge and transport the body to Wood River Chapel, Blaine County's one-stop shop for coroner, refrigeration, and memorial services. Not that Rotter needed refrigeration, having been flash frozen.

While Jack ferried me back to the lodge, unerringly navigating through the darkening blizzard, I considered the irony of Erik Rotter's death. Had he died on an expert slope it might well be renamed Rotter's Ruin or Erik's End. Instead, he bought it below a narrow, flat, easy-to-ski trail. For a former Olympic medalist long past his prime, it was a last missed gate before the pearly ones.

Sheriff Bob Walters was waiting at the lodge, having taken over an hour to cover the thirteen miles from his office in Hailey. He spoke briefly with Stele, and I gave my report. I was pleased when he said he wanted me to assist with his investigation.

I'd been with the Blaine County Sheriff's Office for less than a year, working out of Ketchum. The sparsely populated area—twenty-seven hundred in the town, twenty-one thousand in the county—could in no way be considered a hotbed of criminal activity, likely thanks to the number of county residents with firearms who resided within two miles of one of the three gun ranges in the valley. Locals knew very well what to do with a weapon. Murders were rare—one every eighteen months or so—and then almost invariably drug-related. As the most junior detective in the county, my biggest case had been an FWI—flying while intoxicated: a flock of cedar waxwings drunk on overripe berries engaged in kamikaze attacks on a prominent local businessman.

Sheriff Walters had overseen the well-being of the populace over the past eight years: everything from shepherding the county through a raging, weed-fueled wildfire to riding herd on a weed-fueled hip-hop festival that went on until three a.m., earning the enmity of every homeowner within head-banging earshot. If the sheriff was rattled by the murder of a well-known Olympic athlete, he showed no evidence of it. He ordered every member of the Sun Valley Ski Patrol who had been on the mountain that day to return to the lodge for interviews.

We began with my snowmobile driver, Jack. He explained that the mountain had been closed at noon due to the blizzard's high winds, heavy snowfall, threat of avalanche, and near-zero visibility. As lifts were closed, the ski patrol swept the slopes to ensure all skiers had cleared the area.

Cody and Dustin, Rotter's body duly delivered, were next. Cody, who did nearly all of the talking, explained that the discovery of Rotter's body had resulted from a targeted search.

As a marketing icon for Sun Valley Ski Resort, Rotter enjoyed special perks, including skiing Bald Mountain before and after regular operating hours, when the lifts were officially serving only the ski patrol. Not even the senior US Senator from Idaho (a part-time resident) was allowed such a privilege. When Cody and Dustin headed up the mountain to do their sweep, Rotter had caught a chair with them, determined to ski his regular last run of the day.

Cody told Rotter that only an idiot would be on the mountain if he didn't have to be. "Rotter was jawing like he usually does. He called himself King of the Mountain, claimed he won one of his Olympic medals in worse conditions, and he'd see us at the bottom. What a jackass."

Dustin pointed out that even a jackass was smart enough to stay back in the barn and not saunter out in a storm.

Completing their sweeps by two o'clock, Cody and Dustin returned to the ski patrol office at the lodge to report that their assigned slopes were, as best they could see in a whiteout, clear of skiers. While preparing to leave, Cody noticed that Rotter's conspicuous SUV—vanity plates: OLYMPC—was still parked in the skier-loading zone, another accommodation to his boundless ego. Cody checked with resort employees inside the lodge but no one had seen Rotter and a call to Rotter's cell phone went straight to voicemail.

Grumbling that Rotter had probably been picked up by a friend and was downing a few at a local bar, Cody and Dustin had no choice but to return to the mountain. "Hell to pay if we'd lost Mr. Olympic Ego," Cody said.

They took a snowmobile and started their search from the bottom, a task made easier by a hiatus in the storm bringing better visibility. "I could almost see the front of the snowmobile," Cody said sarcastically.

Cody claimed it was common knowledge within the ski patrol that Rotter had a fixed set of slopes he'd ski at the end of each day; with Baldy free of other skiers, he'd hurtle down the mountain as if he were still the ski god he'd been before a third ACL tear wrecked his right knee and precipitated his retirement. Dustin and Cody backtracked Rotter's customary run as they took a snowmobile up the mountain: River Run to Lower Olympic (a natural half-pipe) and then to mogul-studded Upper Olympic. They were nearing the top of Upper Olympic when eagle-eyed Dustin glimpsed a flash of yellow in the woods.

"Just luck that I saw Rotter's ski jacket through the snow," Dustin said. "We were close to the pines on Olympic when I had a strange feeling and peered into the trees. There he was, where he shouldn't have been, because there's no way he could have skied there from Olympic."

Dustin and Cody agreed that Rotter had to have been on the trail that intersected Olympic just above where the body was found.

"Rotter wouldn't be found dead skiing a beginner's trail," Dustin said without cracking a smile.

"And nobody, including Erik the Egomaniac, would ski through the trees in a whiteout," Cody added. "Someone on the trail must have flagged him down, killed him, and then shoved the body over the edge into the trees. Course, by the time we reached the trail, the snow had covered any tracks. If Dustin hadn't spotted Rotter when he did, we might not have found him 'til April Fools' Day."

Interviews with other members of the ski patrol confirmed that almost everyone knew about Rotter's regular run. And, like Cody, most had no use for Rotter: one patrolman called him a "useless sack of shit, pardon my French." Rotter's privileges around the resort and conceitedness were at the heart of the animus, although I detected more than a whiff of envy at his accomplishments, both on and off the slopes.

Rotter's previous success as a mogul skier had earned him shiny medals and a shinier entourage of ski sluts and boarder babes. Sun Valley's goodwill ambassador spread his own goodwill among rich women. Not that he wouldn't have seduced a poor woman for a quickie, but he specialized in disenchanted trophy wives who could afford to foot his living expenses. By late that night, Sheriff Walters had elicited a lengthy list of women whom Rotter claimed to have conquered, including nearly a dozen in the past year alone.

Between the ski patrol members who envied Rotter and the disenchanted women who may have hated him, we probably had more potential suspects than I could count on both hands. And toes.

* * * *

In the early hours of the next morning, the storm moved out. Dawn brought brilliant blue skies and the sound of snowplows molding massive mounds of white into small mountains. The sun glistened on the crystalline landscape, squint-inducing to anyone without wraparounds.

While the sheriff and I conducted interviews, Cody escorted two deputies from my office to the trail above where Rotter's body was found. They swept the trail and the area where the body was found with a metal detector, eventually locating two nine-millimeter shell casings in addition to Rotter's ski poles. The report from the coroner confirmed that Rotter had died from gunshots delivered at close range; his broken bones and contusions from tumbling down the mountain were merely icing on the cake.

The next day, the sheriff and I closeted ourselves in his office to discuss our findings. We'd talked with Rotter's recent rolls in the hay (and, more discreetly, their husbands and significant others) who'd been in Ketchum the day of the murder. We'd also reviewed the ski-lift ticket scans to determine who had and had not been on the slopes before the murder.

"Well, what do you think?" the sheriff asked. He leaned back in his chair and propped his legs on the open bottom drawer of his desk.

I attempted to appear equally relaxed in the hard ladder-back chair I occupied, although I was keyed up and eager to impress. I'd heard from colleagues that the sheriff encouraged subordinates to share their conclusions so I'd spent hours poring over my notes and, in every way possible, preparing for this opportunity.

"I believe we have two plausible suspects."

Sheriff Walters's thick eyebrows didn't so much as twitch while he waited for me to proceed.

"First, Danny Bridges. His wife, Christina, had an affair with Rotter last spring. Bridges found out and forced her to break it off. Bridges dropped a bundle on a romantic couple's retreat in Rarotonga, on top of six months of intensive couple's counseling. But Christina slept with Rotter two weeks after the retreat and, in a moment of insanity, confessed to her husband. Most men would call Dan the Divorce Lawyer, but Bridges claims he forgave her 'seventy times seven times.'" I consulted my notes. "He said that 'a wife is not to depart from her husband but to be reconciled.'"

"Right," the sheriff said. "It's from the Bible. Though we can't verify the exact number of times he forgave her."

"Nor did he say anything about forgiving Rotter."

"Whom he likely saw as an ongoing threat to his marriage."

"That's what I think. Bridges said Rotter's death was the work of an avenging angel. Maybe he was that angel, deciding in his own twisted way that the sanctity of marriage trumps the sanctity of life."

"Assuming I buy that," the sheriff said, "how did Bridges get from Boise to Baldy in time to commit murder?"

That was a bit tricky. The day of the murder, Bridges had flown from Seattle to Boise and then driven home, not arriving until evening, or so he said. The Idaho State Police confirmed that the heavy snow contributed to numerous accidents along the Interstate 84 to State Highway 75 route, and that the normal three-hour drive from Boise to Ketchum *could* have stretched into a six-hour nightmare.

"What if he didn't take the interstate but drove over the pass?" I said. "I know conditions were poor—heavy snow and near-zero visibility— but Bridges does drive a Range Rover. He could have made it home in a few hours, leaving him plenty of time to kill Rotter."

Sheriff Walters smiled. "You've never driven the pass in winter, have you?"

"No."

"The pass is, well, nearly impassible in any decent amount of snow. During Monday's storm, it hadn't been plowed and the high winds created massive snow drifts. You want me to believe that after landing in Boise, Bridges risked his life driving the pass in order to make it home in time to grab a gun, drive to the slope, slip onto a chairlift without having his ticket scanned—"

"His wife admits she skied a few runs with Rotter that day. If a friend of Bridge's saw them and called him, Bridges might have been enraged enough to risk the pass. And as for getting up and down the mountain, Bridges owns a set of *randonnée* skis," I said, referring to skis that enabled one to climb steep hills.

"My point is whether Bridges would do all that on the off chance he can find Rotter on the slopes, kill him, and escape without being seen."

The sheriff's steady gaze willed me to make the conclusion.

"Okay, it's unlikely, but it is technically possible."

Sheriff Walters frowned. "Who else?"

Maybe it had been a mistake to mention Bridges, but I didn't want to appear close-minded, although I was. I *knew* who killed Rotter.

"Sue-Ann Miller."

Sue-Ann, twenty-nine years old, was an attractive, five-foot-ten former track standout at UCLA who'd been Rotter's near-constant companion for the past four months. She was the fourth wife of Braydon Miller, thirty years her senior, who had made an outrageous fortune building and selling companies in Silicon Valley. I'd seen Braydon for the first time at a fundraiser for the Sun Valley Symphony and was struck by his large head and oversized hands and feet, all of which made him seem much taller than his six-foot frame.

"I agree she's a possible," the sheriff said. "Tell me the why and the how."

"Sue-Ann was in love with Rotter and thought he loved her back. So she asked Braydon for a divorce, he agreed, and they submitted the paperwork. Then Sue-Ann discovered that Rotter had taken up with Christina Bridges again. If the waitress at the Burger Bunker is to be believed, Rotter was hitting on her, too. And there may be others."

"Shall the leopard change his spots?" Sheriff Walters said. "I take it you didn't believe Sue-Ann as the mourning lover?"

Sue-Ann's eyes had been red and her appearance drawn during the interview. I was suspicious of her repeated declarations of a broken heart and avowal that she'd not left the house since she'd heard the news of Rotter's death. It was all too dramatic. "Skillful makeup, soap in the eyes, and dreadful acting."

"Go on."

"Rotter's betrayal gnawed at her. She'd burned her bridges for a man who treated her like another stroll in the park. So she plotted revenge, and when she heard of the blizzard and a possible whiteout, she saw her chance to kill Rotter with impunity. She grabbed a gun—Sue-Ann admitted she and her husband owned nine-millimeter handguns—and headed for the slopes. Sue-Ann denied she saw Rotter on the mountain, but one of the lift-ticket scans has her getting on the chair lift a few seconds before he did."

The sheriff consulted his notes. "I had a little chat with the lift operators at River Run. Rotter came through the lift checkpoint twice with Christina Bridges. The second time, Sue-Ann pushed past them and may have said something to Rotter. So I spoke to Christina myself, after you did. She didn't hear Sue-Ann say anything, but mentioned she saw Sue-Ann on the slope several times Monday, possibly following her and Rotter."

"So Sue-Ann is lying about not seeing Rotter. And I bet she's lying about going directly home after the mountain closed." I leaned forward in the chair, eager to share my theory. "Her last lift-ticket scan was at 11:40, twenty minutes before the lifts closed. I think Sue-Ann saw the way the storm was coming in and knew the mountain would soon close. She found a place to wait until the closing was announced, probably Roundhouse Restaurant, and then hid while the place cleared out. Around one o'clock she emerged and skied the two hundred yards down the slope to wait for Rotter to do his last run. Or she waited outside the restaurant until he came by, and waved him over so they could ski together. In either case, he stopped when he recognized her leopard ski suit. When she got him where she wanted him, she killed him, dragged his body the few yards to the edge of the cat track, and shoved him off. After that, it would have been easy to ski off the mountain in the whiteout without being seen."

Sheriff Walters peered at me thoughtfully. "Do you truly believe Sue-Ann Miller shot Rotter in cold blood?"

I nodded.

"It's a good story," he acknowledged, "and with her having access to the same type of gun that killed Rotter and lying about seeing him, we should have enough for a search warrant."

I was pleased I'd nailed it but tried not to show it.

"Except that I don't believe it for a New York minute, or an Idaho second, either." Sheriff Walters held up his hand before I could say anything. Abruptly he removed his legs from the desk drawer where they'd been resting, swung forward in his chair, and planted his feet squarely on the floor. His eyes bore into me as he delivered his verdict: "I think Sue-Ann lied because she was embarrassed to admit she saw Rotter with another woman, a slap in the face, proving he wasn't ready to settle down after all. A search might turn up something interesting, but I'm telling you now, Braydon Miller did it. He's a vindictive bastard who doesn't merely beat his opponents but humiliates them. A man like that isn't going to let his knockout, much-younger wife divorce him for a good-looking ski bum."

"But how could Miller get up and down the mountain? Sue-Ann mentioned he doesn't ski."

"Braydon Miller runs the occasional half marathon and is easily fit enough to climb halfway up Baldy on snowshoes. And don't assume because a man doesn't ski that he can't ski. A little sleuthing on the Internet will tell you that Miller graduated from a high school in northern Minnesota. No one comes out of the land of wearying, long winters without learning how to ski cross-country at least."

Sheriff Walters stood and stared down at me. "I'm telling you. He's the killer."

* * * *

The next few days didn't unfold quite as Sheriff Walters planned. A search of the Miller home yielded a quiver of skis for Sue-Ann, including *randonnée* and old downhill skis. The ski room was full of her equipment, but there didn't appear to be so much as a snowshoe for Braydon. Sue-Ann's ski locker at the base of River Run was more revealing. In addition to her custom-made downhill skis, poles, and boots, we found a nine-millimeter pistol wrapped in a faux-fur scarf and shoved in a ski helmet. Bullets fired from the gun matched those taken from Rotter's body.

I wanted to fist pump and woo-hoo to the world, but Sheriff Walters wasn't ready to concede that I'd solved the case. He demonstrated that the flimsy ski-locker doors were useless against a hard pull, so the gun could have been planted. Spraying Sue-Ann's equipment and ski clothing with luminol yielded not a trace of blood. Not even a mashed moth. In what seemed to be a spray in the dark, the sheriff used the luminol on the skis and poles at her home but found nothing. The sheriff had all of Sue-Ann's ski equipment and skiwear consigned to the evidence room. "Something is not right," he said repeatedly, but wouldn't say—and didn't know—what the something was.

Sue-Ann reluctantly admitted that the gun was hers, but she'd taken it along on backcountry hikes only because Braydon insisted she have protection against wild animals. She'd never fired it except at a range, and doubted she could ever use it on a living creature.

The gun was clean of prints, and the last time Sue-Ann had seen it, so she said, was in the locked glove box of her car, weeks ago. Braydon backed her up, declaring that they owned several handguns for protection. Sue-Ann's car had been serviced three weeks prior to the murder, and Braydon hadn't remembered to take the gun out, nor did he recall seeing it in the car afterward. "Anyone could have taken it," he admitted. The mechanic, whom we interviewed, appeared to be the only man in town whose wife Rotter hadn't charmed; the wife was middle-aged, middle-weight, middle-class, and hugely in love with her husband. If the mechanic had swiped the gun, it wasn't to exorcise Rotter-related angst.

We sorted through Sue-Ann's credit and debit card receipts. She shared the credit cards with her husband, and the sheriff was hoping a snowshoe purchase would pop up. It didn't. We didn't expend any effort checking with retailers because in Idaho, snowshoes were sold everywhere: sporting goods stores, department stores, big box stores, and the occasional drug store. That trail went cold.

Despite the lack of evidence pointing to Braydon as the killer, the sheriff stuck to his theory. "Here's a guy who devours his business rivals, yet is so big-hearted that when wife number four declares her intent to dump him, he lets her stay in his house and still use a joint credit card. It makes no sense."

I opined that since Braydon was the type who always had to win, maybe he was hoping by keeping Sue-Ann financially dependent, she'd decide to stay. Or maybe he did still love her; he had seemed quite solicitous of Sue-Ann when we'd questioned him about the gun.

The sheriff responded with a withering look.

The district attorney had no choice but to prosecute Sue-Ann. She insisted vehemently that she was not a killer, evidenced by the fact she picked up and relocated snakes on the bike path so they wouldn't become flattened fauna. (To my way of thinking, it didn't mean she wouldn't dispatch a much larger snake like Rotter.)

Sue-Ann was arrested. She made bail, but instead of returning to Braydon, she moved into a ski-in-ski-out condominium while awaiting trial. Despite her primo location, Sue-Ann forsook skiing and all social activities and donned black. To all who would listen, she proclaimed her innocence, but as the trial date drew near, she appeared diminished, drained of vitality, and years older.

To the delight of the town, heavy snowfalls early in the new year brought a record number of skiers to Sun Valley who, apparently, were unafraid of a second murder on the slopes.

* * * *

In late April the ski season came to an end.

So did Braydon Miller.

Sue-Ann slunk into the sheriff's office the Monday after the mountain closed and announced she had shot Braydon with one of his own guns. She waived her rights, seemingly proud to confess to the murder of Braydon, not Rotter.

Sue-Ann explained that her life had been devoid of meaning since her beloved Erik died. Convinced that Braydon had murdered him—although she didn't know how—she grew tired of waiting for the police to figure it out and resolved to avenge Erik's death her own way. That she now faced life in prison for murdering "the bastard who broke my heart" seemed not to matter. Sue-Ann was emphatic that justice had been served, albeit with a side of revenge.

* * * *

The day after Sue-Ann's confession, I found myself in a slightly cold, concrete-block evidence room, where Sheriff Walters had placed Sue-Ann's skis, poles, and boots on a long table. "Look carefully at her *randonnée* skis," he said. "Tell me everything you see."

"K2 skis," I said, referring to the brand. "Blue and white design and a decent length for a good skier, maybe 180s." I was a good skier but shorter than Sue-Ann, and my skis were 165 centimeters long—more than five feet. I continued my inventory. "Bindings are high end. Skis and bindings probably cost fifteen hundred dollars or more."

"Look harder," he urged.

I leaned over the skis, searching for the clue he'd spotted and I'd obviously missed. There were a few dings on the skis, meaning nothing more than they were probably a season or more old. Suddenly I saw it. "The bindings—they're set for a huge boot!"

"Sue-Ann's feet are large for a woman, but not as big as mine. I wear a size eleven and I would swim in these."

"Braydon Miller," I said.

"Yup. Remember what I said about Miller: that he doesn't ski doesn't mean he can't ski? He borrowed Sue-Ann's *randonnée* skis."

"But he must have used his own boots."

"Exactly. He purchased boots and bided his time, maybe hoping he'd catch one or both of them skiing in the backcountry. Instead, the blizzard provided his opportunity. Sometime during the morning he climbed up on *randonnée* skis. Instead of Sue-Ann, it was Braydon waiting for Rotter's last run. Braydon waved Rotter down, killed him, made his way back down the slope, slipped into the nearly deserted River Run Lodge, and planted the gun in Sue-Ann's locker. When he returned home, maybe Sue-Ann was there and it was all he could do to sneak in and quietly replace the skis. I guess in his arrogance Miller thought we'd never suspect him, so he didn't bother to spend the five minutes resetting the bindings."

"If we can find the boots, we prove his guilt," I said.

"Or evidence that he purchased a pair."

Lighter and more flexible than downhill ski boots, *randonnée* boots are sold by a limited number of sporting-goods stores. We contacted every such store in Idaho, asking if they'd sold, for cash, *randonnée* ski boots in a large size in the past year. We hit pay dirt in a backcountry sports store in Pocatello; a clerk had sold a pair of ski goggles and size-thirteen boots to a man three weeks before Rotter's murder. The clerk remembered the transaction because the boots had been in inventory for two years, "waiting for Bigfoot." A photo of Braydon Miller elicited a "yeah, I'm pretty sure that's the guy."

It was good enough for Sheriff Walters and me.

Sue-Ann was unimpressed with our detective work. "I *told* you Braydon was the biggest heel in the Western Hemisphere."

Maddi Davidson is the pen name for sisters Mary Ann Davidson and Diane Davidson, who reside on opposite coasts of the United States. As Maddi they've published three novels in the Miss-Information Technology Mystery Series, available through Amazon: *Outsourcing Murder, Denial of Service*, and *With Murder You Get Sushi*. Their most recently published short story, "Heartfelt," was published in Buddhapuss Ink's *Mystery Times 2015*. More information about Maddi is available on the website maddidavidson.com.

THE HISS OF DEATH
by Lauren R. Silberman

Abby Tillman raced to keep up with Trisha as she trotted toward the snake house. The bouncy director of community engagement towered over the petite Abby, whose legs practically skated across Autumn Hill Zoo's recycled rubber pavement.

"I'm so sorry that Tom couldn't take you through the zoo personally." Trisha tossed the comment over her shoulder. "But the development office arranged a last-minute tour with some important potential donors, so we had to bring out our big guns."

Abby wasn't offended by the implication that she wasn't a big gun—she completely understood. Abby was just a contractor, hired to conduct an audience survey for the zoo. If it was up to her, she'd also reserve the director's time for the people who were willing to pay top dollar rather than someone the zoo was paying. Contractors had to be flexible.

"Goodness, was that a raindrop?" Trisha paused to check the sky, then glanced down as if she worried about droplets landing on her teal polo shirt, embroidered with the zoo's logo. Abby had noticed that zoo staff wore matching shirts in the zoo's colors, appearing slickly professional but still approachable. A nice touch. "Was it supposed to rain today? Well, burnt bread on a stick. I should have checked the forecast. I've got three school groups prepping to come through and that senior tour and..." She counted her fingers as she listed names. Abby felt as if she had been forgotten. Trisha kept running through her to-do list.

Abby coughed loudly.

"Right, right—okay, here we are. They're already inside. I texted our intern Penny that you were coming. Let's hope she updated Tom." Trisha shook her head. "He doesn't like surprises."

Rain began drizzling around them. Trisha gave Abby a quick smile and ran off.

"I'm sure it'll be fine," Abby said, before realizing that Trisha was already out of earshot. Abby paused at the doors of the snake house—or more formally the herpetarium. Each door was decorated with one half of a corn snake in bronze relief. The handles were shaped like garden snakes. She hesitated to touch them. She gazed upward. The entire building resembled a squat ziggurat, like some mythological temple buried in a long-forgotten jungle.

The rain grew steadier. She braced herself, grabbed one of the slick metal garden snakes, and opened the door.

Abby wiped her eyes as they adjusted to the dim light inside the herpetarium. She found herself in a small room lined with display cases housing live snakes, tucked into the walls in three horizontal rows. She tried telling herself that she didn't mind snakes. Right? They were just tiny reptiles doing their snaky thing. Nothing to be worried about here. To be on the safe side, Abby kept her eyes ahead, ignoring the creatures writhing behind the glass.

Thunder crashed outside. She jumped and hurried into the next room, through another door adorned with snake handles. This room was larger and encircled with a single brilliantly lit display that started above her knees and went up to almost the ceiling. She caught sight of an enormous, coiled, chartreuse-colored behemoth before she could look away. She shivered. Then she noticed that a window into the case was slightly ajar.

"He can't get you. I was just about to feed him," said a voice behind her. Abby turned on her heels to gaze up at a young woman with bright blue eyes that matched the bow holding back her perfectly combed blond hair. Abby realized she was patting back her own dark locks, which tended to fall flat and lifeless. The woman wore an embroidered polo shirt identical to Trisha's but in canary yellow; a silver bracelet sporting the zoo's logo dangled from her wrist. Abby leaned in to admire the bracelet and realized it was a medical-alert medallion, not the zoo's logo after all.

"Are you Penny, the intern?" Abby asked.

"At your service!" Penny saluted.

If Trisha had been the epitome of enthusiasm then Penny embodied perkiness. The young woman held out a hand and eagerly grasped Abby's in a robust shake. "You must be Abby! I'm so excited to work with you! I'm really interested in visitor studies! I was into chemistry, but then I wanted to open my own rescue, and then I did open my rescue—when I was only sixteen! And goodness, that was awesome, but I haven't completely given up on the sciences, I promise you! I even work part-time at a vet's office! Trying to decide between becoming one myself and zoological studies! What you're planning for us sounds really interesting and really cool…"

Penny prattled on with Abby only half listening, unable to keep up with the young woman's stream of commentary. When did she find time to breathe? And when was she going to close the case window?

Behind Penny, an enormous, barrel-chested man paraded into the room, followed by a small entourage. His face was buried in a heavy but manicured dark brown beard and a head of thick curls streaked with gray. He dominated the room, both in size and presence. If he'd lived in another time, he would have undoubtedly been a pirate.

"And here we have my dear friend Percy—" He waved his arms.

"Penny!" the intern corrected.

The man turned; his face contorted. Obviously he was not used to being interrupted. "Not *you*. Percy." He pounded on the glass. The monster slithered in response. Penny deflated. Her shoulders turned in. The man ignored her. "Oh my darling, you appear hungry. You there, you, you…" He snapped his fingers at Penny, clearly unable to come up with her name although he'd just heard it. "Go feed my sweetie pie here."

"Yes, sir." Penny sprinted toward a corner of the room. Abby didn't care to watch, but she felt relieved when Penny finished and closed the window. She gathered that the dominating man must be Thomas Flatterly, the zoo's famous—and sometimes infamous—director.

Abby studied Flatterly's entourage. There was a mousy woman, less than half the size of the middle-aged but still handsome, long-haired blond hunk who snuggled up behind her. The couple waited in the middle of the room, near Flatterly but turned away from him as if bored. Behind them was a lanky string bean of a man who peered through the glass at "Sweetie Pie," adjusting his thick glasses every few moments. A few steps to his right stood a heavy-set woman who reminded Abby of her middle-school principal, down to her floral-print dress and sensible shoes. She rested her back confidently against the glass. Abby cringed, but nobody else seemed to be worried.

"So, Tom, you were saying—" the woman wearing the floral-print dress began.

Flatterly waved away her words. "Yes, yes, of course, Jeannie. So Percy joined the zoo about fifteen years ago, which, coincidentally, was the same time that I… Wait, who are you?" He spun around and pointed a thick finger squarely at Abby.

"Abby Tillman, Artifactual Consulting." She put out a hand that was bluntly ignored. Dropping the offending arm back to her side, she continued, "Trisha said that I should—"

"Oh, *Trisha said*." He appeared about ready to explode. Even in the darkened room, Abby could see his face reddening. Then he looked about, apparently remembering his group. "If Trisha said, then, why, of course, you should be here."

"Thank—" The lights flickered in the room. Everyone turned around, as if trying to see the cause. "It's raining pretty hard outside," Abby reminded them. "Starting to thunder and lightning, I believe."

The mousy woman nodded and glanced up at her beefcake—even his blond hair looked anxious.

"Don't worry, Hunter, dear," she said, patting his arm.

Abby's mind clicked. Hunter Jones. Of course. He'd been in a series of low-budget action films about fifteen years ago. They were legendary for their cheesy quality. Was the woman his agent, then, or maybe his wife? Didn't strike her as a mistress, but you never knew.

"Well, then." Flatterly waved away the storm and barreled ahead. "As I was about to say, Percy here is a star of the zoo. He was born in the wilds of the Amazon but nearly killed when—"

The lights blinked off and on again. The group huddled closer together. Abby silently prayed that she would not be stuck in the dark in a building full of snakes. Surely the zoo had a backup generator. Or was that something Flatterly was hoping to get funded by today's potential donors?

The lights flickered once more, off, on, then off again. And off they stayed. *Please let there be a generator.*

"No worries, everyone," Flatterly said. "We just had a team working on the system yesterday. We're ordering a new part or two, but they assured me that everything would work until the new parts arrive." As he spoke, Abby could make out the generator groaning to life outside. "See, there we go. So, lights in three, two, one…"

The lights did not listen to his countdown.

The generator struggled and sputtered before loudly popping and quitting. They remained in the dark. With no windows, all the light was sucked out, leaving only pitch-blackness. What had happened to the emergency lights? Weren't all buildings legally required to have those?

"You need a new facilities management team," a voice said. It sounded like the mousy woman. Abby agreed; this couldn't be safe for the animals. Why wasn't anything working?

Everyone stood relatively quietly, waiting for the lights to return. Thunder crashed above. Abby thought she heard Percy move in his case. She imagined him slithering and hissing through his enclosure. She couldn't suppress a small shriek. She wasn't the only one. Within a minute, the others had apparently given up on waiting around. She heard them moving about in confusion, bumping into one another, trying to find their way toward the exits in the dark.

"That thing… It's moving!" someone cried.

"Tom, are we safe?" another voice asked.

No response.

"Tom?"

Silence pervaded the room.

"Is this some sort of prank?" someone asked.

"Oh, Lord," another exclaimed.

"What?" Abby asked. She stepped forward, tripping over an unseen obstacle at her feet. She screamed. "Percy's loose! Oh, no no no…"

The lights flicked on.

It wasn't Percy at her feet. He was safely inside his cage. Instead, she had stumbled over the slumped body of Tom Flatterly. Abby touched his throat, feeling for a pulse.

"He's dead," she said as she pulled herself up.

"He must have had a heart attack," Jeannie said.

"Did he have a heart problem?" the mousy woman asked. Hunter started to cry.

"Mr. Flatterly!" Penny raced across the room. She dive-bombed past Abby and sprawled across Flatterly's body. "We need an ambulance! Someone call 9-1-1!"

Abby had already pulled out her phone to do so.

"I don't think an ambulance would do you much good, little girl," said the bespectacled bean-pole man as he knelt beside Penny. "I've seen meat in my kitchen more alive than this man."

Abby pursed her lips. What a horrible thing to say.

Penny grabbed Flatterly's limp hand, obviously devastated. Tears flowed freely down her cheeks.

"Come now, Grover," Jeannie said. "That's only because you enjoy killing the little animals immediately before serving them to your guests." Abby couldn't tell if the woman was being snarky or not. And her cell phone wasn't getting a signal yet. Was it the storm or the thick walls of the snake house?

"Everything at Chez Gardner is brought to the table in the most *humane* of manners, I can assure you," Grover replied. Ah, Grover Gardner. Abby had read reviews of his restaurants in the papers. More than a bit outside of her price range. Now if she could figure out the identity of the remaining woman in the room…

"Move aside," ordered the mousy woman, pushing Penny away from Flatterly. She peered close to his body. "I'm a doctor."

"Of pharmacy." Hunter added.

"Shush, Hunter." She went back to examining Flatterly's body.

"I can't get a signal." Abby gave up trying and put away her cell phone. "Penny, do you have a landline in here?"

The intern wiped her eyes. She pointed to the smaller room near the front entrance. A phone was visible on the wall beyond the doorway. Abby started toward it.

"But it doesn't work," Penny said. "I've been trying to tell Mr. Flatterly, but he just…" Penny burst into tears again, backed up against the glass display case, and leaned against it for support.

"Then, I'll go out to the main admin office," Abby replied. "Storm or not, he needs—"

"You're not going anywhere," the mousy woman stated. Abby stopped in her tracks. "None of us are. Tom didn't just die. He was murdered."

Everyone stopped and stared at one another. Abby noticed that they all instinctively backed up a few feet from each other.

"How do you know that?" Jeannie asked.

"Someone stuck a needle in his neck. It broke off—look, the tip is still there."

Abby turned back and leaned over Flatterly's body. She could barely make out the thin spike of a needle sticking out of the zoo director's thick neck. A few inches higher, and no one would have seen it for his hair.

"If it's murder, then we definitely need to call 9-1-1," she said aloud.

"What about the rest of the syringe?" Grover asked.

"I don't know…." The mousy woman shook her head.

"And we're locked in here!" Hunter pushed against the doors in a panic. They didn't budge.

"Not again," Penny said. "Stupid security locks."

Abby wondered if anything worked in this place. The lights, the generators, and now the locks. Mousy woman was right; they did need a new facilities management team here.

"Calm down, Hunter," the mousy woman snapped. Hunter stopped trying to shove the doors open and stood taking deep breaths.

Abby fought her rising panic, switching to consultant mode. So, they were locked in a room with a dead body and a murderer. It was her business to solve problems for museums and zoos. While this wasn't what she had expected, she figured that the logistics were probably the same—assess the situation, research potential solutions, and test theories.

Abby felt as if she had stepped into an Agatha Christie story. She took in the scene. Flatterly lay on the floor in roughly the center of the space. The room wasn't particularly large, and no one had been more than a few steps from anyone else when the lights came back on. She tried remembering who had been standing where before the power was restored.

Besides Abby, three other people had knelt beside Flatterly's body: Penny, Grover, and the mousy pharmacist. Any one of them could have picked up the syringe. But who had plunged it into Flatterly in the first place? What poison was used? And where had the syringe gone?

She wasn't the only one who had thought of that last question.

"Show us your hands!" Jeannie ordered. "Turn out your pockets! Your purses!" She grabbed Grover by the upper arms and shook him.

"Unhand me, Jeannie. I don't have a purse."

As Jeannie loosened her grip, Grover turned his pockets inside out to prove that he didn't have the syringe. Everyone else followed suit. The syringe wasn't anywhere to be found.

"Well, that wasn't helpful," the mousy pharmacist said. "Even in a room this small, there must be a million other hiding places."

"Who would want Mr. Flatterly dead?" Abby asked. She hadn't actually meant to say the words aloud. Everyone turned and examined one another suspiciously.

"Well, I was surprised to see *you* here," the pharmacist said to Grover.

"Me?" Grover threw his hands up in mock surrender. "Why is that?"

"I remember those articles in the paper about Tom protesting Chez Gardner when it first opened. How he'd secretly videotaped the farms you operated and the cruel conditions of the animals cooped up there and given those drugs." She wagged a finger at him.

"That was years ago. Besides the restaurant is a success, and Tom and I have… come to an understanding since then. He's been known to dine with me," Grover replied.

"Protesting the animals…" Hunter jumped in, and then just as quickly stopped, apparently confused midthought. He held a finger to his lips as if it would help his thinking. "Oh. That's like what he did to you back in college," he continued. "Isn't that right, sweetie?" He seemed pleased with himself for remembering.

"Hunter…" The pharmacist's voice trembled with anger.

"Oh, yes, Hunter, what?" Jeannie asked, obviously intrigued.

"When Molly was in school, she conducted experiments on lab animals. Rabbits and mice, you know. Anyway, Tom went to the same school, and he released them all! She got in so much trouble because of him." Hunter laughed at the thought. He slapped Molly on the back, apparently thinking she would also be amused. She stiffened but said nothing.

"Well, isn't that something," Jeannie said to Grover. He nodded.

"No, no, it isn't something," Molly replied. Her voice was tinged with fury. "It was just a silly incident years ago. We were kids. We're not kids anymore. Now I run one of the largest pharmaceutical companies in the country."

"My family's company," Hunter added helpfully.

"Yes," Molly nearly growled. "Your family's company. We're a leader in the industry, and our record is spotless. Really."

Abby might have thought that Molly protested too much, but then again, they were each being accused of murder. How would she react if someone suggested she had done Flatterly in?

"And you—who are you?" Jeannie asked, spinning toward Abby as if reading her mind. Now she'd find out how she'd respond to accusations.

"I'm a contractor. Abby Tillman, Artifactual Consulting. I'm supposed to conduct a visitors' survey to help the zoo better gauge how they're addressing the needs of their current audiences and begin identifying new—"

"I don't need the whole backstory." Jeannie waved away Abby's explanation. "So, basically you're a stranger and could have any host of reasons to kill Tom."

"Oh, and like you don't, Jeannie?" Molly sneered.

Jeannie paused. Her painted-on eyebrows crept up the vast plain of her forehead with a "What, me?" expression.

Molly squared her shoulders and invaded Jeannie's space. "Really? And that whole faux-faux fur fiasco happened to someone else?"

Abby glanced at intern Penny, who shrugged. At least she had stopped crying.

"Faux-faux fur?" Abby asked.

"So, yes, some of the fur was real. Okay, okay, all of it was real fur. But my clients want the best, the freshest, and the most envelope-pushing designs. And sometimes envelope-pushing means, well, envelope-pushing," Jeannie replied, as if that somehow excused her deception. Abby wouldn't have taken her for a fashion designer, but then again, some of the dresses she saw superstars wear in the glossies looked remarkably cheap for their price tags. Maybe that was the point? The irony of a $3,000 peony-print dress that seemed like something from the bargain bin?

"And Mr. Flatterly protested?" Abby asked. She was beginning to see that Flatterly was prone to very public demonstrations against any perceived ill treatment of animals. Or at least, he used to be, since it sounded as if everyone had made nice over the years. She wouldn't be surprised if he had softened a bit, even changed his tune when he realized the money that these folks could bring into the zoo.

"Maybe a little." Jeannie rolled her eyes. Molly and Grover stared pointedly at her. "Okay, maybe a lot. But I got rid of the fur—for real this time—and we made up at a dinner at Chez Gardner." She motioned toward Grover. He didn't appear pleased to be noticed again.

"Fine, so everyone here had some sort of beef with Tom," Grover said.

"He never seemed to mind my pet tiger," Hunter said. Everyone turned to him. Abby had forgotten to include him as a potential murderer, but maybe she had overlooked him too easily.

"Hunter!" Molly stomped her right foot. Abby would have wondered what she saw in him, but then his baby blue eyes flickered in the dim light. Even a few years past his prime, his body remained in great shape, his skin was nicely tanned, and his hair... Oh, his hair. Abby caught herself salivating a little.

"He played with Kitty all of those times he came over for dinner," Hunter continued. "He even liked the photos of that big hunt we went on a few years ago. You know the one where you shot that cheetah."

Molly put a hand to her forehead. She put the other one against his enormous bicep, steadying herself. Jeannie nearly fell over, laughing at the pair of them. Abby decided that Hunter really had to be an innocent in all of this. Goodness gracious—what had all those movie stunts done to him?

"I guess you all have gotten past these, uh, incidents," Abby said to the group, "especially if you're willing to consider donating money to the zoo now."

"Bygones are bygones," Jeannie said. Abby thought she was going for magnanimous but instead she sounded saccharine. Nonetheless, the rest of the group nodded in unison.

"The zoo needs us, and the good press doesn't hurt," Grover said.

"Agreed," Molly said.

A win-win, Abby thought. Funny how money could turn former enemies into kindred spirits. But that didn't mean that one of them might not have still killed Flatterly, but which one?

Abby paced across the room, refusing to look at Percy, who lurked inside his case. As much as she tried ignoring him, she still managed to catch every pulse of muscle beneath his shiny green scales, every flick of his forked tongue, and every flash as the light caught his flat, lidless black eyes. He seemed to be taunting her, as if he knew the answer.

She breathed in deeply. No one knew how long they were going to be stuck in this room. The only way to conquer a fear is to face it, she thought. Bizarre how the dead body in the middle of the room didn't faze her, but this creature—who did nothing wrong except be born creepy—was making her cringe. She wasn't going to be able to think straight until she dealt with her phobia. Abby walked up to the nearly ceiling-high glass, practically sticking her nose against it like a five-year-old kid.

"You saw it all, Percy," she whispered to the snake. "Tell me what happened." She stepped back, not truly expecting an answer.

"What are you doing?" Penny asked, inserting herself between Abby and the display, partially blocking her view.

"Want to know a secret?" Abby offered.

Penny nodded.

"I'm afraid of snakes."

Penny laughed. "Well, you wouldn't be the first. Lots of people are terrified of them. But I love them. The vet I sometimes work for isn't just for dogs and cats but also snakes and lizards and rabbits and squirrels and salamanders and…" She turned as she spoke, heading back toward the others.

Abby was about to follow when something in the case caught her eye. She leaned forward and squinted, paying little attention to what Penny was saying. Then she turned back to the intern.

"Hey, Penny," Abby asked slowly, interrupting the young woman's dissertation. "I'm sorry to be all nosy, but what is your medical alert for?" She gestured toward the young woman's bracelet. "I mean, is it anything that could be a problem if we're stuck in here a while?"

Instead of being offended, Penny perked up. "Oh, I'm a diabetic. I have to be careful about my sugar intake, and I have all this insulin that I need to…"

Again, Abby stopped listening. She didn't need to hear what Penny was trying to hide with her babble. Everything became obvious to her now. The intern was good. Too good. The only person not questioned by the group.

"Molly," Abby said, while again turning and ignoring Penny's ongoing chatter, "I think it's safe to call for the authorities now."

"How are we going to do that?" Molly replied. "No one's getting service, and Penny said the landline is dead. And I'm not letting any of you out of my sight until we figure out who killed Tom."

"I think you'll find that the cord is simply removed from the phone. It may even be working fine," Abby replied.

Hunter went to check. He held up the limp, dangling cord for everyone to see. After plugging it in, he picked up the phone and gave a thumbs-up.

"Oh, wouldya look at that?" Penny laughed nervously. "I don't really know how those old phones work. Always had a cell phone myself. Can't remember a time before them—"

"I bet she's also the one who locked the door," Abby added.

"You think that *she* killed Tom?" Jeannie asked Abby, not quietly. "Then where is the rest of the needle?"

Abby pointed at the display case's closed window. The intern scrambled to stand in front of the window and flung her arms wide.

"Nothing to see here, folks…." Her voice betrayed her nervousness. "Just a giant python. He sure is handsome, isn't he?"

Although significantly shorter than Penny, Molly easily pulled the girl away with a single tug. Sure enough, inside Percy's case, lying atop of the grass was a syringe with a broken needle.

"When did she do that?" Jeannie asked.

"Probably when she was fake crying against the glass," Abby replied. She was a little amazed at how calm she sounded, but the moment felt remarkably natural—as if she was giving a presentation on her visitor studies' findings. She even had visuals, and a syringe in a snake pit was definitely more interesting than any Powerpoint slide she'd ever created.

Penny's eyes flashed. In place of the young, helpless, and naïve intern she'd pretended to be, Penny's scowling countenance now appeared dark and penetrating. Abby had no trouble believing that she was the murderer.

"You accuse me of murder? Me? You all…" She pointed around the room for emphasis. "You're the real murderers. Killing innocent animals for what? Fine dining? Clothing? Pills? You all disgust me." She spat at the floor. "And then you clomp through the zoo, as if your petty money would forgive your sins, like some sort of indulgence?" Penny shivered with apparent revulsion.

"Then why kill Tom?" Jeannie asked.

Abby suspected she knew what Penny would say.

"That rotten excuse for a man was the worst of you. He turned his back on the good fight, started sleeping with the enemy—cozying up to all of you, bestowing clemency if you would just support the zoo. Support him and his oversized salary and ego, really," Penny spoke with zeal, confirming Abby's hypothesis. The intern peered down at Flatterly's fallen body and kicked it hard. Everyone gasped. Hunter turned away, burying his face in his large hands.

"I guess you have pretty lax security around here," Molly said. "If no one even notices you walking around with syringes—"

Abby interrupted to explain. "Medical bracelet. Penny claims she's diabetic—"

"I am diabetic."

"So even better. Who's going to think twice about her carrying syringes or anything else medically related?"

"Don't diabetics use EpiPens these days?" Grover asked.

"For emergencies, sure, but not all of them use them daily," Molly the pharmacist said. "There are now several ways to treat juvenile diabetes. Syringes are less common, especially among younger patients, but far from unheard of."

"So he was killed with insulin?" Jeannie asked.

"That would take a long time. Much longer than the lights were out," Molly replied.

Abby remembered Penny's work experience. "She's worked at a vet's office."

"Ah," Molly jumped in, "so she probably used barbiturates or a similar drug—like those used in animal euthanasia."

"Yes," Abby said. She turned to Penny. "You were looking for a moment like this, weren't you? Perhaps you even messed with the generators, knowing about today's storm. Maybe the security locks too and the phone cord so we couldn't run or call for help in case your drug didn't work as fast as expected. Did you really think you could pull all of that off without anyone realizing what had happened?"

"And you all have been yammering around here without noticing for how long?" Penny said.

Touché, Abby thought.

"There you all are."

Everyone turned.

Trisha strutted into the room, covered in a bright yellow poncho and flanked by a host of matching staff members, some of whom carried extra ponchos and flashlights. And one was a security guard. The cavalry had arrived.

Within minutes, Penny was subdued, the authorities called, and everyone was escorted out by an army of zoo staff. Before Abby left, however, she paused in front of the python's tank and put her hand against the glass.

"This entire time, I was scared of you, when really I should have been worried about a seemingly innocent and sweet intern. I'm sorry. While I'm not quite ready to snuggle up with you yet, I do get that not every monster is what they seem," she said.

Percy flicked his tongue in what Abby decided was appreciation. He was majestic, really, with his brilliant sheen and strong, supple body. She could envision painting her kitchen the same shade as his lime-green scales. She blew a good-bye kiss at Percy. He rubbed up against the glass and hissed back.

Lauren R. Silberman is the author of *Wild Women of Maryland: Grit and Gumption in the Free State* (History Press, 2015), *Wicked Baltimore: Charm City Sin and Scandal* (History Press, 2011), and *The Jewish Community of Baltimore* (Arcadia Publishing, 2008). She serves as the deputy director of Historic London Town and Gardens in Edgewater, Maryland. She lives in Greenbelt, Maryland, with her husband and enjoys researching, drawing, and writing in her free time. Learn more about her at www.lsilberman.com.

FROZEN ASSETS

by KM Rockwood

"Hey. It's me. Marcos. Let me in."

Bert struggled out of the blanket, rag, and bubble-wrap cocoon he'd wound around himself and crawled over to the Styrofoam panel that served as the door of his makeshift shelter. He moved it aside.

Icy fingers of wind crept down the neck of Bert's jacket, through layers of hoodies and the unraveling wool sweater someone's grandma had knit years ago.

Marcos ducked in, a blanket wrapped around himself. Sharp pellets of snow swirled inside. He carried two plastic shopping bags, which he dumped into a cardboard box in the corner.

Marcos was just a kid, sixteen, maybe seventeen. A runaway. He was supposed to be at the shelter. What was he doing out in this weather? Not Bert's business. In his years on the street, he'd learned not to ask questions. The answers were likely to be lies.

"What you got there?" Bert asked instead as he fixed the door panel back in place.

"Some food. And a good blanket."

Ranger, Bert's big black dog, didn't rise from her pile of newspapers and rags in the corner, but she did sniff at the box.

Bert tried to peer into it himself. With the streetlights shining a soft glow through the walls, the inside of the shelter wasn't totally dark, but Bert pulled out his tiny flashlight and aimed its beam at what Marcos had brought.

"Bag lunches," Marcos said. "From that kid with the North Star jacket who hands them out."

Bert knew who he meant. A rich kid, snugly dressed with warm boots on his feet. Occasionally, he'd park his big, fancy SUV at a street corner and hand out the food from the back until he ran out, then climb back in and drive away. He said this was his "community service."

Whatever it was, the food was usually pretty okay and very welcome.

"I ate at the Rescue Mission," Marcos said. "Chili and corn bread. So you and Ranger can have most of this."

Bert opened the bags. Marcos had managed to snag five lunches.

"How'd you get so many?" he asked. Usually the rich kid was pretty uptight about giving more than one to a person.

Marcos shrugged. "There weren't a lot of people out. It's too cold and windy. And beginning to snow hard. I told him I knew a couple of other people who'd like them. They were the last ones he had, and he wanted to get going. So he asked me if I was sure I wasn't going to pig out on them all myself." Marcos laughed. "When I said no, he gave me the rest."

Each bag contained two bologna-and-cheese sandwiches, an orange, a baggie with celery and carrot sticks, some chips, a carton of milk, and a juice box.

"Good haul," Bert said, selecting one of the sandwiches. He stuffed half of it into his mouth and tossed the other half to Ranger, who caught it in the air and gulped it down. She looked longingly at the rest of the sandwiches. Bert took another one and gave it to her. "We can save the rest for morning. The chips, too. We may as well eat the fruit and veggies now. And drink the juice and milk. How much do you want?"

"Can't we save some of the milk cartons for the morning, too?" Marcos asked.

"Probably not. It's down in the twenties, and it's only gonna get worse. We got no way to keep them from freezing. So if we don't drink them now, they're likely to go to waste."

Marcos took a baggie, an orange, and one of the juice boxes. "You can have the rest."

"You sure?" Bert asked. But he was already gathering the oranges into his lap. He took off the socks that covered his hands, revealing grimy hands in fingerless gloves, picked up one of the oranges, and started peeling.

"I'm sure."

"Here you go, Ranger," Bert said a few minutes later, ripping open the top of a milk carton and holding it so she could lap it up.

He drained the remaining milk cartons himself and started on the celery and carrot sticks. Then he yanked his jacket closer around his shoulders and nodded at the blanket around Marcos's shoulders. "Looks like a nice warm one. Where'd you get it?"

"The Rescue Mission," Marcos said.

"You steal it?"

"Not really. They handed it to me. So they must have wanted me to have it."

Bert raised his bushy eyebrows under his watch cap. "I thought you was gonna stay at the Rescue Mission tonight. It's not a good night to be sleeping rough."

"*You're* sleeping rough," Marcos said.

Bert shook his head. "That's different. The Rescue Mission won't let me bring Ranger. Neither will the emergency shelter at the church. I can't leave her out alone. And I got this place fairly well insulated. Besides, I got a good warm jacket, even if it's a bit worn."

Marcos's jacket gave more of a nod to fashion than to warmth. It was short and it didn't even have a hood. He had good gloves, but when Bert had found him a few days ago, sitting on a curb and shivering, the kid hadn't even had a hat. Now he had a ripped wool stocking cap, but without a hood over it, it couldn't really be keeping his head warm.

"I got this blanket," Marcos said, "so I ought to be okay."

"Well, we're not likely to freeze to death in here, but we're not gonna be exactly toasty, either. Why'd you leave the Mission?"

Adjusting the blanket a bit tighter around himself, Marcos said, "I got spooked. They asked me for my name and how old I am."

"And you gave them your real name?" Bert was incredulous.

"Yeah. Stupid of me. But I'm still pretty new at this. I told them I'm seventeen."

"A minor. Not good. Did they say anything about it?"

"Not then. So I figured they was cool with it. But later, when I was getting a refill of my coffee, I heard one of the staff on the phone. I don't know who she was talking to, but she said my name."

The idea of a hot cup of coffee was too painful for Bert to contemplate right now. He forced the idea out of his mind. "Who do you think she was calling?"

"I dunno. But I bet my parents have me on every missing-person list they could find."

"So you gonna stay here?"

"Maybe. If you'll let me."

"Of course I'll let you. I just don't think you're gonna like it."

Marcos drained his juice box. "You know that Reverend Henry? Who's got the apartment attached to the old church?"

Bert snorted. "Yeah. He gives me the creeps."

"Well, he said he'd drive by the end of the alley on Ninth Street later tonight. If I changed my mind about staying at the Mission, I could go stay at his place. He's got room, and he's got food."

"Yeah. And booze. And maybe some of the evil weed. And who knows what else? But that stuff don't come free, y'know."

"He knows I don't got any money."

"Not money. But if he gives you stuff, you're gonna pay, one way or another."

"He says he's writing an article about homeless youth. For a magazine. He says he can interview me and use some stuff for his book."

Bert couldn't believe how gullible this kid was. "That's just a line he uses. He likes boys, if ya know what I mean. For sure you won't be the first one, and you prob'ly won't be the last."

Marcos's jaw tightened. "You don't know what you're talking about. I'm not dumb. I can tell the creeps from the good guys."

Bert shook his head. If the kid didn't want to hear the truth, wasn't much he could do about it.

Marcos crawled over to the entrance. "You mind if I take this new blanket with me? It's frigid out there, and I don't know how long it will be before he comes by."

"It's *your* blanket. You got it. You need anything else?"

"I don't think so." Marcos tucked his hands under his armpits. "I'm gonna go see if I can find him."

"Suit yourself." Bert reached over to move the door panel again.

"If he don't show up, can I come back here?"

"Of course. Any time."

After Marcos left, Bert set about blocking any place in the little cardboard and Styrofoam shelter where he could feel the breeze blowing through. It used to be a lot easier, when everybody read newspapers. But people read newspapers on their cell phones now, and they sure didn't get done with them and throw them away where anybody could retrieve them and use them for stuffing in holes in the walls. Bubble wrap didn't work nearly so well, but it's what he had.

Ranger crept over next to him. Lying on the layers of discarded packing materials that kept them off the frozen ground, she put her head in his lap and whined.

"I know, girl. It's cold. But at least we got a little supper. And I'm gonna wrap everything around the both of us. We'll be okay."

Not a night for the luxury of taking off his boots, Bert decided. He tucked the remaining food back in the cardboard box. He gathered the coverings around them as best he could and lay down himself.

Ranger stretched out next to him, her head lying next to his on the old cushion Bert used for a pillow. He flipped off the flashlight, snuggled up against her warm body, and dozed.

* * * *

"Bert! Let me in!"

Damn. The kid was back.

Bert crawled over and moved the door panel.

Marcos stumbled in and banged into one of the walls, followed by a flurry of snow.

After he replaced the door panel, Bert switched on the flashlight. He tried to rearrange the bubble wrap where Marcos had hit the wall. The kid lay down on the other side of Ranger.

"Hey, dude." Bert moved the narrow flashlight beam over to where Marcos lay. "We're gonna have to move some of them blankets. If you're gonna stay here, we got to get us all wrapped up together."

Marcos nodded, but he didn't move. Or say anything.

Looking closer, Bert saw that his shoulders were shaking. And his face was wet. Marcos made a choking sound.

"You crying, dude?" Bert asked. "What's up?"

Marcos sniffed loudly and wiped his heavy glove against his running nose. "You know what he wanted."

"Reverend Henry?"

Marcos nodded again.

"That son of bitch," Bert said.

"You ever hang around him?"

"Can't say as I ever have. I'm too old for his tastes. "

Marcos sniffled. "He unzipped his pants and wanted me to *touch* him."

"Yeah, well, I can't say as I'm all that surprised. A lot of that going around. Was this in his car or what?"

"No. Right out in the alley, behind the dumpster."

"A bit chilly for outdoor activity, I'd think. Make it all shrivel up."

"Yeah. He said he wanted me to warm it up. Make it all hard. He said then we could go back to his place and *do* something with it."

"So what'd you do?"

Marcos rolled over. "I shoved him away."

"I prob'ly would've done the same thing. Only I wouldn't have gone there in the first place."

"Why didn't you stop me?"

"What was I supposed to do, handcuff you to the wall? I tried to tell you, and you blew me off. So I figured maybe you didn't mind."

"How could I not mind?"

"You gonna live out on the streets, it's something you got to make up your mind about. Somebody makes you an offer, you gonna put out or not? And it ain't pretty women who're gonna be looking for it."

Marcos lifted his head and considered Bert with red and swollen eyes. "Would *you* put out?"

"Nah. Ain't my thing. But I don't put nobody down for doing whatever they need to do to get by. Things are tough all over."

"Oh."

"Why don't you just stay here for now? Things have a way of looking different in the morning. We'll get those blankets wrapped up around us and Ranger, and it won't be too bad."

"Okay. And Bert?"

"Yeah?"

"When I shoved him, Reverend Henry fell back. Hit his head on the dumpster."

"Was he hurt?"

"I dunno. He was just lying there when I left."

"Was he moving?"

"I didn't look to see."

"Any blood?"

"Maybe. There was a security light, but it was pretty dark."

Bert shivered. It was not a good night to leave a man lying out on the ground, maybe unconscious. Even a predator like Reverend Henry.

"Look," he said. "I'm gonna go out and check on the reverend. You and Ranger stay here and try to get some sleep."

"You think that's a good idea?"

"Going to check? I dunno. But I'm gonna go do it."

"Okay." Marcos sat up. He wiped his nose again and started rearranging the coverings. Ranger licked his face.

"Close the door panel good behind me."

The night air was so frigid it stung wherever it hit Bert's bare skin. The wind and snow inched down his collar. He shivered and hunched down in his old jacket. The snow spun in little eddies on the pavement, piling up for a few seconds in one place before the wind picked it up and churned it again. Bert hurried the few blocks to the alley at Ninth Street. It was an old industrial area, a few occupied warehouses and manufacturing plants among the abandoned buildings. But none of them was operating now. No traffic moved on the icy streets.

When he turned the corner onto Ninth Street, Bert saw a car idling at the end of the alley, parking lights on. He almost turned back. But the dome light was on, too. And the driver's door was open.

He crossed to the other side of the street, intending to walk by and see what he could without appearing too interested. He glanced as he passed, but the car blocked his view down the alley.

Hell. A car idling at this time of night by an alley—of course it would attract attention. Bert didn't need to look disinterested. He turned around and walked back to it.

Nothing moved but the swirling snow. Light from the interior of the car puddled on the asphalt and sidewalk. At the end of the alley, a security light cast another murky ring of light. In between were darkness and shadows.

Stepping around the car, Bert fumbled with his sock-covered hands to dig his flashlight out of his pocket.

Beyond the dumpster, Reverend Henry lay on his back, spread-eagled. His coat was unbuttoned, the flaps flung to either side. His pants were unzipped, the fly gaping. A dark pool of liquid—probably blood—surrounded his head. The flashlight beam glinted off the teeth in his open mouth, and he stared at the sky with sightless eyes.

Bert shivered again, but not from the bitter air. Without touching anything, and being especially careful not to step in the blood, Bert squatted down next to the body. He worked the sock off his hand and held his fingers under the reverend's nose. He didn't feel anything, but his hand was so numb he couldn't be sure there wasn't a breath. He stood up and went to the car.

A box of tissues lay on the passenger seat. Pulling the sock back over his hand, Bert leaned in and snatched a tissue out of the box. He squatted again next to the inert form and held the tissue by the nose and mouth.

Not even a flutter.

Reverend Henry was probably dead. If the fall and the blow to his head hadn't done it, the cold might have. And if he wasn't entirely dead now, he certainly would be before long if he continued to lie outside in this storm.

Could be any of them, lying unconscious in the arctic weather. Bert himself. Or Marcos. Or any of the street folks he knew from the soup kitchens. If they didn't help each other, who would?

But this wasn't somebody with no place to go and no one to care. This was Reverend Henry, who took advantage of kids who were already down on their luck. He didn't deserve the same consideration.

Hunched into his jacket, Bert stood over the reverend, trying to think. How many people had heard Reverend Henry asking Marcos to meet him? Even one could be too many.

The wind died down a bit. Snow began to settle on Reverend Henry, including his face. It didn't melt. In the lull, the car's engine purred softly. Bert got in the driver's seat and shut the door. The dome light went out.

In the army, Bert had driven some light trucks. But he no longer had a license, and he hadn't driven anything since. Still, it was a skill that, once learned, came back almost instinctively. He put the car in gear and let it coast slowly down the street, away from the alley.

Reverend Henry's church coordinated a ministry for the homeless, providing showers and donated clothes. They accepted mail and sometimes let people use the phone. The reverend lived in a small apartment behind it. It was only a few blocks farther.

With his sock-covered hands on the steering wheel, Bert guided the car toward the church, not stepping on the accelerator at all. When he got there, he steered toward the curb. The front tire bumped the curb, and the car stopped.

Bert removed the keys from the ignition and climbed out of the car, closing the door quietly behind him. He carried the keys to the door of the church office and pushed them through the mail slot. Then he trudged back toward his shelter.

The bitter wind picked up again. The snow changed to freezing rain, pelting him with crystals of ice. As he walked away from the parked car, the faint tire tracks the car had left on the street gradually faded, and by the time he got there, the ones in the alley were totally obliterated. He saw no sign of his footprints entering the alley. He slowed down, but he was careful that the footprints he left now didn't give any indication that he interrupted his journey.

When he got to the shelter, the only sound Bert heard was Ranger's snoring. He maneuvered the door panel out of the way and slipped inside, trying not to step on Marcos or the dog. He replaced the door and crept up next to Ranger, who stirred and made snorkeling noises.

He rubbed her ears. "Some watchdog you are, huh?"

Ranger's tail thumped once under the blankets, and she licked his cheek.

"Too nippy for kisses," Bert said, wiping his face with his sleeve. He tucked the covers over the three of them again and closed his eyes.

He slept fitfully, and it was still dark when he woke up. Someone was moving, so he fumbled for his flashlight and turned it on.

Ranger and Marcos were sitting together, sharing a sandwich.

Bert sat up.

"You want a sandwich?" Marcos said, holding one out toward him. "They're a little frozen, but you can still sink your teeth into them. I ate half of one, and gave Ranger the other half. I figure I can get a decent breakfast, though, so I'm gonna leave the rest for you."

"Where are you gonna get a good breakfast?" Bert asked.

"I'm going back to the Rescue Mission," Marcos said.

"The Rescue Mission? Aren't you afraid your parents are gonna find you if you go there?"

"Yeah, well, I've been thinking. Maybe it's time for me to go back home."

Bert, who didn't have a home to go back to, nodded. "Maybe that's a good idea. Why'd you leave, anyhow?"

Marcos shrugged. "One of those things. I wasn't supposed to take my dad's car. But I snuck out of the house one night and took it. And I wrecked it."

"Anybody hurt?"

"Nah. Just property damage."

"You left home over a *wrecked car*?" Bert said.

"Yeah, well, my folks were gonna be mad about it."

"Of course they were gonna be mad. You took their car when you wasn't supposed to and you wrecked it. But is that worth running away for? Wasn't that worse? They're probably worried sick."

Looking down at his hands, Marcos said, "I suppose."

Bert sat up straighter. "You got a warm place to stay, enough food to eat, and folks who care about you. A future. And you decided you'd rather stay out here on the street because they might be mad at you?"

Marcos shrugged again.

Bert peered around. Not much light was making its way through the walls of the structure. It was still night. "The Rescue Mission don't unlock the doors until seven."

"I can sneak in the back door."

"Sneak in the back door?"

"Yeah. That's how I got out. With the blanket. And I rigged the door so it wouldn't lock behind me."

"Isn't that an emergency exit? There should be an alarm on it."

"I rigged that, too. It won't sound. When they notice it, they'll just think it's broken."

"So." Bert tried to think. "They may not know you didn't spend the night there?"

"Not unless they made another bed check. I was way over in the corner, right next to the door where it's really dark. I waited until they turned off the lights and everybody was asleep. I heaped up the covers and the pillow so there was a lump in the bed."

"Well, then," Bert said. "Maybe you ought to take the blanket and see if you can't sneak back in before they notice an empty cot."

"I guess. Maybe I should leave the blanket for you?"

"No. Take the blanket back. If you can pull this off, you don't want them to be asking you what happened to the blanket."

Marcos sighed. "You're right. As usual. But I hate to leave you like this."

"Just go," Bert said. "Put this whole thing behind you. Forget it. Like a bad dream." He closed his eyes and could see Reverend Henry's body lying in the alley.

"Okay," Marcos said. "But I'll be by to see you sometime. Maybe bring some food and clothes."

Bert knew that would never happen, but he said, "You do that. But no hurry. Good-bye, now."

Marcos moved aside the door panel and slipped through. He looked back at Bert and Ranger. "Good-bye, dude. And thanks. For everything."

Bert fit the door panel back in place behind Marcos and lay down next to Ranger. He, too, would put this out of his mind. As soon as they ate up the food Marcos had brought, there would be no sign that the kid had ever been there, nothing to remember him by.

KM Rockwood writes stories that give voice to people living on the fringes of society. Their lives, their hopes and dreams, and the situations they encounter, often beyond their control, form the basis for the tales. A varied background, including work as a laborer in industrial settings, supervising an inmate work crew in a large state prison, and teaching special education courses in an alternative school and GED courses in county detention facilities, provide a background for KM's short stories and novels. *Abductions and Lies*, the sixth in the Jesse Damon Crime Novel Series, was recently released.

THE STORM IN THE TEACUP
by Linda Ensign

"I didn't know the genie living in the teapot was murderously insane," I said.

Tommy straightened in his chair and rubbed a hand across his jaw. It wasn't hard for me to concentrate on his face; it was hard not to. The timing of this conversation totally sucked, but timing wasn't really the issue. The issue was what I knew, and what I was going to tell him.

"But, Samantha, you knew—what's her name—was a genie?"

I nodded. "Felicity."

"Right, Felicity." Tommy frowned, the three lines between his eyebrows deepening into ruts. "How long did you know—Felicity—was in the teapot?"

Wrong question. Right question would have been *"what* did I know about Felicity?" But I wasn't going to correct him; I was going to answer his question. Starting at the beginning would give me time to decide what version of the truth would ease my conscience.

* * * *

I have a passion for all things tea, and I have since my mother gave me a chipped Royal Doulton teapot and two mismatched cups as a consolation prize for her not being home for my eighth birthday. Exactly one year later I bought my second teapot with the first money I earned hawking cotton candy on the Ocean City boardwalk, a chipped and paint-speckled brown beauty from the local thrift store. From there my obsession with the trappings of this civilized ritual grew. I hid my penchant for collecting crockery for years until the day Kate found me rooting around in her family's curbside donation for the missing lid to a discarded porcelain tea canister. She had said nothing when I rode my bicycle away from her house, my ears red with embarrassment. I stayed out of school the rest of the week, fearful of what she might say when we passed in the hallway. That Saturday a knock at the door revealed Kate, with a shy smile, holding out the lid to the canister. From that day she seemed to delight in each new find almost as much as I did. Our shared interests expanded to include bike rides to the lighthouse, campfires on the beach at midnight, and cheering for the local high school sports teams at all their games.

Everything started to change the year we both turned eighteen. My parents were killed in a traffic accident on Ocean City Gateway, and I felt drawn to the soft-spoken policeman whose dark-brown eyes appeared filled with sorrow when he broke the news to me. The policeman, Tommy, kept me updated about the city council's plans to install traffic lights at the busy crossroads. Kate was dismissive of him, but I was grateful for his thoughtfulness, and it took me many months to realize that Kate was the reason he kept coming around long after he had a valid reason to. As I watched their relationship bloom, I poured my feelings into building my stash of tea paraphernalia. When I received the inheritance from my late parents the year I turned twenty-one, I had enough inventory to open my store, The Teacup.

Although it was not quite prime real estate, being on a narrow street at the very southern tip of the boardwalk, it was a store nonetheless. I believed that amongst the throng of vacationers who swamped our small Maryland town in the summer months there would be at least a small percentage of tea lovers. These tea lovers would also appreciate the history and the craftsmanship of a teapot, especially one steeped in history. They would look past the patina and dents to the real beauty underneath. I didn't realize that what I termed a much-loved teapot wasn't the average seaside vacationer's cup of tea. There were the occasional connoisseurs who shared my passion, but the majority of the shoppers wanted something cheap, chintzy, and flower-patterned in which to brew their organic fair trade tea leaves.

Owning the shop often provided a convenient excuse for avoiding Kate and Tommy. The rapaciousness with which I had built my collection allowed my small store to fill my time, hiding my growing loneliness and disillusionment with life, love, and people in general.

Kate was so happy when she stopped by the shop the morning of my twenty-second birthday that she didn't realize I'd been crying. She prattled on about Tommy, and how she would be a mother to Tommy's son, Matthew, and kept holding her hand up to the light so that the diamond on her ring finger would sparkle. When she finally stopped dancing around the shop and asked about my silence, I feigned concern about an upcoming buying trip to England, a lie that led me down the path that sealed both our fates.

I simply had to escape; I needed time to think and to figure out a way to separate my pain from her happiness. I hoped that by the time I returned, the sight of my best friend marrying the man I'd been in love with for years would bring me only joy. That evening I booked a four-week trip to England, leaving the following day.

By the last week of my visit, I had already shipped two large boxes home and was nearly finished filling the third. Every day had brought more amazing finds, but the jumble sale at the small church in Langford, Nottinghamshire, held the largest collection of tea paraphernalia I had ever seen. There were at least two dozen tea sets in pristine condition, twenty-five silver teaspoons, and a teetering pile of ornate silver trays, all stacked haphazardly on the bare wooden tables amidst the mismatched glassware, worn children's books, knitted doilies, and stretched-out sweaters.

The thrill of the bargain hunt over the previous weeks had lifted my spirits, but after opening countless boxes and finding one exquisite flower-patterned tea set after another, my mood began to turn as gray and cold as the weather. I'm still not sure if it was the rain, the smell of dust, or the general feeling of malaise that permeated the air of the small church, but the realization dawned that my vast collection was destined for a similar fate.

I was about to give up and head for the station to begin my long train ride back to London when I walked over to a table wedged into the back corner and moved aside a stack of sweaters to reveal a tattered green silk box that had been hidden from view. I ran my fingers along the worn edges of the green box, feeling the nub of the silk threads. A strange tingling sensation started in my fingers, traveled through my wrists, lifted the hairs on my arms, and settled at the back of my neck. The lid slid off to reveal a battered copper teapot nestling in a bed of what looked like pencil shavings, but smelled like old tea leaves. The teapot lifted easily out of the box, although some of the packaging clung to it and had to be brushed off.

The teapot felt heavier than it looked. I held the lid down with one hand, while I turned it over to check the markings on the bottom. It was too dark in the corner of the church, and I moved toward the stained-glass mullion windows to my left to take advantage of the light struggling through them.

"What are you doing?"

If I hadn't been holding on to the teapot with both hands, I would have dropped it. I'd been so absorbed that I hadn't noticed anyone else in the room, let alone the tall redhead who stood in front of me and blocked what little light there was.

"How much?" I asked, instead of explaining that I had been trying to check the manufacturer's mark.

She studied me thoughtfully, and then the teapot. "A lot more than you think."

"You have no idea how much I'm willing to pay." I waited for her to move out of my way, but she stayed where she was, staring at the teapot.

"I hope you do." She finally looked up at me, her expression unreadable.

I was about to ask what she meant when she pivoted on one heel and hurried toward the church exit. I waited until the door closed behind her before I took the teapot back to the table and returned it to the box. I carried the box over to the small gray-haired man sitting at the high table near the entrance.

"How much?" I placed the box on the table.

"One hundred and four pounds." He put his hand protectively on top of the tattered green lid.

I removed my purse from my jacket pocket and counted the colorful bills. I didn't have enough cash.

He tapped his long, scraggly fingernails on the green silk.

I was tempted to grab the box and make a run for it, but I handed him my credit card instead.

"What's this?" He peered at both sides of the card, and then stared at me with suspicion.

"My credit card."

"We don't take credit cards." He handed it back to me.

"I only have seventy-five pounds." I bit down on the sudden and unexpected surge of anger that raced through me.

"It's from the Turkish Ottoman era." He crossed his arms.

"There's a cash machine in town," someone behind me said before breaking into a coughing fit, her hot breath ruffling the hair on the back of my neck.

I didn't turn to see who the owner of this helpful information was. The old man held up his index finger as he reached into the pocket of his cardigan and removed a small mobile phone. He turned away, and I could not hear his muted conversation.

"Seventy-five will do." He turned back to me and slid his phone back into his pocket.

I threw the bills down on the table and scurried out into the churchyard, the green box clutched in both hands. I should have realized then that my overreaction had something to do with the teapot, but at the time I attributed it to homesickness.

* * * *

"So you've known about Felicity since you went to England? For *over a year*?"

The harsh edge in Tommy's voice brought me back to the present. He had been doodling on the yellow notepad on the table between us—dollar signs, teapots, daggers, and hearts. Hearts?

"I didn't say that," I said, instead of asking him why he was drawing hearts. Why does anyone draw hearts?

He drew another ornate dagger. "When did you find out there was a genie inside?"

I looked over his shoulder at the photos of the missing, as well as wanted murderers, bank robbers, and petty thieves that were tacked to the police station's notice board.

"Sam?" His voice jogged me out of my reverie.

"Yes?"

"Tell me when you first found out about the genie."

"The middle of May, right after I returned from England." How much of what we realize we now know have we always known, but simply ignored for one reason or another?

"How?" He added the final artery to the small heart at the bottom of the page before he looked up at me.

Some things are forever etched in my memory. May fifteenth was one of them.

* * * *

I brought the copper teapot back in my checked luggage, the green silk box wrapped in my best wool sweater and layers of wrinkled underwear. The first of my shipped boxes had already arrived and I dallied over its unpacking, letting the anticipation of my most prized purchase, the battered copper teapot, wait until last. I cleared a space for it in the front window, where the sliver of morning sun that reached my store above the roofs of the adjoining buildings would find it.

I gently opened the lid of the box and slid the teapot out of its unusual packaging. I held it up to the morning sunlight, which shimmered and glided over the contours of the vessel, making it glow in my hands. I looked at it from all sides, trying to figure out what about it drew me to it so strongly. It was shaped nothing like a modern teapot, but had a long, thin spout, an equally thin handle, an hourglass-shaped belly, narrow shoulders, and a hinged lid. There were at least four large dents in the surface of the teapot, and traces of oxidization were evident in the hinges, joins, and flanges. But then, I had bought it for its patina and its aura, not its utility or beauty. I rubbed my fingers along the surface of the teapot, savoring its warmth and texture.

I tilted it toward the sunlight to inspect the markings underneath.

"What the bloody hell?"

I glanced up in surprise. There was no one else in the store. Had I now resorted to talking to myself out loud? I turned the teapot back upright and lifted the lid. A wave of nausea washed over me, accompanied by a buzzing in my ears. I sat down on the floor, closing my eyes to stop from falling over. The nausea slowly ebbed, but the buzzing morphed to an incessant ringing sound.

I soon realized the ringing wasn't in my ears, but emanated from my cell phone. I searched the area around me and spotted it on the windowsill next to the teapot. I stumbled to my feet, groggy and disoriented, and answered it. It was Kate, calling to welcome me home and invite me to Matthew's sixth birthday party. She babbled on, so excited that Tommy had finally agreed to let her organize his son's party that her voice squeaked. I had the unpleasant thought that if she were a mouse I would drown her in the nearest teacup. Kate was like a cancer eating away at my own happiness. I quickly finished the call and sat down on the windowsill, wondering where this surge of animosity had come from. She was my friend, my best friend. I had been jealous of her, annoyed with her, irritated by her, and disappointed in her, but I had never hated her. I picked up the teapot and stared at its reflective surface, as if searching for the answer.

"You won't find the answer there," the voice said. Strange. I could almost believe the voice was coming from the teapot.

"Where are the answers then?" I lifted the teapot lid and peered inside. It was empty. What had I expected?

"You can only see me when I want you to." It was a woman's voice, but the age was hard to determine.

With my heart beating fast, I said, "Well, I want to see you, whoever you are." I did not like my petulant tone.

"My name is Felicity." Now she sounded annoyed.

"Okay, Felicity. Now, where *are* you?"

"In the teapot, of course—where *else* would I be?"

"Then let me see you." I turned the teapot to the light but most of its interior was still shadowed.

The laughter that filled the store made my skin crawl. I only just calmed the urge to throw the teapot against the nearest wall. Instead, I stored it under the front desk. It was three weeks before I heard from Felicity again. Long enough to think I had imagined the whole episode.

* * * *

"You were acting strangely when you returned from England. I should have realized something was wrong." Tommy's voice was soft, edged with something that sounded like regret.

"Why?" Was it regret for not intervening then? Intervention would have been futile. The final act had already been scripted, the stage designed, the actors cast. Even if nothing else had happened that summer, that first wish would have led us here.

"Perhaps if I—" His brows drew together as he pondered what he would have done, what he could have done, what he probably should have done.

I shook my head.

"I'm sorry—I interrupted you." He gestured for me to continue and dropped his gaze to his notepad, starting to draw a web in the top left corner.

I stared at his hands. What type of spider would inhabit the web he was so carefully constructing? Hopefully not a black widow.

* * * *

Even before my trip to England I had seen that the downturn in the economy was catching up with our insulated seaside community. Across the street the only stores also gearing up for the tourist season were the Oceanside Gallery, Kermit's Kones, and Bikini Beach Babes, with its eclectic collection of popular summer staples, including condoms and after-sun soother. On my side of the street, only Carmichaels Candy remained, although there were rumors that the youngest Carmichael was considering selling and moving to Oahu.

I was almost pleased when Rat's Tat Parlor opened across the road early that spring, although the graphics plastered in its front windows, and the innuendos in its signage, were widely interpreted as the writing on the wall for the family-friendly inclusivity of our small section of the boardwalk. Rat himself was a decent guy, soft spoken and friendly, and it turned out that the majority of his clients were as well. They just weren't the kind of people remotely interested in bone-china teapots and antique silver teaspoons.

And a formerly vacant store next to mine was getting a new tenant. I was too busy feeling maudlin to pay attention to the equipment being delivered, and I felt only a mild annoyance at finding the new owner's large black SUV parked in my spot when I returned from shopping trips or visits to the lighthouse. Then a flyer taped to *my* store window, garish and grammatically incorrect, informing me that Caraway Street was now the proud home to the Fun Stuff Arcade, started the rumblings of dissent in my belly.

Within a week of the game arcade opening on Memorial Day weekend, my initial annoyance had turned into intense aggravation. The loud music seeped through walls that were thinner than they appeared. The vibrations from the thumping music caused my most delicate teacups to rattle in their saucers. I had to close my bedroom windows at night and miss the fresh ocean air because the arcade visitors stood outside my store and smoked. I reported the sound violations and Garry was forced to lower the volume of the music to an acceptable level, but the vibrations continued.

Garry. The owner of the arcade was overbearing, acrimonious, and spiteful. In early June, I finally ventured into the arcade to investigate the vibrations, and he was overly friendly—obsequious even, revealing all his teeth in his welcoming smile. The split-second after I introduced myself as the owner of The Teacup, he puffed out his chest and sneered at me down his pitted, bulbous nose.

"What do you want?" He blew the smoke from his cigar straight into my face.

I stared at him. "We've never been formally introduced, I'm—"

"Yeah, I know," he spat out, then turned on his heel and walked away.

I stared at his retreating back, wiped my face with my sleeve, and then wedged my hands into the arms of my sweater. I walked around the arcade, looking at all the games, and trying to avoid being bumped into, knocked over, or elbowed by the players and onlookers. As I reached the wall adjoining my store, I realized what was causing the vibrations.

The machines weren't just near the wall but pushed right up against it. Not only that, but the wiring for all the machines in the vicinity were routed behind an asbestos duct directly against the wall they shared with The Teacup. If a fire started in this area, it could engulf my store along with the arcade. When I turned from examining the wall I saw Garry glaring at me from five feet away.

Although I didn't look behind me, I knew he followed me to the exit. While Garry may have suspected me of reporting the noise, if any fire code violations were reported he would immediately know I was the whistleblower. I had no doubt that finding his truck in my parking spot, his cigar butts in my flower boxes, and dog (or human) pee on my front door would seem like a walk in the park compared to what he was capable of if he became really angry. I rubbed my temples, trying to ease away the tension that merely thinking about him brought on.

I retreated to the sanctity of my own store and made myself a nice pot of Earl Grey tea from Harrods. There were over five hundred ordinances for local businesses, and halfway through reading them, I developed a headache. The vibrations in the floor and walls, the ambient noise, and the waves of animosity rolling off Garry were detrimental to my mental and physical health. I couldn't swear to it now, but I think I was looking down at the copper teapot under the counter when I said out loud, "I wish he would just go poof and vanish into thin air."

One hour later, I accepted Tommy's invitation to join him and Matthew for double-scoop waffle cones at Kermit's Kones. Kate was, he reported, being fitted for her wedding dress and he was more than happy to be excluded. I wasn't sure if I was or not, and was pondering my split feelings over a pistachio-chocolate concoction when I smelled smoke and saw arcade visitors running from the building. Minutes later we heard the sirens and watched as the brave men of the volunteer fire department first battled the roaring blaze and then ordered everyone to retreat to a safe distance on the beach. Tommy rushed to assist the firefighters, and Matthew and I walked over to the beach and watched from a safe distance. I found myself curiously calm, even though I knew full well that my own shop could be damaged or destroyed in the conflagration. I was considering walking back to the confectionary and ordering a strawberry-vanilla cone when the arcade exploded, sending a fiery plume high into the night sky and raining hot ash down on the startled crowd.

It took a week for the heat in the building to dissipate, and Garry's remains were never found. I declined Kate's offer to stay with her and Tommy and chose instead to stay at a hotel until the fire department declared my store safe. I found my shop remarkably unscathed, although my small apartment above The Teacup had to be thoroughly cleaned as soot and smoke had seeped in through the partly opened windows.

I polished the copper teapot and placed it on a small footstool in my front window so that it was always within view. If the explosion had claimed anyone else I would have melted it down and forged it into a plaque in remembrance, but I couldn't feel any remorse for the demise of the owner of the game arcade.

* * * *

"Why would you think that Garry's murder has anything to do with you?" Tommy paused in mid doodle and looked up at me.

"You're calling it murder?"

"Foul play is suspected." Tommy looked down at his desk. He seemed to realize that he had been filling the notepad with doodles, and ripped off the sheet with a frown.

"Why?"

"Stores don't explode on their own." His frown deepened as he looked up at me.

I felt an overwhelming urge to reach out and smooth the lines in his forehead with my forefinger. I folded my hands in my lap instead. "Who do you suspect?"

"You know I can't discuss a case with you." He drew a heart in each corner of the new page.

"Can't or won't?"

He put down his pen and sat back in his chair, folding his arms. "Why would you even think his murder is your fault?"

"I wished him gone." It was the most honest thing I had said that day. As I'd discovered, voicing specific wishes wasn't even required, only the mere inference of a desire. Felicity knew my thoughts.

"You were with Matthew and me when the fire started." He unfolded his arms and studied his hands, then leaned forward on the desk again.

"I know."

"You said you wished him gone." He ripped off the sheet of the note pad and wrote *WISHES* on the top of a new one.

I nodded.

"That is not the same as wishing him dead." He underlined the word three times and sat up straighter in his seat. "Which brings me back to my original question. Why do you think Felicity was murderously insane and why did you wait until now to tell me about this?"

"That's two questions," I said. He closed his eyes briefly, and when he opened them I saw that the mask of his profession had slipped into place.

* * * *

Hordes of tourists were attracted to the burnt-out shell of the game arcade, perhaps in the hope of finding some fragment of bone. Often they wandered into my store. The doorbell chimed so frequently that I considered removing it. I moved the more expensive Wedgewood and Royal Doulton tea sets to the mahogany display case after yet another oversized beach bag had knocked over and chipped a teacup. While it is perfectly acceptable to have a "nice to look at, nice to hold, if you break it, consider it sold" sign prominently displayed, it's not well received when you request the klutz who broke the teacup to ante up for the whole set, despite its modest hundred-dollar price tag. I removed the sign and my efforts at exchanging inane pleasantries led to a modest increase in sales.

The frequent customers, even if they didn't become buyers, helped to take my mind off the looming death of my romantic dreams—Kate and Tommy's wedding. But every upside has its downside, and this silver lining was indeed tarnished. By the end of July, I had suffered five broken teapots and at least a thousand dollars in losses due to shoplifting.

Garry's heirs were suing our landlord, hoping to prove that some fault in the building's wiring had caused the fire. I had grown tired of telling both sets of lawyers that there was nothing I could tell them that would be of any use, and the thought that I might be called to testify unsettled me. One particular day started with the appearance in my email inbox of an animated male stripper inviting me to Kate's bachelorette party. Her maid of honor, a position she had not offered to me, had chosen to hold the festivities in a local strip joint on the edge of town. I had deleted my third inflammatory response when my phone rang. It was the landlord telling me that he was raising the rent because, as he put it, commercial property was a large liability.

I'd barely set the phone back down when the front door to the shop was thrust open, and the smell of coconut oil oozed in. A scantily dressed woman entered the store, her oversized orange beach bag swaying perilously close to the teacups on the display table. I watched her in the wall-mounted mirrors as she browsed around the store, picking up one item, and then another. She didn't turn the items over to look for prices, nor did she stop at any one item for longer than a second, but somehow she managed to flash the large diamond on her ring finger with every movement. I worked hard to unclench my jaw as she approached the counter.

She looked over her sunglasses, seeming to notice me for the first time and smiled, revealing perfect teeth that matched the large white sunhat shielding her eyes. Long blond hair curled over her tanned bronze shoulders. A bright green bikini top peaked through her white crocheted top.

"Can I help you?" My voice sounded polite despite the spark of homicidal rage I felt ignite in my soul.

"You're the owner of this quaint little shoppie?" She waved her hand in a circle, the diamond on her finger winking at me in the overhead lights.

"Yes, I am the owner of The Teacup." I straightened my shoulders; the honey in her voice was not going to catch this fly. A movement behind her caught my eye. The teacups on the display table were hovering two inches above their saucers as if lifted by an invisible hand.

The woman rummaged around in her beach bag with one hand, keeping her eyes on me. The teacups moved counter-clockwise three inches above the table. I felt my heart beating faster. The invisible eddy that held the teacups in its grip gained speed.

Finally she pulled a piece of white paper from her bag. The teacups blurred with the speed of the eddy. She unfolded the paper with a flick of her wrist and glanced down at it. "Samantha Owens?"

"Yes?"

"You've been served." Her smile broadened as she slapped the paper down on the counter.

I should have known. The lawsuit. I didn't know which side had sent her, but it didn't matter. The spark of rage ignited a roaring fire of hatred toward the perfect woman standing before me, and I wished I could wipe that smile off her face.

The teacups stopped moving and dropped onto their saucers with a crash.

"What was that?" She spun around.

The display table wobbled, lifted three inches off the ground, and then slowly fell over. The blue floral teacups and saucers, bright blue miniature milk jug, and pale blue polka-dot sugar bowl slid off and shattered on the concrete floor. The lid of the sugar bowl rolled to within a foot of where she stood and stopped, spinning slowly on its pointed lid like a top.

She stared down at the lid, her mouth a perfect O. "That wasn't me."

"It could have been your beach bag." I crossed my arms and pretended to be angry. I wasn't; the blue polka-dot set had been my least favorite purchase this year.

She shook her head, her eyes wide, and hugged her beach bag tightly. As the lid finally came to a rest she moved quickly to the door, circling as far as she could around the broken crockery and upended table. The door shuddered in its frame as she yanked it open and rushed outside.

"Did you see the look on her face?" Felicity's laughter echoed around the shop.

"That little incident cost me a couple hundred." I tried to hide my amusement, but a small giggle escaped, releasing some of the tension inside.

"Good riddance—you know you hated that tea set. And talking of a little, I think she peed herself. Just a little." Her laughter filled the air again, and this time I joined her.

A sudden screech of tires outside jolted me out of my amusement. A split second later a car door banged, and I ran to the store window. The blonde was lying spread-eagled in the road, blood soaking into her white crocheted top. Her head was obscured under the front left wheel of a delivery truck.

"I guess that wiped the smile off her face," Felicity said, with a chuckle from somewhere behind my left shoulder.

My laughter died as the fire of anger inside me was extinguished in an icy blast of fear.

* * * *

"So you're saying that Felicity caused the accident." Tommy was doodling again, a bigger spider this time, one with dozens of eyes.

"If she could move things and make the display table fall over, I have no doubt she caused the delivery van brakes to fail."

"Why would she have wanted to murder the process server?"

I studied the crown of his head, slightly off center, sprinkled with gray, and felt an urge to admit that it was because *I had wished the woman dead.* I clenched my hands together and counted to ten before answering him. "I have no idea. I told you, she was insane."

"*Murderously insane* were your words."

"Yes."

Tommy frowned. "That is two deaths she's responsible for. Tell me," he said, drawing dagger-shaped legs on the spider, "who else?"

I shook my head. *If only I could, Tommy, if only I could.* A version of the truth would have to suffice though.

* * * *

"Hey, you."

I looked up as the newly reattached doorbell dinged. It was Kate. I hadn't seen her since her bachelorette party the previous month and her appearance shocked me. She had lost so much weight she looked skeletal. The whites of her eyes were yellow, and her once luxurious black hair was peeking out in wisps from a cheerful blue and yellow scarf. I hurried to her and we hugged like the friends we used to be in high school, before Thomas Robert Anderson came into our lives and turned them upside down.

"I have some Bahrain green tea already brewed." I took her hand, feeling the papery thinness of her skin and the brittleness of the bones beneath.

"I probably couldn't keep it down," she said. A spark of her spirit peeked through her smile but was quickly dimmed. "But I'll watch you drink it. We need to talk."

"Hold on," I said and went to lock the front door and turn the *open* sign to *closed.* Since the process server's accident, even more gawkers thronged the street outside. We walked to the small tearoom at the rear of the store and settled in our seats.

"Sam, will you promise me something?" Her eyes were serious when I finally gathered enough courage to meet them.

"I'll try." I could be nothing but honest with her now. I poured myself a cup of tea, trying to keep my hands steady.

"It depends, right?" A brief smile transformed her death mask to a faded facsimile of the joyous and vibrant person she once was.

"It depends," I agreed.

"It's about Tommy," she said.

My eyes fell. Oh God no, Kate. *You don't know how I still feel about him; please don't make me promise to take care of him.* I felt the coolness of her hand on mine and looked up again.

"I know you love him, Sam." Her eyes were full of compassion.

The tea soured in my belly. I slowly put the teacup down in the saucer and folded my hands in my lap. I could feel the heat rising in my face.

"You are both like family to me," I said.

"I know. We love you too," Kate answered.

I lifted the teacup and forced down another sip of tea. Love has different meanings, different shades, different perspectives, and different depths. It is also the flip side of hate. I once loved Kate like a sister, but I had loved Tommy more. Witnessing their love grow had twisted and churned that sisterly love, pushing it down into the blackness at the pit of my soul.

"What do you need?" I asked.

Kate closed her eyes. I watched her blue-veined lids tremble and the irises move behind them. I poured myself another cup of tea and waited.

"Will you help him with my funeral arrangements?" she finally said.

"You're not—"

"I am." Kate opened her eyes and straightened her shoulders. "We all go eventually. It's my time."

No, Kate, it was not your time. You were meant to have a long and fruitful life with Tommy. I was meant to watch and wane.

* * * *

"Here."

I looked at the tissue Tommy was holding out to me. I dabbed at the wetness on my cheeks. What was I supposed to tell him?

"You wished for her to live?" His voice broke on the last word.

"Maybe if I had, she'd still be here." I felt the anger in my voice and regretted it slightly when I saw him recoil a little.

"What did you wish for then, Sam?" He was drawing daggers on the paper. The daggers were all protruding out of the large heart in the center.

I wondered if he could read my mind and was just toying with me, and I felt a surge of anger. "It's not like Felicity said, 'I'm a genie. You have three wishes.' And I ticked them off my fingers as I made them. If she had, I would have wished for peace, wealth, and happiness." I felt the truth inch its way to the surface.

Tommy put down his pen and tore the sheet of paper off the pad. He looked up at me, his eyes serious. "Kate had cancer, Sam. No one would wish that on anyone else."

I didn't answer.

"Where do you think Felicity is now?" He tore the piece of paper into strips.

"It doesn't matter anymore." I picked up the strips of paper and started forming them into flowers.

"She destroyed your store. How do you know she won't come after you, or me, now?" A hard edge entered his voice.

I laid the paper flowers in a row on his desk. "Because she's gone."

"How do you know that?" He picked up a flower and pulled it apart.

"She got what she wanted." Had he believed me or was he just humoring me? I avoided his eyes.

"She destroyed The Teacup."

"Yes."

He sighed and leaned back in his chair, his hands behind his head. I picked up the flowers and threw them toward the trash can in the corner of his office. They landed with remarkable accuracy. The clock above the filing cabinet ticked loudly in the silence. I willed myself not to think, not to ponder, not to wish.

Tommy ran his hands through his hair and sat forward. "Peace, wealth, and happiness, right?"

"Yes." My voice cracked on the truth of it. The words trembled, sounding to my ears like a plea for forgiveness.

"I know you have an alibi for the night it all happened, and I can't imagine you'd do that to your own store, but I have to file the report. It's already weeks late. I was hoping you might remember something, but I can't very well write that a genie destroyed your store."

"I wish I could be more helpful, but Felicity's the only one I can think of." I tried not to shiver when I said *wish*.

"That's okay, you've been very helpful. I'll see you when I get home." His voice was soft, and his smile slow, but genuine.

* * * *

When I returned to the small cottage we now share, I made a pot of Bahrain tea in my new porcelain teapot and took my cup outside to sit on the deck overlooking the ocean. A slight breeze stirred the sea grass and set the copper wind chimes attached to the overhang to singing. I sipped my tea and closed my eyes, the melody of the chimes a contradiction to the cacophony of the memory of the storm in The Teacup that played in an endless loop in my mind.

The morning we buried Kate, I'd returned to my small apartment above the shop and buried myself under my blankets. The tears would not stop, and my chest hurt so much I thought my heart would explode with grief. I eventually fell into an exhausted sleep but woke with a start just after midnight. My thought on waking was that I had to destroy the teapot.

I rushed downstairs, and as I reached the bottom step, the mahogany display cases starting tipping slowly over, their doors opening, and teapots, teacups, and saucers sliding off onto the floor. Then the display tables all tipped over, sending their wares crashing to the floor. Teaspoons danced in the overhead light before volleying into mirrors. Doilies danced and whirled, joining the floral teapots, cups, and saucers as they careened off the walls, smashing every mirror in the store. Plastic wrap writhed off cardboard boxes of tea, joining the teabags and loose tea leaves in their undulating dance around the solitary item in the eye of the storm—the copper teapot.

Felicity is inside me now. I can't remember if she always was, or if she really lived in the teapot before I met her. Did she enter me the night her power wrecked The Teacup or was it before?

It doesn't really matter anymore. The teapot was melted down and transformed into a beautiful set of wind chimes.

I now have unlimited wishes.

Linda Ensign is busy shopping her contemporary fantasy novel and polishing the first in her mystery series. She manages MostlyMystery.com, a blog that features glimpses inside the mostly sane world of mystery writing, and is the editor of the *E-Nunciator*, official newsletter of the Virginia Writers Club. She is a member of Sisters in Crime, as well as its Chessie Chapter, and is president of the Northern Virginia Writers Club. Linda is the founder of Yellow Hare Inc., a technology company specializing in developing eLearning games and apps. This is her first published short story. Her website is www.LindaEnsign.com.

STORMY, WITH A CHANCE OF MURDER

by Alan Orloff

Chief Meteorologist Mike Morgan smoothed his tie and stepped in front of the green screen. As Channel Six's top weather guy, he was the news team's point man on those half-dozen occasions every year—blizzards, hurricanes, ice storms—when the weather became the top story.

Tonight's big weather story: a violent series of thunderstorms.

Mike plastered a small smile on his face, careful not to look too happy; he wasn't delivering welcome news, and maintaining an appropriate demeanor was part of the gig. "Good evening, everyone. I hope you've purchased your bread and milk and charged your batteries. Looks like we're in for some very severe weather for the next eight to twelve hours." He gestured at the blank screen behind him, one eye on the monitor where he could see his hand superimposed upon an actual map.

A graphic materialized on the monitor, complete with menacing title: *MegaStorm*. Mike had lobbied hard for *Stormpocalypse*, but he'd ceded to the objections of his staff and settled for the slightly less sensational and easier to pronounce *MegaStorm*. Either way, Mike knew the marketing guys would eat it up.

"Let's look at the radar. As you can see, we have a huge front coming in from the west, which will drench us with up to two inches of rain per hour…"

With visibility approaching zero.

"…leading, in turn, to some serious local flooding…"

Obliterating any tell-tale footprints.

"…along with the high probability of a vicious electrical storm, the likes of which we've rarely seen."

Enough to keep most people—and their prying eyes—off the streets.

"Expect widespread power outages and other service disruptions throughout the entire viewing area, possibly lasting for several days."

Keeping police departments very busy.

For the next five minutes, Mike detailed his forecast, repeatedly invoking the hallowed name of Doppler and tossing around terms like *derecho* and *squall lines* and *supercells*, warning his viewers to take this one seriously. When he finished, he mopped his brow and threw an *I'm-not-kidding-this-storm-is-the-real-deal* look at the camera, accompanied by a breathless, "More details at eleven. Now, back to you, Rick."

"Thanks, Meteorologist Mike. I'm sure all our listeners will heed your warning about the, uh, *MegaStorm* and take appropriate precautions." Rick cleared his throat and lowered his voice. "And now, in other news…"

No longer on camera, Mike unclipped the mic from his shirt, flashed a thumbs-up to the anchors, and waited by the studio door until they broke for commercial. When they did, he slipped out and headed to his office.

He had a murder to commit.

* * * *

Murder was such an ugly word. He hoped his confrontation wouldn't lead to that ultimate solution, but he wanted to be ready for whatever might be required. The perfect window of opportunity had opened, and Mike was planning to shimmy right through it.

He had almost five hours before he went on again during the eleven p.m. newscast. Ordinarily, he'd be manning the radar and interpreting the computer models and monitoring the National Weather Service alerts, but he'd trained his staff well. They could do without him for a little while. If need be, his number-one assistant, Amber, could go on-air with a weather bulletin. Hell, her Q rating was almost as high as his. Of course, she was a thirty-year-old stunner, which didn't hurt her popularity one bit. When he poked his head into the staff bullpen to announce he'd be going outside to check on the latest conditions, they barely glanced up from their computers.

Mike grabbed a dark-blue slicker from the freestanding coat rack near the door, and left without another word. Walked down the hall with purpose—just another harried newsman with someplace important to go. Little did they know.

Big Dan Donovan, news director, barreled around the corner, almost plowing into Mike. "Hey there, Mike. Where's the fire?" He raised an eyebrow when he spotted the slicker in Mike's hand. "Oh, out to get a firsthand forecast? Brave the elements? Nice. I like to see my people get personally involved."

"Right, right. Just going outside to peek on things. Won't be going far, not with this storm."

"I hope you're on the money about this one," Big Dan said, scowl gaining traction on his doughy face. "And *MegaStorm*? Don't you think that's a bit much? I believe Casper Wells described it as just a bad summer thunderstorm."

"Don't worry. We're in for a violent one, that's for sure. I'd stake my reputation on it."

Big Dan's scowl deepened. "The last time you screwed up we heard about it big-time from our viewers. You've been on an unlucky streak, I'm afraid. Too many more misses and…" He let it hang.

"Trust me, boss. Trust me."

Big Dan glared at him, then bustled off.

Mike *had* been on a bad streak, a really bad streak, and he'd been getting an earful about it. From the viewers, on local talk radio, even from that jerkwad Casper Wells, the weather guy on Channel Two. Unfortunately, the run of bad luck had extended beyond his weather forecasts. His house needed a new roof, he'd broken his wife's big toe when he accidentally stepped on it, and a friend's restaurant he'd invested in had gone belly-up. Not to mention…

He shook it off. He shook it all off. His luck was about to change. He could feel it in his bones, just as he could feel the fury of the gathering *MegaStorm*.

Mike strode down the main hall past the cafeteria, then turned left toward the side entrance, pausing long enough to don his slicker before easing through the door out to the weather patio where they sometimes shot storm footage and forecasts. He paused for a moment, glanced around to make sure none of his weather grunts happened to be outside experiencing the deluge firsthand, then clanged through the gate separating the patio from the parking lot.

He hustled to his car, parked nose out on the far end of the lot behind one of the station's news vans. When he finally shut the door behind him, he exhaled, allowing a small smile—this one real—to emerge. *Phase one, successful.*

Mike paused a moment to take inventory. Under the passenger seat he'd hidden a hunting knife, one he'd purchased at a yard sale five years before while he was on vacation at the beach. Untraceable. He also had a dorky pair of thin rubber rain boots, the kind you could buy at any Walmart, Target, or Sears in the Western Hemisphere. Also untraceable.

Mike started the car, jammed it into *drive*, and sped off, windshield wipers going full throttle. He forded a giant puddle by the parking lot's entrance and turned left onto the main drag. Traffic was almost nonexistent, a far cry from the usual evening crush of commuters. Thanks to the frenzy-fomenting media—himself included—most rational people were too scared to venture outside, content to ride out the treacherous storm in the comfort of their homes.

Perfect.

Mike didn't have far to travel. Heather Prine, his hot little flame, lived about fifteen minutes away. A recent college graduate, she'd started at Channel Six as a weather department gofer, and they'd hit it off immediately. Theirs had been a torrid affair; Heather once said she'd always had a thing for weathermen. Usually the girls went for the news anchors or the sports guys, so Mike was proud of his conquest... if a little perplexed.

About three weeks ago it had all gone to crap. Overnight, Heather had become an *ex*-fling and wannabe blackmailer. She'd quit her job, then cut him off and threatened to go public with their affair unless he forked over some cash. Even if he wanted to pay her off, she'd asked for more money than he could scratch together in a dozen years, especially without access to his wife's bulging trust fund.

Such an exposé would ruin his marriage. His career. His life.

He needed to talk some sense into Heather, and he was prepared to be as persuasive as necessary.

Mike leaned forward, trying to glimpse the road ahead of him, headlights struggling against the darkness. The rain poured down in sheets, and an eighteen-wheeler could have been parked ten yards in front of him and he wouldn't have seen it.

Despite conditions that called for the utmost in concentration, Mike's thoughts kept drifting back to Heather. Though twice her age, he still felt they had a special connection. She had a unique way of looking at the world, and she brought out the playfulness in his soul, much more than his staid wife ever did. He refused to believe that the only reason Heather slept with him—about thirty times—was to get ahead in the business.

He recalled the way she smelled. The way she smiled. The way she kissed. The way she did that thing with her—

Mike jerked the wheel hard to his right as he bore down on a trash can that had blown into the street. His front tire bumped up onto the curb, and he mauled some poor guy's mailbox. *Shit!* He hoped his car hadn't been damaged—if the cops got involved, he didn't want to be nabbed by some CSI hotshot matching paint smears off a mangled mailbox post.

Mike straightened his car and bounced back onto the road, now going barely twenty miles per hour. At least he'd been right with his hurricane-like forecast. The bad-luck streak had ended, and he could breathe a little easier about his job security.

Ten minutes later, he turned onto Heather's street. It was located in an older neighborhood, where the houses were modest, but well maintained. Heather didn't exactly choose the area—she'd taken up residence in her grandmother's house after the old lady got shuffled off to a nursing home. When you were a recent college graduate, you took what you could get. She'd talked about saving enough money to afford a down payment on her own house someday. She *hadn't* discussed blackmailing him to augment her bankroll.

Sometimes plans go awry.

Mike rolled to a stop five houses down and parked in front of an empty lot. Although the rain had slowed a bit since he'd wiped out the mailbox, it was still coming down hard enough that anyone peeking out their window wouldn't be able to identify his car—at least not beyond a vague description. Dark sedan.

He reached beneath the passenger seat, removed his knife, and tucked it into the ample pocket of his slicker. Then, with great effort and an unwelcome chorus of rubbery squeaking, he pulled on the cheap galoshes. He flipped his hood over his head, hopped out of the car, and sucked in a deep breath.

The torrential downpour had eased a little more, and the sky had lightened a shade.

Head down, Mike walked briskly toward Heather's house, the knife in his pocket weighing heavier with each step. Water flooded low spots on the sidewalk, and he kept veering to the side to avoid splashing his pants. A nearby lightning strike illuminated the area, creating an otherworldly aura.

Mike pressed on.

When he arrived at the edge of Heather's yard, he stopped behind a large oak tree to survey the situation. A car was parked in front of her house, and although he didn't have a good angle, it appeared to have a Channel Two News logo on the door. Had Heather gotten a job with their competing station? That would explain a lot. The abrupt departure. Her squirrelly behavior. Her decision to end their affair.

Time to find out what that girl was thinking. Time to change her mind, if he could. If not…

Mike glopped through the muddy yard to the front door. Rapped on it once, twice, three times, then stepped back and waited.

He didn't have to wait long. The door swung open, and Heather appeared, dressed only in a silk robe, clutching a twenty-dollar bill. Her pupils dilated, then quickly shrank to normal. "What are you doing here?"

"We need to talk. Can I come in?"

Heather glanced over her shoulder. "Do you have the money?" she asked, voice lowered.

"The money? Sure, sure. Let me in, and we'll discuss it."

She hesitated, then opened the door and beckoned him in. "Come on. Let's be quick about this."

Mike wiped his boots on the mat, then stepped into the foyer. Put his hand in his pocket and felt the cold steel. Wondered if he had the guts to carry through, if it came to that.

Heather shut the door behind him and cinched the belt on her robe. "Okay, then," she said. "You know the deal. Your money for my silence. Let's have it."

From the back of the house, Mike heard a shower running. "Is someone else here?"

Heather's gaze flitted toward the source of the noise, then back at Mike. "My cousin is visiting. For a few days. Now, do you—"

"We had a good thing," Mike said. "Hell, we had a great thing."

"*Had* is the operative word."

"We could have it again. Just because you went to Channel Two doesn't mean it has to end. In fact, I—"

The doorbell rang.

"Crap. Just a second," Heather said. As she moved to open the door, Mike circled behind her, not wanting to be spotted. A witness was the last thing he needed.

"About time," Heather said to the person at the door.

"Can I come in? Wouldn't want your pizza to get wet."

"Uh, okay."

A young man stepped inside, toting his insulated plastic carry-case emblazoned with the words *Hot Pizza*. "Whassup," he said, nodding his greeting at Mike.

Mike nodded back and mumbled, "Hello."

The pizza guy removed a cardboard box from his case and gave it to Heather, and she handed him the twenty. "Keep the change. It's nasty out there."

His face lit up. "Thanks." He turned to leave, then spun around, pointing at Mike. "Hey. You're that weather dude. On Channel Six. Meteorologist Mike!"

Mike nodded. He'd been made. His hand unclenched from the knife in his pocket. A tiny surge of relief pulsed through him, now that he realized he wouldn't be killing anyone. Then his anger rose. Heather would rat him out, and his life would be ruined. He gripped the knife again.

"Hoo boy. You're in some kind of ginormous slump. Haven't you blown like five major forecasts in a row?" The pizza guy stood up straight and smoothed out an imaginary tie. "This is Meteorologist Mike," he said in an exaggerated nasal voice. "I predict we'll have twenty inches of snow. No, no, make that three feet of snow." He slumped back into pizza-guy mode. "I think we barely got a dusting on that one. Heh, heh, heh."

He glanced around, saw that nobody else was sharing in his fun, and erased the smirk from his face. "Uh, okay. Thanks for the tip." Clutching his case under one arm, he opened the door and slunk away.

Heather closed the door, set the pizza down on a nearby table, and turned toward Mike, sporting her own little smirk. "Now, *Meteorologist Mike*, where's my cash? Or do I have to let the entire world know how much you like handcuffs and feather dusters?"

"Seriously, Heather? I thought I knew you better than that. We meant something to each other." Mike parsed his options. The pizza guy had recognized him. But could that be used as an alibi somehow? *Think, Mike! You're a smart guy. Think!*

"A girl's got to do what a girl's got to do. Being a weather lackey doesn't pay very well, and you know how much I like nice things. If it makes you feel better, consider it payment for services rendered. Of course, if that's the case, then maybe I should ask for more, considering how much you enjoyed my *services*."

Mike stepped forward.

"Hey, there. Didn't know this had turned into a party," someone said from behind him. Mike recognized that deeply modulated voice; he'd been hearing it in his nightmares for months. He whirled around to see weather rival Casper Wells, Channel Two, with only a pink towel wrapped around his waist. Mike's blood began to boil. Heather was screwing Casper? That's why she dumped him? Was sleeping with weathermen the only way she knew to advance her career? But with that skunk?

No demure smirk for Casper; he sported a clown-like grin. "What are you doing here? Shouldn't you be at your station working on some erroneous forecast? Maybe you should call for snow. I mean, the temperature *has* dipped into the low nineties."

Mike opened his mouth to respond, but nothing came out. Next to him, Heather's eyes sparkled, as if she enjoyed watching her two lovers face off.

Casper padded to the window, pushed aside the drapes with his forefinger, and gazed out at the sky. "Based upon the latest projections, I *predict* this storm is going to peter out in the next hour or so. After a few last isolated cells pass, it'll be *smooooooth* sailing." He turned back toward Mike. "Just as I've been predicting all day long. How you could have called for such a prolonged deluge is beyond me. *MegaStorm*? Ha! Seems like you're still mired in your mongo slump, buddy boy."

Mike's mind revved into overdrive, and a plan coalesced. A desperate one, but it was all he had.

He stepped toward the window and drew the curtains back, inching to one side to make room for Casper. "You can tell when the storm will dissipate just by looking at the clouds? Will you show me how you knew that?"

Casper glanced at Heather, then shrugged. "Sure. Be glad to give you a few pointers. You could use all the help you can get." Casper crossed in front of Mike and began talking about the cloud formations as he gestured skyward.

Mike tuned him out, all his concentration on the knife in his hand and the task before him.

* * * *

Five minutes later, Mike could breathe easier. He'd surprised Casper from behind, left arm around his neck while the right reached around and stabbed him in the gut—a move his rival never *predicted*. Then, after a short but energetic chase, he'd managed to dispatch Heather, too. It took him another fifteen minutes to stage the tableau so it looked like Casper had committed *hari-kari* after offing Heather in a lovers' quarrel.

Details were important: Mike wiped his own fingerprints off the knife and placed it into Casper's hands, maneuvering them into just the right position. Then he made sure he washed the few splatters of blood off his slicker and galoshes.

The pizza guy would certainly place Mike at the scene, so he needed to gin up a plausible scenario. Mike turned off his phone, then quickly found Heather's phone. With a knuckle, he tapped out a cryptic text message to his number: *Cspr stabbe*.

Then he placed Heather's phone near her dead hands and mentally rehearsed his alibi. He'd tell the cops he'd just swung by to ask Heather about some research she'd done for him a while back, but he'd left on the heels of the pizza guy. A half hour later, he'd gotten a weird message from her, but when he'd texted back, she hadn't responded. Now that he knew the awful truth, he guessed Heather was trying to tell him what Casper had done to her. Mike would be sure to choke up a little when he said it.

Although his story was a little shaky, Mike felt it just might hold up if he could summon his inner thespian and be convincing—he minored in theater in college. It wasn't like he had a real choice; if he hadn't silenced Heather, she would have turned his life to shit for sure. He suppressed a grin. Taking care of his rival was a little bonus for a job well done.

He had one more thing to do.

Get the hell out.

Mike glanced around the living room a final time, then, confident he'd taken care of all the particulars, bolted through the side door. The sky had darkened once again, one of the last few storm cells Casper had so pompously predicted. The rain pelted Mike as he crossed Heather's yard on his way to the car, and a bolt of lightning struck almost at the exact time thunder boomed. Too close!

Mike picked up his pace.

Another bolt of lightning, even nearer.

Mike began to jog.

Yet another lightning strike, impossibly close.

He broke into a flat-out sprint, splashing through puddles in his galoshes.

Twenty-five yards from the safety of his car, Mike's scalp tingled and his hair stood straight up and the smell of ozone flooded his nostrils. The sky flashed a brilliant, blinding white, and in that instant, in that final split-second of rational thought, Mike realized his streak of bad luck had indeed continued.

And ended.

Alan Orloff's debut mystery, *Diamonds for the Dead*, was an Agatha Award finalist for best first novel. His seventh novel, *Running from the Past* (Kindle Press), was a winner in Amazon's Kindle Scout program. His short fiction has appeared in *Needle: A Magazine of Noir*, *Shotgun Honey Presents: Locked & Loaded, Both Barrels*, Vol. 3 (One Eye Press), *Jewish Noir* (PM Press), and *Alfred Hitchcock Mystery Magazine*. He's been a guest editor for *SmokeLong Quarterly* and served on the editorial panel for *Chesapeake Crimes: Homicidal Holidays*. Alan lives in northern Virginia and teaches fiction-writing at The Writer's Center in Bethesda, Maryland.

THE LAST CAVING TRIP

by Donna Andrews

"You'll love this cave, man," Roger said, dropping his backpack at his feet.

My shudder had nothing to do with the cold mountain air. But Roger was rummaging through his pack, not looking at me, so I didn't have to fake enthusiasm. I wouldn't have fooled him anyway. He might have been monumentally self-centered, but he'd known me for ten years, and after several caving expeditions together in the last few months, even Roger probably realized that I didn't exactly get off on caves the way he did. I had claustrophobia—not enough to keep me from going into a cave but enough to keep it from being any fun.

Typical that Roger never seemed to wonder why a man with claustrophobia kept forcing himself into caves. I had an explanation ready in case he ever asked: I wanted to test my limits. Push beyond them. See if I could overcome them. I could rattle it off with great sincerity if I had to.

But Roger never asked.

My stomach tightened when I spotted the cave's entrance. Entrance. To me, it just looked like a ragged hole in the side of the hill. Or possibly the mouth of some hungry, lurking creature, with a few patches of unmelted snow like uneven teeth.

No. Just a hole in the side of the hill. No use letting my imagination run wild.

"Get your gear on!" Roger jabbed me with his elbow.

I let my pack slide to the ground and hauled out my gear. Faded army-surplus fatigues, still shedding bits of dried mud from our last trip. A windbreaker for extra warmth. Backup batteries and lights. Energy bars. Plastic water bottles. Gloves to protect my hands from cold and sharp rocks. Knee pads in case we had to crawl for a while. Finally I put on my caving helmet and adjusted the strap.

Actually, it was Roger's old helmet. I'd promised to buy it from him if I decided to keep on caving. We'd been out so many times now that I was surprised he hadn't already hit me up for the money.

I checked the wire that connected the battery to the light at the front of the helmet and smiled. I wouldn't be buying Roger's helmet after all. I planned to make this the last caving trip.

For both of us.

I stuffed my clothes in my backpack, along with spare shoes, socks, my down coat, and a black plastic garbage bag for the muddy cave gear after I came out. I left the backpack near the cave mouth.

"Don't put it there," Roger said. "What if someone sees it and reports us?"

I glanced around and shook my head. We were on a small ledge, halfway up the side of a hill so steep we'd had to pull ourselves the last few feet by holding onto roots and tufts of grass. So even if a stray hunter or hiker passed by on the trail below, odds were he wouldn't spot the entrance, much less our packs. And with the forecasters predicting eight to ten inches of new snow by morning, passersby were even less likely than usual.

But I moved the pack anyway. You didn't argue with Roger. When we'd planned this expedition, he'd seemed quite blasé about the idea of an unauthorized, out-of-season visit to a controlled cave, but now that we were doing it he didn't seem as self-assured. His anxiety secretly amused me.

Besides, I didn't want our expedition interrupted. I'd waited too long. Not just the months since I'd decided to kill him, but the whole time since I realized what a menace he was. Looking back, I was almost grateful for the episode with Jeanine. At first I told myself maybe he hadn't known I was interested in her. But of course he'd known, and he went after her anyway. If he hadn't, I might never have seen through him. Never have realized how many other scummy things he'd done to me and to so many others over the years. And always gotten away scot-free. Just to save face, I'd managed to pretend I'd never been that interested in Jeanine anyway. But as I silently seethed, it hadn't taken me long to realize that I'd have a better chance of getting back at Roger if he believed we were still friends.

When Roger revived his old college interest in caving, he assumed I would go along with his plans, the way I always did. The first trip was hell. Only my determination not to look weak in Roger's eyes got me through. The following night I awoke from a nightmare where everything that could go wrong in a cave *did* go wrong, and I knew I'd found the answer.

I endured several more caving trips after that, waiting for a chance like this—just Roger and me, no one else along. No witnesses. No dialing 9-1-1. Cell phones were prone to damage from the damp and mud and were useless underground in any case, so we always locked them in the car trunk. All of Roger's other caving friends had been scared off by the weather forecast. But not me. I wasn't afraid of snow. Just caves.

I smiled as I hoisted the pack onto my shoulders, took a deep, steadying breath, and stooped to follow him into the cave.

It was wide at first, but too low to stand for the first twenty or thirty feet. Bent almost double, we scrabbled over a series of broken rock slabs that curved slightly to the left, only to stop short at a gate made of square steel bars, secured with a combination lock on a thick chain.

"Damned property owners." Roger rummaged through his pockets. "They ruin the caves with these stupid contraptions."

Seemed like a very useful contraption to me. The bars were drilled deep into the rock and welded fast, with spaces between them wide enough to let bats through while keeping out stray humans. Curious children. Teenagers in search of a place to party. Out-of-season cavers who didn't care if they interrupted the bats' breeding season.

I offered up a silent apology to the bats. It's for a good cause, guys.

"Good thing I have a friend who got me the combination." Roger fished out a piece of paper with writing on it. I leaned over so I could read the numbers as he punched them in.

"Afraid we'll get separated inside?" Roger jeered. "Don't worry, I won't leave you behind. Here, you keep it. I can remember it."

He wadded the paper up and flicked it at me. I caught it, smoothed it out, and reread the combination before tucking the paper into the back pocket of my pants.

We had to remove our backpacks to pass through the gate. Roger went in first, of course. I handed him both packs before crawling through myself.

I squatted near the entrance, where it was still bright enough to see without my helmet light, and watched Roger. He carried our backpacks around until he found a dry place to stow them, then checked several times that they couldn't be seen in the unlikely event anyone stumbled into the outer passage. He tightened his bootlaces and broke one, then searched unsuccessfully in his pack for a replacement before finally knotting and relacing the old one. He ran outside to take another leak before we got started, even though we'd already done that half an hour before. Then he put the chain back on and snapped the lock closed so no one would barge in and interrupt our trespassing. Any other time, I'd have been annoyed by his hyper behavior, but because we were entering a cave, I welcomed the delay.

I did my usual routine, too. Different from Roger's. Pretended to be studying the rock formations, making minute adjustments to my helmet strap, anything to fool myself about what I was really doing: forcing myself to go farther in—as far as I could bear—then stopping to breathe before pushing a little farther. By the time Roger had finished his preparations and slid down the sloping, gravel-strewn floor toward me, strapping on his helmet as he slid, I was ready. I could do this as long as I stayed focused on the immediate task at hand. Find solid footing for each step, and a good handhold when needed. Take it one rock at a time.

No time to dwell on how many tons of rock lay between me and the surface. Remind myself that the rock around me hadn't moved for years, even centuries. It should stay put a few hours more. Not that logic helped much when the dread kicked in.

I could do it, I knew, and I'd never have to do it again. No one would think any the worse of me if I lost all interest in caving after the horrible ordeal of my friend's death. Everyone would be sympathetic. Hell, maybe Jeanine and I would get together after all. Drawn together by our shared loss. And then—

"Ready?" Roger said. "Let's hit it!"

He didn't wait for an answer. I took a deep breath and followed.

Roger's nonstop chatter kept me from getting spooked by how silent the cave was when we weren't moving. Before my first cave, I never paid much attention to ordinary sounds around me—birds, traffic, or the refrigerator kicking in—until they were gone, replaced by the strange half-muffled echoes of our progress through the cavern.

And at least so far, this cave was living up to its advance billing.

"The first hour or so is a straight shot," he'd said. "Dead easy."

By which he meant dead boring, for him. One main path, so not much chance of getting lost. Not many side passages to explore, which meant fewer of those anxious moments when Roger would say, "Hang on—you stay here. I want to see where this goes," and disappear for five minutes or ten, or even an hour, leaving me to wonder what had happened. Was he lost? Hurt? Or had he found another way out and decided to see how long I'd wait? He'd tried that trick on another caver once. No wonder so few people would go caving with him, even before the caving club kicked him out. I was almost the only person who'd still cave with him. Didn't he ever wonder about that?

And what was my function here, anyway? Safety, officially. "You cave alone, you die alone," cavers always said. But Roger didn't give a damn about safety. Probably just wanted an audience, a witness to his exploits.

Or maybe he just liked having someone to pick on. He knew I was always good for that.

"Don't look so anxious," he said, with a snicker, as he returned from one of the few side tunnels. "If I got lost, even *you* could find your way out from here. Wait till we get past the big crawl. It's like a maze after that. Really cool."

I didn't plan to get that far. Roger had more than his share of faults, but even I had to admit that cowardice wasn't one of them. He thought nothing of crawling through eighty or ninety feet of a tunnel so low we could only inch forward on our bellies and so narrow we couldn't turn around until we reached the exit. If there was an exit. The only thing worse than doing a narrow crawl was following Roger into one, hearing him shout "Dead end!" and knowing I had to scuttle out backward, with his boots smashing into my face if I wasn't quick enough. I hated any kind of crawl, and I didn't want to endure something Roger called a big crawl, much less the maze beyond. I had to act soon.

Roger went off, still snickering. I got up more slowly from the rock I'd been sitting on and was surprised to find I was shivering. I knew that was dangerous in a cave. No matter what temperature it is outside, in the cave it's between fifty-five and fifty-seven degrees. Pleasantly cool if we walked in from a summer's day, and warm after the snow and twenty-something temperatures outside today. But a good forty degrees below the temperature of the human body. Walk around generating heat and we'd be fine, thanks to our layers of clothing, as long as we didn't get wet. Sit on a rock too long and we'd feel the cold seeping into our bones. Was my shivering psychological or the first sign of hypothermia? As many cavers die from hypothermia as from cave-ins, Roger had told me. Or was that just another way to scare me?

I hurried after Roger. The winding, downward slope became steeper, more like a half-vertical tunnel. I caught up with him at the point where it became almost completely vertical. He had turned around and begun descending.

"You've got to watch this part," he said. "Fall here and you'll hit some really sharp rocks below."

I could tell from how slowly he moved that this wasn't an easy descent. Maybe now?

But when I stuck my head over the edge to shine my helmet light down, I saw that the steep part was only about eight feet deep. That short a fall probably wouldn't kill him, unless he landed just right. And I couldn't rely on that.

Then it was my turn, and I had to pay attention to the descent. Not just to keep from falling but to make sure I could do it by myself on the way back. After the descent came a twenty-foot stretch of narrow passage. Passage wasn't the right word for it. More like a vertical crack that had opened in the rock and could snap closed at any moment, with any slight shift in the earth around us. I knew that wouldn't happen short of an earthquake, but down here the knowledge never seemed convincing.

There wasn't really a floor, either. When I looked down, I saw that the crack just narrowed gradually until it finally closed again in a V some ten or fifteen feet below. It was so narrow there was hardly any way I could fall. All I had to do was shuffle along, inch sideways holding my breath, hands and feet pressed against the sides. Chimneying.

I hated it. I was breathing hard by the time I got past that stretch.

"You look like you could use a break," Roger said. "Let's take five in this room."

I glanced around. In caving terms, yeah, it was a room. Fifty feet underground, any place tall enough to stand and wide enough for two people to pass each other counted as a room.

And why the sudden concern about me taking a break? I distrusted his occasional benevolent moods. Half the time they were just his way of setting someone up for a cruel prank.

He flopped down on the one flat area of rock and pulled out his water bottle and an energy bar. Then he snapped off his helmet light.

"Might want to save your battery, too," he said.

I ignored him and pretended to be looking around for a comfortable perch. If I turned my light off, too, we'd be in absolute darkness. Gave a lot of people the creeps, me included. Probably why Roger did it. The five minutes it would take for Roger to bolt his energy bar wouldn't make much difference to our battery consumption anyway, but he loved to show off how little the complete absence of light bothered him.

I found an almost comfortable place to stand, leaning slightly against a rock face, and played my helmet light over the rocks around us, pretending to study them. Should I do it now? I could see several large loose rocks. I hefted one, a heavy one the size of a grapefruit. Would that work, or should I find something larger? I had my gloves on; there'd be no fingerprints.

But maybe they could figure out from an autopsy that he'd been hit with a rock so his fall wasn't accidental. That was the whole purpose of doing this in a cave—making it look completely plausible as an accident. I reluctantly put the rock down.

I closed my eyes and imagined the snow that must be falling outside. Soft white flakes as far as the eye could see. And the way snow-covered fields reflected every bit of light so it was never really dark.

"Show time."

I opened my eyes to see that Roger was standing, stuffing the energy bar wrapper in his pocket and starting off again.

He set a fast pace, obviously impatient to get to the interesting part of the cave. Half walking, half sliding, I followed him through more steep, downward-twisting tunnels. If the slanting tunnel suddenly turned into a vertical shaft, Roger'd be the one who plummeted down, I thought with relief. And if I fell, I'd have Roger to land on. Maybe he'd keep me from having to do anything after all.

It was all downhill now. That worried me. A couple of times before, Roger had scrambled down a steep slope and then found he couldn't climb out again without help from a fellow caver. What if he was doing that now? Roger was taller, stronger, and much better at free climbing than I was. I went as slowly as I could without getting left behind, testing each handhold and foothold as I went. And while Roger seemed happy to scramble down in the dark, I liked to see where I was going. I'd never forgotten the time I'd reached out for the next handhold and instead of the cold, clammy surface of the rock I'd felt the warm, soft flesh of a cluster of hibernating bats, molded against the cave wall.

We hit a crawl, a tight one. No room to use my legs, so I could only brace my feet while I pulled with my arms. My windbreaker's pockets were so crammed with stuff I had to take it off and push it ahead of me, adding to the closed-in feeling.

Stopping halfway to catch my breath, I panicked, lying there in the crawl, with the damp, wet stone of the ceiling dripping on my back, even touching it in places. The dim beam from my helmet light pooled on the stone an inch or two from my face. Like being facedown in a coffin. For a moment I wanted to shout for help, flail my arms and legs, push myself backward out of the crawl, and make a dash for the surface. Light. Air. Freedom. Safety.

"You stuck back there?" Roger called from the other end.

I took deep breaths and forced myself to stay still and silent, but what saved me from completely losing it was a sudden surge of utter hatred. I wasn't sure if it was for Roger or the cave. Maybe both. It left me shaken, but the worst of the panic had passed, and I began creeping forward again.

I emerged into a large chamber and breathed more easily at the sudden sense of space around me. I glanced up at the rock formations overhead—too jagged and irregular to call a ceiling, but they gave between ten and thirty feet of welcome headroom. Ceiling, chamber, passage—the words were meaningless. I'd entered a wholly alien geometry; a place not hostile to the frail humans who invaded it, but worse—profoundly indifferent.

I pushed the thought away, shivering on the rock floor, puffing to catch my breath. Only it wasn't really much of a floor. More of a ledge, a few feet wide. We'd emerged into another, larger crack in the rocks. I glanced at Roger, who stood at the edge of the ledge, gazing down.

As I watched, he dropped a pebble. We both listened as it fell, bouncing against the rocks at least a dozen times before landing.

"Deep," Roger said. "Want to take a look?"

"No thanks," I said, pressing back against the rock. "Shouldn't we keep moving?"

"Plenty of room to stand," he said.

I glanced up, and my helmet light hit his face like a spotlight. He was grinning, the way he always did when he knew he was getting to me. He knew how I felt about heights, too.

"Stow it," I said. "Which way now?"

"Hmmm." He pretended to think. He turned, squatted, and peered over the edge, as if mapping out our route.

"What if I said down?" he called over his shoulder. He was smirking, I knew, even though I couldn't see his face, only the mud-stained seat of his pants.

"If you say so." I lifted my right leg and slammed my foot into him, hard.

I heard a sharp sound—more like "Oof!" than a cry or a scream; maybe I got him in the kidney—and he toppled over the edge. I closed my eyes and tried not to listen to the thuds his body made on the way down. Eight, nine, ten. The last one squelched slightly, as if he'd landed in mud. Smaller rocks continued to rattle down for a few seconds. And then, in the silence that followed, I strained to hear.

"Roger?" I called.

No answer.

I held my wristwatch in the beam of my helmet light and checked the time. Should I wait?

"Roger?" I called again.

No noise. Nothing at all.

Should I peer over the edge? My stomach churned at the idea.

The hell with waiting, I thought. If the fall hadn't killed him outright, he was certainly badly injured, and hypothermia would speed things along. I was impatient to get outside and start my drive—or hike—to the little town where I could sound the alarm.

I grabbed my windbreaker, shoved it into the crawl, and wiggled in after it.

The crawl was worse going back. I'd gotten through once, so it should have been easy, but I must have taken a slightly different angle this time. My bundle got stuck once, and I ripped a hole in my windbreaker, shoving until I got it moving again.

When I got out of the crawl, I sat for a few minutes until my heart slowed. Nothing left but a long, slow climb, a couple of narrow places, and then the open air.

A minute or two after I started climbing again, my helmet light flickered a few times, then went out.

"No!" I fumbled at the helmet for a few minutes, flicking the on/off button. Definitely dead. Perhaps the wire had been disconnected. I took deep breaths, reminded myself that I had spare batteries, a slender Maglite, and as a last resort, a little key chain flashlight. Never go into a cave without three sources of light—another cavers' maxim.

I felt my way carefully back down to the flat place outside the crawl and rummaged through my windbreaker's pockets. I found the Maglite and used it to check the cord between the battery and the helmet light. It was still connected.

I found the spare battery and slotted it in.

Still nothing.

Had the bulb gone bad? Or had Roger—stupid, careless Roger—not bothered to give me properly charged batteries?

Stupid, careless Roger or cunning, manipulative Roger? Just the sort of practical joke he'd find hilarious. Stupid, careless me for not checking my own equipment.

I swore and threw the helmet against the wall. I took deep breaths to fight off the panic.

Calm down, I told myself. Blessing in disguise! Once I got out, the malfunctioning cave helmet would add realism to my story of how poor, careless Roger had his accident.

I used the Maglite to search till I found the helmet and put it back on—it was still protection for my head, after all—and started the long climb again. I held the Maglite in my teeth to free both hands for climbing. Going down, we could half climb and half slide, letting gravity do some of the work. Climbing up, I had to grope for handholds and footholds and pull myself up a few inches at a time, praying I was going the right way. What if I'd missed a side passage? I could be crawling slowly and steadily up the wrong route, headed for some distant dead end. From this new angle, nothing looked familiar.

I breathed a sigh of relief when I reached the tight passage I remembered. It no longer felt like a dangerous, narrow trap. More like a welcoming hallway with an exit sign at one end.

Until my foot slipped and I dropped the Maglite while grabbing for a handhold.

The light died on the second bounce.

I braced myself with my back and legs and fumbled in my pocket for the key ring flashlight.

It didn't give much light. I'd had it a couple of years—was the battery going dead?

And what if I dropped this light, too?

My hand started shaking at the thought.

I pulled the string from my windbreaker's hood and used it to tie the little flashlight around my wrist. A bit awkward, but at least I wouldn't drop it.

I started to climb again when I felt a hand grab my ankle.

"Get away from me!" I kicked frantically to free my foot.

I heard the rasp of fabric ripping and realized that no battered, bleeding hand had reached up from the depths of the cave to drag me down with it. What I'd felt was the tug of my pants leg catching on a sharp rock. Nothing more, and certainly not the macabre vision my mind had conjured up.

"Idiot," I said in a shaky voice. Roger wasn't following me. Roger wasn't going anywhere. But it took a few minutes before my hands stopped shaking and I could move again.

Another steep climb, and then the last long stretch of relatively gentle uphill slope. The little flashlight began fading in and out, brightening when I shook it, but only briefly. Before the battery died completely, I spotted the metal gate.

Weak with relief, I sat down by the gate. My knees were shaking, and I hadn't realized how dry my mouth had gotten. I fished in the windbreaker's pockets and pulled out my water bottle.

Better than Champagne, I thought, taking a sip.

"To absent friends," I said, lifting the bottle, and then I took a long, satisfying drink. The bottle was almost empty, but I could eat snow once I got out. Fresh snow. I couldn't see outside, but from the quality of the light coming from the entrance I could tell the snow was falling.

I reached into my back pocket and pulled out the paper with the combination, unfolded it, and punched the numbers into the combination lock.

Nothing happened.

I tried again, more carefully, but the lock didn't budge.

I shook the little flashlight and added its feeble glow to the light from the entrance. Had I read the paper wrong? No, it definitely said "combination: 7938" in Roger's bold, sprawling hand.

I tried it a third time.

Nothing.

Had Roger changed the combination? Why?

It was colder near the entrance. I searched my pack and Roger's, donning an extra layer of clothes. I found a few energy bars. No more water, damn it. And while the whole cave was damp and clammy, I hadn't seen any pools or puddles of water.

I had to make the quarter bottle I had last.

But last how long? How often did someone come by during off season? Off season and in the middle of a major snowstorm?

Maybe not for days. Or weeks.

I went back to the combination lock and punched in Roger's birth month and day. His birth year. The numeric part of his license plate.

I tried a few number sequences at random, but then stopped myself. Random numbers weren't going to help. I needed a method. Start at 0-0-0-0 and keep going till I had it.

"Damn you, Roger," I muttered. Even dead he'd figured out a way to double-cross me.

I settled into a comfortable position, Roger's pack under me as a cushion and a buffer against the cold, and began methodically punching in combinations. Punch the numbers and pull the lock. 0-0-0-0 and pull. 0-0-0-1 and pull. 0-0-0-2. 0-0-0-3.

I glanced at my wristwatch and timed myself. If I got a good rhythm going, I could punch eight combinations in thirty seconds. Make it fifteen a minute.

0-0-1-4. 0-0-1-5. 0-0-1-6.

How many possible combinations were there? Four numbers—ten to the fourth power. Ten thousand combinations. And at fifteen tries a minute, the ten thousand combinations would take me... ten or eleven hours. If my math was right. And if I could keep up the pace.

At 0-3-0-0 I stopped to warm my fingers. At 0-5-5-0 I stopped to put on all my spare clothing and Roger's, too. The wind was starting to gust into the mouth of the cave. The temperature was definitely dropping. And the light was fading. By 0-9-0-0, I couldn't see to punch the numbers. I had to go by feel, which cut my speed significantly. Should I go deeper into the cave where it was warmer? At least until morning? No, going deeper wouldn't let me warm up; just slow down how fast I lost heat. My only real hope was to keep punching numbers as long as I could and hope I hit the right combination soon.

1-2-3-1. 1-2-3-2. 1-2-3-3.

If only I'd waited till summer to do this. Or at least spring. The changed combination would only be an annoying delay then.

As I punched numbers with dead, cold fingers, I obsessed over why Roger had reset the combination. To guard against someone discovering us? As a practical joke?

Or maybe not a joke at all. Maybe Roger had seen through my act. Maybe I hadn't fooled him after all. Maybe we'd both been planning more than an ordinary caving trip today.

A beam of light lit up the combination lock.

"Having fun?"

Roger was squatting just outside the bars. His face was bruised and crisscrossed with gashes, some crusted over and some still seeping blood. His coveralls were coated with mud and ripped in several places. But he was wearing his usual sarcastic smirk and brushing snowflakes off his windbreaker.

"Did I forget to tell you I'd discovered a back entrance to this cave?" he sneered. "You might want to try it. Of course, you'd have to rappel down that cliff you kicked me off and get through the maze. Took me three trips to find my way through it, but hey! You might get lucky."

He threw back his head and laughed. I winced and closed my eyes against the sound. When I opened them again, he was gone.

"Roger? *Roger?*"

No answer. No footsteps. Had he really been there, or was I hallucinating?

1-3-9-9. 1-3-9-... 1-3-9-

I couldn't remember what came next. I tried to care, but I just wanted to curl up and go to sleep. And wasn't the air getting a little warmer?

I had a feeling that was a bad sign.

Last caving trip. Yeah. Guess the joke was on me after all.

Donna Andrews was born in Yorktown, Virginia, and now lives in Reston, Virginia. *Lord of the Wings* (August 2015) is the nineteenth book in her Agatha, Anthony, and Lefty award-winning Meg Langslow series, to be followed by *Die Like an Eagle* in 2016. *Storm Warning* is her lucky seventh outing as one of the editors of the Chesapeake Crimes anthology series. She is an active member of Mystery Writers of America and Sisters in Crime. She blogs with the Femmes Fatales at http://femmesfatales.typepad.com/. For more information: http://donnaandrews.com.

INNER WEATHER

by Carla Coupe

Johanna sat facing the mirror, pinning up her hair. *Was that a wrinkle?* Leaning forward, she peered into the glass, frowning.

"Where're you off to tonight, babe?"

Her breath caught for a moment. He grinned at her, his reflection wavering a little in the glass. He relaxed among the rumpled sheets, long-limbed, naked. Her frown didn't soften as she brushed mascara on her lashes—upper, lower, upper again—then blinked three times. Her lashes didn't stick together. *Good.*

"So, it's a secret," he said, stretching his arms overhead, warm brown skin dark against the white sheets. "Mmmm, let me guess. You're packing your overnight case, so it's a quick in-and-out. Passport. A black skirt and low heels, starched white shirt. Very chic."

Her gaze met his in the mirror as she put on her favorite pearl earrings. She quickly looked away, but he chuckled softly.

"Paris, of course. How romantic. April in Paris." He stared at the ceiling. "The forecast is for showers. Don't forget your umbrella."

She paused, then rose and pulled her camel-colored trench coat from the closet, added an Hermès scarf. *That would have to do.*

* * * *

Water poured off the awnings, flooded ankle-deep down the gutters, sprayed out from car wheels over unsuspecting pedestrians seeking shelter in doorways and under canopies. Johanna squished up to the fifth floor of the apartment building, leaving a trail of damp footprints, as well as drips from the brown attaché case she carried. She scanned the numbers on the doors until she reached twenty-one, then pulled out the key she had been given and unlocked the door.

The flat was furnished in castoffs. A battered Louis XIV chair sat next to a small wrought-iron bistro table in the kitchen. The window overlooked a narrow street and a block of flats.

Stripping off her soaked trench coat and scarf, she shivered. *Oh, for a space heater*. She opened the case and removed the pieces of the rifle, fitted them together, then quickly checked it over. All was well. Maurice was reliable with equipment, if nothing else.

She smoothed her thin black gloves, making certain they fitted snugly over each finger. Then she pulled the chair over to the window, slid up the sash, and settled herself as comfortably as possible, given the wind-driven spray that occasionally dampened the rifle and her face, and the cold air that permeated her bones. Should she put her coat on again? She sighed. No, it was too wet for comfort. She set down the rifle.

A quick check of her watch. Her employer said the man would arrive by five. *Good.* She picked up the rifle, positioned herself. Exactly eight minutes later a black limo pulled up. Johanna sighted carefully, waited. He would be exposed as he mounted the stairs to the entrance, presenting his back for a clean shot. *Easy.*

The driver's door swung open and a uniformed man got out, snapping an umbrella wide as he dashed around the vehicle. He opened the rear passenger door and held the umbrella high. Rain pockmarked his gray cap and jacket.

The leaden sky darkened. A gust of wind barreled down the street, caught the umbrella, sending the driver staggering. Another gust hit, then the downpour intensified. Rain sheeted down as the driver hurriedly recovered, the umbrella again shielding the open car door.

Damn. Johanna squinted. She could barely make out the man clambering from the limo, barely see him as he dashed toward the steps, the driver following on his heels, still holding the umbrella overhead.

She let out her breath, aimed, and fired.

The driver stumbled, twisting to face her as he fell. The umbrella, caught by another gust, sailed from his grasp to land in the flooded gutter. *Shit.*

Her target dashed inside. His driver lay on the steps, red staining his uniform, crimson sluicing down the steps. No second chance today.

The rain eased as Johanna hastily broke down the rifle and packed it into the attaché case, then shrugged on her damp coat and grabbed the case. A minute later, she walked out the door of the apartment building into weak, watery sunshine. A crowd had already gathered around the driver, and sirens sounded in the distance. She turned and headed in the opposite direction.

She had missed another target, because of *him*.

* * * *

Two weeks later, Johanna perched on a stool at a hotel bar, slowly sipping her bourbon. The place was nearly empty; it was late on a weeknight, so late even the drunken stragglers had retreated to their beds. At the far end of the long mahogany bar, the bartender rested his head in his hand, eyes at half-mast. From her seat, Johanna could see the whole room reflected in the mirror behind the shelves of bottles. Occasionally the front door would open and one of the cleaning staff would glance around. When they spotted her still at the bar, they'd frown and duck back out. She took another sip, warmth trailing beneath her ribs, and smiled. She'd do the job before breakfast and be home in time for dinner. *Perfect.*

The door opened, but she didn't bother looking. *The cleaners can damn well wait for me to leave.* A finger of cold brushed her back.

"Hey, babe."

Her spine stiffened, her head lifted. He stood right behind her, grinning into the mirror.

She forced herself to relax and breathe evenly, refusing to meet his gaze.

"So, what're you doing in Cleveland? Got something planned?"

Ignore him. She glanced at the bartender, still dozing the length of the bar away.

He leaned forward, his lips almost brushing her ear.

"Better bundle up. It's chilly out."

He winked.

She swallowed hard, squeezed her eyes shut, and slammed back the rest of her drink. It burned down every inch of her throat.

When she opened her eyes, he was gone.

* * * *

The following morning, she propped her foot on the bench and retied her running shoe in the glow of the street light. To her right, wind whipped the lake into whitecaps, blew hard and fast across the granite and concrete plaza, pushing at her like an impatient child.

April? It feels more like February.

Shivering, Johanna pulled her knit cap closer, then tucked her hands into her jacket pockets, fingertips touching the knives hidden in special sheaths. She could barely feel the handles—her thin black gloves prevented fingerprints and improved her grip, but were not for warmth. Tucking her hands under her armpits, she jogged past the huge glass pyramid of the Rock and Roll Hall of Fame, speeding her steps until she joined a knot of other runners.

She nodded to a couple of women, familiar faces now after a week of early morning runs. One nodded back, one waved.

Her target, wearing a bright blue jacket and cap, led the pack. For the moment. That wouldn't last long.

The sky brightened slowly as the joggers passed the little commuter airport a couple miles into the run. Warm now from the exertion, Johanna kept a steady pace and remained toward the back of the group. She knew her target's pattern by now. As every mile passed, blue cap slowed and she drew closer. By the time they reached the marina, the blue cap bobbed only a few runners ahead of her.

The wind picked up, a cold blast of air that blew across the lake and chilled Johanna's damp neck and cheeks. Gray clouds gathered overhead, blocking the sun, deepening the shadows.

Almost time.

They approached Gordon Park, and the woman wearing the blue cap and jacket now huffed and puffed a few paces in front of her, five yards behind the last runner. The sky darkened and the wind blew harder as Johanna slipped the thin knives from their sheaths, holding them carefully. She narrowed her eyes, studying the woman's back.

The right blade will go... there. The left... there.

She moved forward.

Another gust smacked into her, hard as a brick wall, sending her reeling. Sleet pelted down, blinding her, insinuating icy fingers in every crevice of her jacket. Her target yelped and put on a burst of speed, hastening to join the others, already headed toward shelter.

Johanna sheathed the knives.

The target would board a heavily guarded flight this afternoon, out of reach. Her window of opportunity had slammed shut.

Sleet coated her head and shoulders as she jogged toward the nondescript sedan—what was *supposed* to be her getaway car—in the park's lot. Once inside, she shrugged off her wet jacket and pulled off her ice-coated knit hat.

She'd been so careful; her plan had been perfect.

Except for the damned weather.

* * * *

Johanna walked briskly along the path, dodging clumps of students and the occasional professor. Six months. Actually six months, one week, and three days. That's how long it had taken her to get another job after the previous fiascos. Between the murmurs about incompetence and whispers of ill luck, no one would hire her. But now she had a job, and she was damned if some ridiculous weather-related incident would botch it for her. Her plan was perfect.

She shifted the sheaf of music scores from one arm to the other as she skirted the university's performing-arts building. Windows glinted in the autumn sunlight, reflecting her striding form.

"Well, babe, I never pegged you as a music lover."

She swallowed a gasp and glanced at the reflection in the windows.

He walked beside her, in jeans and a sweater, his long legs easily matching her pace.

God damn him!

Taking a steadying breath, she released the tension in her jaw, let her shoulders drop. Now was not the time to get distracted.

"So, where are you headed? Inside?"

She ignored him. Ignored his questions as she turned the corner and headed for the entrance of the building. But she couldn't help looking at the reflection out of the corner of her eye.

He raised his arm in a casual wave and laughed. A bank of heavy clouds boiled up behind him and raced across the sky, blotting out the sun. "Too bad your day is growing darker."

Fat raindrops hit the ground as she pushed open the door and ducked inside.

She was safe, and her job would go as planned. He couldn't bother her in here.

Crossing the spacious lobby decorated with concert announcements and photographs of previous shows, she descended the uncarpeted steps and moved briskly along the cinder-block corridor. Wooden doors to practice rooms lined the walls, a metal plaque with the room number to the right of each door.

Johanna stopped before room eight and pretended to shuffle through the papers she held as she glanced up and down the empty corridor. She set down the papers and pulled on her thin black gloves. After a quick check through the long window to the left of the door, she opened the door.

Piano music spilled from the room and filled the corridor, something loud and vigorous, full of dissonance. She glanced around the room. Music stand on the left. Piano in the center. Shelving on the right. The man seated at the instrument had his back to her. She stepped inside and carefully closed the door before pulling a small metal spool from her pocket. She unwound two feet of thin wire: a perfect garrote.

A monstrously loud bang echoed through the room, the walls, the floor shaking from the sound.

Thunder?

The music stopped. Her target—young, broad-shouldered—turned on the piano bench. His eyes widened when he saw her, and he leapt up with a yell.

The fluorescent lights in the ceiling flickered once, twice, then went out.

Darkness enveloped her, complete, Stygian. She dropped the garrote and stepped back until the wall pressed against her spine. Her target's harsh breaths betrayed his location, still beside the piano.

"Who sent you?" he whispered.

She reached for the knife hidden in her jacket. Not her preferred method for this job, but needs must.

He grunted and a faint breeze brushed her cheek. *What was he...*

Something hard—the music stand?—smashed into her left arm and ribs. Pain crashed through her as she lurched to the side, her legs giving way. She reached out, her hand sliding down the wall as he struck her in the back. Why couldn't she feel her legs? A starburst of pain exploded in her head. The door opened, shut, she was alone in the black.

She closed her eyes and let the pain wash over her.

* * * *

Another cold day, one of so many since she had arrived here. *How long has it been? Years?* She held up her hand, studied it for a minute. Wrinkled, spotted skin. *Many years.*

Johanna turned her face to the late afternoon sun, a woolen blanket pulled tight over her legs and lap. She tucked her chilled hands under the blanket as two men approached her up the winding gravel path. She knew one. The other was a stranger.

"Good afternoon, Johanna," the familiar man said. "This is Dr. Hernandez."

She nodded once.

"Johanna is our longest resident," the familiar man continued. "She's been here almost fifty years."

She let their words trickle by, words like "brain damage" and "aphasia." She'd heard them before. Meaningless.

When the familiar man grasped the handles of her wheelchair, she looked up, opened her mouth. The sound that emerged was harsh, imperative.

"No, I'm not taking you inside," he soothed, his voice gentle. "Not yet. I'm just moving you to the courtyard where you'll be out of the wind. Your lips are blue with cold."

She settled back, the gravel crunching beneath the chair's wheels. The garden was past its best, only a few flowers braved the winter chill.

She would finish her daily vigil in the relative comfort of the courtyard, where stone walls and pavers held the sun's warmth.

The two men continued to speak as they walked, and when they angled her wheelchair into a patch of sunlight next to the building, the familiar man touched her shoulder briefly. "I'll let Margaret know you're here. She'll come for you in about twenty minutes."

Johanna watched them cross the courtyard and disappear inside the building. She turned to the window beside her, ignored the frail figure in the wheelchair reflected in the glass.

Her heart gave a little lurch.

He stood beside the wheelchair, grinning at her.

"Hey, babe. Long time, no see."

She nodded, then squeezed her eyes shut. A tear trickled down one cheek. When she opened her eyes, he was still there, his reflection smiling at her from the glass. He leaned over to press a kiss to the top of her reflection's head. She could almost feel it.

She opened her mouth. Moved her uncooperative lips and tongue and said with great care, "I'm sorry."

"I know," he said. "I forgive you."

She leaned her head to one side; her reflection's grizzled gray hair brushed his arm. He lifted a hand, stroked her reflection's face. The faintest sensation caressed her cheek.

"It's time, babe."

He walked slowly away.

The sun dimmed, caught behind a single dark cloud. Fat raindrops left dark circles on her blanket, dampened her withered hands and face.

Johanna took one shuddering breath, then another. She had killed him, but he had stopped her from killing again. He had used the weather to save her soul.

Her heart beat once, twice, then stopped.

Carla Coupe fell into writing short stories almost without noticing. Two of her short stories—"Rear View Murder" in *Chesapeake Crimes II* and "Dangerous Crossing" in *Chesapeake Crimes 3*—were nominated for the Agatha Award. She has written a number of Sherlock Holmes pastiches, which have appeared in *Sherlock Holmes Mystery Magazine*, *Sherlock's Home: The Empty House*, and *Irene's Cabinet*. Her story "The Book of Tobit" was included in *The Best American Mystery Stories of 2012*.

SHELTER FROM THE STORM
by Shaun Taylor Bevins

Silvia had heard the predictions, but not even a blizzard—and that's what the weathermen were forecasting—could deter her from the two-hour drive to the cabin, not now with so much at stake. Pulling her front door shut, she confronted the expanse of gloomy gray. The air possessed a dense quality, a foreboding that seemed to penetrate to the marrow of her bones. She took a deep breath to calm her nerves. She wriggled her cashmere scarf up over her mouth, taking comfort in the moist warmth of her breath. The heaviest snowfall wasn't expected until after midnight, and by then she'd be at Drew's cabin, safely out of Tom's reach.

She heaved the large suitcase into the trunk of her Camry. Susan, her lawyer, had assured her they would arrange a time when she could collect the rest of her belongings, at least the belongings Tom hadn't destroyed once he understood she wasn't coming back. Silvia couldn't care less. Let him burn, shred, smash, trash whatever he could. What few clothes and trinkets she had collected over the past seven years were a small price to pay for her freedom.

She slammed the trunk closed and shuffled toward the driver's side door, leaving a set of fresh tracks in the light dusting that already covered the asphalt. By the time Tom arrived home from his shift, it would be too late. She'd be gone, like the song—long, long gone. She pictured him opening the envelope she'd taped to the refrigerator, his name written neatly in cursive across the front and book-ended between two red hearts. She imagined the angry flush of his cheeks and the prominent flare of his nostrils when he discovered its folded contents were copies of her petition for a divorce and not some sappy note of endearment. It wasn't necessary, of course. The official papers along with the restraining order would be served to him on Monday by an officer of the court. But this was her stand, her chance to break free on her terms and show Tom he didn't own her and never had.

She took one last glimpse at the little Cape Cod with its perfectly weathered cedar shingles, cozy dormers, and red brick chimneystack. It looked especially charming viewed through the kaleidoscope of gently swirling ice crystals and dusted in snow. The quaint three-bedroom house located on a quiet but happy street symbolized everything she had hoped her marriage to Tom would be but had never become. Still, she allowed herself a moment of nostalgia, regret even, for the good times because there had been a few. And at least she was escaping while Tom was at work, avoiding a confrontation. She glanced at the glove compartment where the little .22 Beretta had been hidden in the months since she'd bought it at a pawn shop. Just in case. With a heavy heart, she shifted the Camry into reverse, easing it down the driveway, yet once on the open road, she didn't look back.

She dialed her best friend, Alice, put the phone on speaker, tucked it into the holder, and headed down Main Street.

"You're what?" Alice sounded incredulous.

"Leaving."

"Now? In the middle of a blizzard? Are you sure that's such a good idea?"

"It's the best idea I've had in a long time."

"Where are you going?" Alice let the question hang for a moment. "No, scratch that. It's probably better I don't know. That way if he calls—and I'm sure he'll call—I won't have to lie to him or to Jack."

"Okay. Listen. Don't worry. I'll be okay. I'll be with Drew."

"Jesus, Silvi. Are you crazy? What if Tom finds out? He'll kill you."

"He doesn't own me."

"You're right. He doesn't. But still, why add fuel to the fire?"

"You know that Drew and I are just friends."

"Honey, I know you think you and Drew are just friends, but I'm not so sure about Drew."

"Now you sound exactly like Tom."

"Sorry, but I've got to call 'em like I see 'em. I mean, just because I'm married to his brother doesn't mean I can't see how crazy jealous Tom can be, but maybe this time he'd be right."

The snow picked up, and as Silvia merged onto Route 10, a gusty wind hurled grape-sized flakes toward the Camry. A thin, slick layer of snow blanketed the blacktop, and she jimmied the wheel slightly left then right, checking for traction. "I've got to go."

"Okay, but promise me you'll call when you get to wherever it is you're going so that I know you're safe."

Silvia promised.

* * * *

She turned onto Cabot Lane, the private gravel drive that according to GPS would deliver her to her destination. The snow had temporarily abated, and Silvia did her best to follow a shallow pair of old tracks not yet obliterated by the fresh snowfall.

As the Camry crested the hill, a contemporary A-frame cabin, whose front wall consisted almost entirely of glass, came into full view. Lights lit up its interior so that it resembled an oversized beacon, and a gray haze of smoke billowed tentatively above the black stovepipe chimney jutting out of the cabin's roof.

"You made it," Drew said, meeting her at the door. The tantalizing smell of sautéed onions wafted past her. Drew, who was wearing a chef's apron, took her suitcase and leaned it against the wall. "Any trouble finding it?"

Silvia held up her phone, which still displayed the GPS function.

"Great. I'm surprised you have service. On a good day, a connection can be spotty up here, but with a storm we're lucky to have service at all."

Silvia shoved her gloves and her phone into her coat pockets and loosened the scarf around her neck as she glanced about the cabin's cozy interior.

The floor plan was open. From where she stood she could see a modest but adequate kitchen, a living room with a faux bearskin rug stretched out before a glowing wood stove, a narrow hallway she imagined led to a couple of bedrooms and a small bath, as well as stairs leading to the loft.

Drew had told her that the cabin belonged to his parents. Now retired and living in Florida, they had given him exclusive use.

He helped her with her coat, hanging it and her scarf on a coat rack by the door. He placed his hand on the small of her back and shepherded her toward the fire. "So what do you think?"

As they walked past the kitchen, she saw a small round table set for two and a bottle of Champagne propped in a stainless steel chiller. "I think you're awesome."

Drew smiled, and it occurred to Silvia he had the smile of a boy, sweet and innocent. Definitely not handsome like Tom but cute in a nerdy sort of way.

He led her over to the couch and motioned for her to sit. Silvia sank into the warm and toasty cushions. Drew grabbed a log from a neat pile next to the stove and fed it into the fire, which spit and hissed as it sucked residual moisture from the wood. "Dinner's almost ready," he said, closing the stove's door.

"Whatever it is, it smells delicious. But really, you shouldn't have. I don't want you to think that you have to wait on me while I'm here. I'm more than capable of taking care of myself."

"Of course you are. But I like to cook, so it's really no trouble. Plus I figured tonight was sort of special. Now you sit back and enjoy the fire. I'll be right back."

Pots and pans clanked and rattled in the kitchen as Silvia glanced around the living room. A huge pair of antlers flanked by two rustic paintings with wildlife themes hung on one adjacent wall, while the stove and its stacked-brick backdrop dominated the other. Combined with the high ceiling and the glass wall, the room's earthy décor gave the impression that the cabin's interior was a natural extension of the wooded landscape outside.

Silvia's eyes eventually settled on the owl-shaped clock located to the right of the wood stove. Ten past four. Tiny pricks of perspiration tingled all over her body. At any moment Tom would be walking through the door of their Cape Cod, expecting to find her and his dinner like he did every night. Except tonight, as he carefully placed his meticulously polished boots by the door so as not to soil the bright white carpet he had insisted upon, there would be no meatloaf browning in the oven or dutiful wife to serve it.

When Drew returned he had lost the apron but held a glass of red wine in each hand. "A merlot," he said as he handed her one of the glasses.

"Ooh, my favorite." She took a sip.

"I remember."

She must have looked puzzled because he added, "The Christmas party."

"Christmas party?"

"Yes, Dahlia's Christmas party."

Dahlia was a librarian at the library where Silvia volunteered. As always, Tom had insisted on accompanying her to the party. *To keep an eye on you*, he had said. As if she needed a chaperone. Then he'd been the one to get plastered and threaten Dahlia's brother with bodily harm simply because he'd accidently bumped into Silvia. Thankfully, she had been able to calm Tom down before he did something stupid that they'd both regret. Still, she'd been so humiliated that she had declined to attend again, despite receiving an invite.

"But that was…" She paused to do the math. "Over five years ago."

"I know."

A rush of warmth flushed her cheeks as Silvia recalled Alice's comment, but she couldn't be sure if it was the fact that Drew remembered such a small detail, or the wine. Nonetheless she relaxed a little when Drew took a seat in the chair opposite her rather than beside her on the couch. Her gaze wandered to the glass wall, and she could see the snow had started again. *You silly girl*, she told herself. *Drew is just a thoughtful person, the type of person who pays attention to the smallest detail. He's a writer, isn't he? It's his job to notice what others overlook.* Then thinking of Alice, she suddenly remembered her promise to call.

"Is something wrong?" Drew asked as Silvia popped up from the couch.

"Alice, I forgot to call her. I told her I'd call her when I got here."

"You told her you were coming to the cabin?"

"No, no. I just mentioned you were giving me shelter. Not that I wouldn't have told her if she had asked. Alice is my best friend. I trust her completely. The truth is when I started to tell her I was coming here, she said that she'd rather not know."

He looked confused.

"She knows the first thing Tom will do when he finds me gone is have Jack drag her into a game of twenty questions. I guess she figures they can't get out of her what she doesn't know."

"Ah."

"But I promised I'd call to let her know that I arrived safely." She had started for the hallway to retrieve her phone from her coat when Drew's next comment stopped her.

"I wouldn't bother," he said matter-of-factly.

She turned to face him.

"I checked my phone for messages while I was in the kitchen and there was no service," Drew said.

"Maybe it's back on."

"You can check, but I doubt it. I told you service is spotty up here even on a good day. Chances are the service is out until this storm passes. Sorry."

"What about a landline?"

"Don't have one. Doesn't make sense since I'm the only one who uses the place these days, and primarily as a retreat for writing." Silvia's concern must have been evident because he added, "But don't worry. We'll be fine. I've weathered more winter storms here than I can count."

Silvia sat back down. Drew seemed so adamant about not checking, and she didn't want to be impolite, so she decided to wait until after dinner.

The two of them sat in silence for a while, sipping their merlots and basking in the stove's heat, which seemed even more inviting because of the blustery weather outside.

"So, how is it?" Drew said, his hand resting on the chair and the rim of his glass sparkling with reflected light from the deer-antler chandelier overhead.

"It's nice. Must have been a good year." She took another sip.

"I'm glad you like it, but I was referring to your freedom. How does it feel?"

Silvia glanced down at her glass then back up at Drew. "Nice. It feels nice."

He raised an eyebrow. "Really?"

"Really."

"No last-minute second thoughts? No regrets?"

"Maybe a few right before I left, but nothing that could change my mind. Not now. Not ever."

"Good," he said. "That's good."

* * * *

Later Silvia proclaimed that Drew's artistic abilities weren't restricted to the written word, for the dinner he had prepared was culinary poetry—grilled salmon with fresh dill and lemon butter served alongside a wild rice pilaf with celery, onions, carrots, mushrooms, and almonds. It was not only beautiful, but also delicious and a perfect complement to the expensive Champagne Drew had chosen to celebrate her new life without Tom. Silvia was never much of a cook. She rarely ventured beyond traditional staples like chicken soup, spaghetti and meatballs, beef stew, and if in an adventurous mood, she might attempt a stuffed chicken with all the trimmings. A basic meat-and-potatoes kind of man who often frowned at what he called froufrou food, Tom had never complained. Now the idea of creating a gourmet meal from scratch, limited only by imagination and personal taste, seemed liberating, and she decided she'd ask Drew for some pointers during her stay at the cabin.

Following dinner Drew suggested a game of Scrabble, and after getting slaughtered several times, Silvia volunteered to clean up in the kitchen where, she joked, she could nurse her wounds privately. Drew attended to the fire, deciding it would be a good idea to bring up another load of wood from a large woodshed at the edge of the property to a smaller overhang closer to the cabin. He explained that while his parents had installed central heating, power outages were common, and it was always better to have a back-up plan just in case. Though deceptively small, the little stove was capable of warming the entire cabin should the power fail.

Done with the dishes and waiting for Drew to finish up, Silvia finally checked her phone. She smiled. The signal indicator vacillated between one and two bars. She toggled through the calls, surprised to find there was not one single call from Tom, but at least a dozen from Alice.

She immediately called Alice.

"God, Silvi. Where have you been? I've been calling every five minutes for the past two hours."

"I'm so sorry. It's just the phone service here is horrible."

"It's okay, but there's something I have to tell you." Silvia could hear the distress in her friend's voice and it worried her. "It's about Tom."

"Don't tell me he's blaming you?" she interrupted. It was the last straw. Any doubt that she'd made the right decision vanished. "I knew this would happen. Listen, you can tell him from me that I left because I wanted to. Nobody had to convince me, and if he wants to get in touch with me he can contact my lawyer—"

"Listen, sweetheart. You don't understand. Tom didn't call."

"But you just said…"

"There was an accident, Silvia. When the police couldn't get a hold of you at home, they called Jack."

"Is he all right?"

"I'm sorry."

"Sorry?"

"He's dead, Silvi. They think he fell asleep at the wheel. There were two witnesses, and both claimed it was as if he never saw the bend in the road, and with the ice and snow… The driver who pulled him from the wreckage found a pulse, but by the time the ambulance arrived, he was gone."

Long, long gone…

Silvia shivered. Dead. Tom, with his big burly hands and robust physique, sinewy muscles that pushed the sleeves of his shirts to their limits—that bull of a man who exuded strength and symbolized vitality. He was only thirty-two for Christ's sake.

"Honey, I'm sorry. I know this must be strange considering… well, you know."

Silvia did know. She immediately thought of the note. Had he read it and in a blind fit of rage stormed out of the house, determined to track her down? Could her cruelty, her childish need for revenge, have contributed to his death?

"When?"

"After work."

"So, he never made it home?"

"It doesn't seem so."

Relief washed over her, as if her vindication in his death somehow made it more palatable, more digestible.

"That's good."

Alice said something, but her voice faded in and out so that it was unintelligible.

Silvia glanced down at the phone's screen and saw that the signal now barely registered.

"Alice, I'm losing the connection. I'm going to hang up and try again. Alice, can you hear me?" The connection went dead before she could get a response.

She turned the phone off and on several times as she moved around the cabin searching for a signal. Nothing.

Finally, she switched the phone off, and with a trembling hand stuffed it back into her coat pocket. A light tap on the door startled her. It was Drew, his hands filled with wood. She opened the door. His cheeks were ruddy from the cold and physical exertion, and his wind-swept, snow-capped hair had a wild quality.

He dropped the logs into a carton he'd brought in earlier to hold the extra wood.

"We're all set," he said, plucking some debris from his sweater.

That's when he must have noticed Silvia's expression. "Is something wrong?"

Silvia couldn't answer, simply hugged herself tightly, tears trickling down her face.

He reached out and placed his hands around her waist, drawing her toward him. Silvia didn't resist.

"You're shaking."

She buried her head into his sweater, tears gushing like water through a broken dam.

Drew didn't ask for an explanation—merely held her, rocking her slowly. After several moments she attempted to speak.

"It's Tom."

"Tom? So that's what this is all about? Don't worry. I told you you'd be safe here. He can't hurt you anymore."

"You don't understand," Silvia stuttered. "Tom, he's... he's... God, Drew. Tom's dead."

Drew hugged her more tightly.

"The note I left. It was so spiteful, so cruel. To think it could've been the last thing he saw."

He stroked the length of her hair. "Shhh. Everything will be all right, I promise."

She wriggled free and took a step back. "You don't understand. I wanted him to suffer. God, how I wanted him to suffer. But not... not like this."

He took her face between his hands. Unlike Tom's hands, which were thick, coarse, and calloused, Drew's hands were slender, soft, and finely manicured. The hands of a banker, she thought, or a writer. He tilted her head back, forcing her gaze up. "You," he said, with a conviction that was almost frightening, "are not to blame. Now, I know this must be a shock, but accidents happen. The roads are slippery. You can't honestly blame yourself for the weather, can you?"

Silvia stared into his eyes. The two had never been this intimate before. Their time together at the library—those afternoons when Drew came to complete research for his books—were spent with the respectable distance of the checkout counter between them. Perhaps it was her distressed state, but the only thought she could form now was that Drew's eyes were actually more of a hazel green with flecks of gold than a hazel brown with flecks of green.

"You're upset," he said. "Why don't you come into the other room, and I'll get you a glass of wine."

Drew stepped back and offered his hand.

"It's all right," he said in a soothing voice. "Everything's going to be all right."

Silvia stared at his hand, then up at his face, the kind, solemn face of her dear friend Drew. She grabbed hold of his hand, finding solace in his touch.

He led her into the living room, leaving her on the couch as he went to find a blanket. When he returned he carried not only a crocheted afghan, but also another glass of the merlot. He handed her the wine then draped the afghan over her lap, tucking it in around the contours of her body. She had since stopped crying and thanked him. She brought the wine glass to her lips, this time not bothering with sips, but instead gulping the mellow liquid in greedy mouthfuls.

Drew sat on the coffee table directly in front of her so that their knees touched. He reached for her empty glass, placing it on the table, then moved onto the couch beside her. He slid his arm behind her neck, hooking it around her shoulder, and she allowed herself to be eased into his body, her head coming to a rest against his chest, the *thub-dub* of his heart thumping beneath her ear.

"You okay?" he said, his mouth only inches from her face and his soft reassuring breath caressing her cheek.

She pulled at a loose string on his sweater. "I don't know."

"That's okay."

"It's just, you know, I wanted to leave. I had to leave. He was suffocating me. I was miserable, and he knew it."

"I understand, Silvia. It's okay."

She tilted her head back so she could see his face. He looked different from this position: the sharp angle of his chin more pronounced, stronger, more decisive.

"The really sad thing is that there's a part of me that's relieved."

"Of course, you're relieved. The man was a tyrant."

"But doesn't that make me a bad person?"

"I don't think so. And who knows. Sometimes things happen for a reason."

"Reason?" Silvia wasn't sure she was comfortable with the insinuation.

"You said a thousand times yourself. A control freak like Tom wasn't going to let you walk away without a fight. It's why you got the restraining order and came here to hide out. A man like Tom is capable of almost anything when it comes to keeping the woman he loves."

Drew's hand slid over hers, interlocking their fingers. She squeezed gently. That's when she noticed them, the scabbed-over patches covering the knuckles of his right hand.

"Your hand," she said, sitting up straight.

"Those? Just a few scratches."

"Are you sure? It looks painful."

"Nah, doesn't hurt at all. Probably happened when I was splitting wood yesterday."

"Yesterday?"

"Ummhmm."

"But I thought you had that big meeting with your editor yesterday?"

"I did. But I decided to cancel so I could come up early and get things ready for us."

"Oh. That was so thoughtful," Silvia said, her words starting to slur and fade.

The vague impression of an idea still too remote and unformed to qualify as a thought stirred in the deep dark recesses of her subconscious. Perhaps if she hadn't been so exhausted, she might have possessed the energy to coax it toward the surface. Instead, her consciousness homed in on the fluffy white flakes outside, which glistened like miniature crystal balls under the cabin's floodlights. The unblemished purity of the whitewashed landscape had a cleansing quality, as if the blanket of snow had conveniently buried all the bad things in the world safely beneath its frosty cover.

She barely noticed the lights flickering off and on. "Good thing I brought up the wood," Drew mumbled into her hair. "It looks like we may end up losing power after all."

Silvia snuggled closer.

"Not that I'm complaining," he added. "I can't think of anyone I'd rather be stranded here with than you." He kissed the top of her head, and the lights clicked off, the orange glow of the stove, the room's only light. "It's just you, me, and the fire from here on out," he whispered, but Silvia's droopy eyelids had already eased closed.

* * * *

When Silvia awoke the next morning she found herself still cradled in Drew's embrace. She carefully lifted his arm and wriggled herself free. Standing, she felt woozy, no doubt the result of the wine and Champagne she had consumed the night before. The power still appeared to be off, and the room felt chilly. She wrapped the afghan snuggly around her shoulders and meandered toward the window, where she marveled at the icy tundra outside. A soft golden light filtered through the barren trees, giving the untainted snow a magical quality.

That's when it hit her. Tom. Dead. She shivered, pulling the afghan tighter. It didn't seem real, any of it.

Her gaze settled on her car and Drew's truck: both nearly buried under a colossal snowdrift. *Trapped*, she thought, *or safe, depending on how you looked at it*. Without cars or a phone, she could postpone dealing with Tom's death, at least for a little while.

Thirsty and suffering from a severe case of cotton mouth, she headed into the kitchen for a drink. The faucet wouldn't work, but Drew had stocked the refrigerator with bottled water. "Just in case," he had said, tapping the side of his head with his index finger. "Thinking ahead and always prepared."

She thought about Alice. She stopped to check her phone, but when she hit the power button, nothing happened. *Damn. The battery.* After checking in with Alice she must have forgotten to turn it off, and now it was dead.

She entered the kitchen and noticed Drew's phone plugged into its charger and sitting on the counter. The power had been off all night, but it was possible his phone still held a charge. She hadn't intended to snoop, yet after verifying the phone service was still out, the icon for his photo app caught her attention.

Family portraits, vacations, old friends, landscapes? She wondered what images she'd find in the folder. Or maybe there'd be no photos at all. It suddenly occurred to her how little she knew about Drew, other than he was a modestly successful mystery writer. "I think of original ways to kill people for a living," he had once joked. Yet most of their time lately had been spent at the public library talking about her and her problems with Tom. Drew, the incredible listener, and she, the unhappy wife with a need to be heard. It was the perfect friendship, yet what did she really know about him?

Curiosity finally prevailed, and she glanced tentatively over her shoulder like a child who knows she shouldn't but couldn't resist. Her index finger was about to tap on the photo icon when Drew's voice startled her.

"What are you doing?"

Silvia dropped the phone on the counter. The *clang* as it hit the Formica echoed throughout the kitchen.

She put a hand over her heart as she turned to face him. "Christ, Drew. You scared me to death."

He walked over, picking up the phone from the counter. "Sorry," he said, staring down at the screen before turning it off. Wrinkles creased his forehead.

"I was just checking for service. I must have left my phone on and now the battery's dead...." She gestured toward the hallway.

"So?"

Her heart was pounding. *Guilty,* she thought. *You're a big, fat snoop, and he caught you. Silvia Marie, you might just be the worst houseguest ever. Not even here twenty-four hours and already putting your nose where it doesn't belong.*

"You were right about the spotty service," she said, trying to sound casual.

Drew smiled, and she relaxed. "Don't worry. Like I told you, this isn't the first storm I've weathered at the cabin."

Silvia seized the opportunity to delve into his past. Besides, talking about Drew would prevent the inevitable—talking about Tom's death—and she really wasn't up to talking about Tom's death, not today. "I guess you spent lots of winters up here as a kid."

"That's for sure."

"So, did you come with family?"

"Sure. Like I told you, the cabin belongs to my parents."

"I mean like the whole family—aunts, uncles, cousins? You know, a big ole family retreat? I bet the relatives never missed an opportunity to come hang out."

Drew opened a drawer and placed his phone inside. "Not really. My parents were both from small families out west."

"Really, I didn't know that."

Drew leaned against the counter in front of her. "Listen, Silvia. You don't need to do this."

"Do what?"

"This."

She immediately felt something inside give, and she wanted to crumble.

"If you don't want to talk about Tom, I won't push." He reached out and brushed her hair away from her face. "I'm not going anywhere. There's no pressure. Whenever you're ready, we'll talk."

Silvia could feel the heat flush her cheeks as the stew of emotions bubbling under the surface threatened to boil over. She swallowed hard and somehow managed to keep her feelings contained, but barely. She sighed. It was going to be a long day.

* * * *

The power returned by ten, and on Silvia's insistence, Drew spent the day writing. "I told you, I didn't want to interfere with your work, and I'm serious."

Drew claimed repeatedly that he didn't mind keeping her company, but she refused to be a distraction. Plus, she needed time to think. That's when he had reached up and stroked her cheek and reassured her that of course, he understood.

She plugged in her phone so at least she'd have power if she ever got a signal, and then spent most the day on the couch snuggled in the afghan. Drew had given her an advanced copy of his latest novel, *Murder, My Love*. Yet her heart just wasn't into reading, and by page ten she found it impossible to focus. Instead snapshots of Tom and their life together filled her thoughts. Memories of their first date, the night he proposed by tracing "Will you marry me?" in the sand during their weekend get-away to Bethany Beach. Their cozy wedding and even cozier wedding night. Funny how the good times can sometimes overshadow the bad, she thought, no matter how bad the bad, and there had been plenty of bad. Tom's outrageous jealousy and his controlling nature. His compulsive neatness that extended beyond an orderly house. His tirades when she'd put the toilet paper facing the wrong direction or failed to perfectly center the crease in his pants. Sure, he'd never abused her, at least not physically. Yet, in some ways what he had done was worse. He'd kept her prisoner in her own home, her only freedom—those afternoons she spent volunteering at the library.

And now she was free and Tom was dead, and her relief in the first seemed to overshadow her grief in the latter. She was increasingly okay with that, and increasingly okay with being okay. Drew was right. It was probably better this way. Tom would never have let her go, not without a fight, or worse.

* * * *

The owl clock indicated it was half past two when Drew announced lunch was ready. Feeling somewhat optimistic, Silvia decided to check her phone. She almost squealed when she discovered a signal. She'd never admit this to Drew for fear of appearing ungrateful for his hospitality, but there was something disconcerting about being cut off from the rest of civilization. The ability to connect with the outside world was reassuring.

She had just hit speed dial when Drew appeared in the living room. "I said, lunch is served."

She raised her hand in an appeal for patience. "Be right there. Just want to call Alice while I've got a signal."

The phone rang once before it was eased from her hand. "Lunch," he said. "I made roast beef on rye."

Silvia stared at her phone in his hand, feeling unsettled. She lunged for the phone, but Drew pulled it out of reach.

"Sorry. No can do," he said playfully, yet despite his lighthearted disposition, Silvia was getting a little peeved.

She reached higher. "Drew, give me the phone," she said firmly. "I really need to call Alice. She's probably worried sick."

Silvia struggled for the phone, but Drew, a good foot taller, had no trouble keeping it away.

"Drew, I'm serious. Give me the phone."

"I told you, lunch is ready."

"I know lunch is ready, but I need to call Alice. Plus, I'm really not hungry, so if you'd just give me the phone."

Drew's whole expression changed, and suddenly he resembled Tom before one of his tirades. Stunned, Silvia could only watch in disbelief as Drew marched over and opened the door to the wood stove. By the time she understood his intention, it was too late. He had already chucked her phone into the fire.

"What the hell are you doing? That's my phone."

He calmly closed the stove's door then walked over to her. He placed a hand on each shoulder. Her first impulse was to shrug them away, but something in his eyes stopped her. Then the something disappeared almost as quickly as it had appeared. "Listen, I'm sorry about that. But it had to be done. I thought running your battery down would be enough, but apparently you can't take a hint. Sweetheart, you've got to let this go."

Sweetheart? Since when had Drew referred to her as sweetheart? "What are you taking about? Let what go?"

"Your life with Tom."

"My life with Tom? Drew, you're not making sense."

"Alice. She's all part of that life. Surely you understand now that Tom is gone how important it is to make a clean break? I really didn't want to have to do that, but you left me no choice."

"Drew, please. Listen to me. Alice is my friend. My best friend."

Drew shook his head. "Really? Alice? Tom's sister-in-law? You can't be serious?" His grip on her shoulders tightened. "You don't think I see what this is all about. You're having second thoughts, aren't you?"

She tried to step back, but his hands were clamped down onto her shoulders, and he wasn't letting go. "You're hurting me," she whimpered.

"Hurting you? I'm trying to help you. That's all." He shook her as if to reinforce his point. "Understand? Help you."

"Please, Drew. Let go. I'm serious. You're scaring me."

He thrust his arms up into the air. "Scaring you?" He brought his hands to his head and clutched two fistfuls of hair in a gesture of frustration. "You, you, you! Does everything always have to be about you? My God, Silvia. What about me? Don't you think I was scared? I risked everything for you. For us!"

Silvia took a step back, but he matched her step for step, backing her up into the wall. He placed his palms on the wall, boxing her in. His chest was heaving and his face was red and bloated. Then it dawned on her, and she felt her heart sink. The accident. She never said it was an accident, but Drew had known.

"Oh my God, Drew. What did you do?"

I think of original ways to kill people.

"Only what needed to be done."

"But why?"

"It's what you wanted. How many times did you tell me you wanted him out of your life? Say that your life would have been so different if you had met someone like me instead of someone like him."

"Of course, I wanted him out of my life. It's why I left. But I never said I wanted him… dead?" She thought back to their conversations. Sure she had joked that it would save her a lot of pain and heartache if Tom could have an unfortunate accident, but she had been blowing off steam. She hadn't been serious. And as far as finding a man like Drew, she had meant it figuratively, as in "a nice guy"—what she'd thought Drew was—not literally.

"Listen, Silvia. I simply did what you didn't have the courage to do." He clenched and unclenched the scarred knuckles of his right hand. "I cut the brake line on his car."

Silvia was sobbing now. "Oh God, no." She tried to duck under his arms, but he was too quick for her.

"Please, Drew. Let me go."

"I'm sorry, but I can't."

She knew he was being sincere. Just like Tom, he would never let go. She felt sick, as whatever fight she had managed to muster slipped away. *You silly, girl,* she thought. *It's long, long gone.*

She didn't bother resisting as Drew pulled her close, only turned her head and stared at the icy landscape outside.

The snow, she thought, *it really is pretty.*

Drew stroked her hair. "It's for the better, Silvia. You should be thanking me. After all, you're finally free."

The word *free* reverberated in her thoughts, igniting a spark somewhere deep within the frozen tundra that had become her heart. It was then she remembered the gun. The one she had never seriously contemplated firing. The sleek black pistol that from a distance resembled a child's toy and was hidden in her glove compartment along with a box of bullets. Yes, Silvia thought. Soon, I will be free.

Shaun Taylor Bevins is an aspiring novelist and a writer of short stories. When she isn't working as a physical therapist (her day job) or mothering her four adorable and extremely active children (her twenty-four-hour-a-day job), she is reading and writing. She is thrilled to have another short story published in a Chesapeake Chapter Sisters in Crime anthology.

THE SECOND STORM
by Marianne Wilski Strong

I really love a rainy day, especially with a good book and a cup of orange herbal tea. But I didn't like the rainy day, I should say days, last month, caused by Tropical Storm Frank. Nobody did. At least, I didn't like the storm right away. Now I think of it with great fondness.

Frank reminded everyone of another storm, known as Agnes, that had blown into my hometown of Wellsboro, Pennsylvania, fifteen years ago, causing so much damage, the National Weather Service permanently retired the name Agnes and established the Federal Emergency Management Agency. Frank wasn't as bad, but it uncovered what I thought were only tall tales from Agnes.

The first tall tale was grim. The Susquehanna River had broken through the dikes at the city cemetery and washed coffins and bodies out into the streets. That story proved true.

According to the second tale, the Susquehanna had broken its banks and flooded the coal mines that lay beneath the city. That story was also true, except that it was ice floes that had drifted downriver and smashed the walls of the mines several years before Agnes.

The third tale maintained that everyone in the city had drowned. That was patently false.

The fourth tale claimed that the Susquehanna had broken through the dikes so suddenly, people had to be rescued from their roofs by helicopter. That was true. My Aunt Sophie was one of those people.

The fifth tale added detail. The Susquehanna had broken through so suddenly, stores hadn't had time to clear out their inventory. Tons of products, everything from meats and vegetables, to sweaters and coats, to diamond jewelry and paintings, had floated into the city and made their way down the Susquehanna to the Chesapeake Bay. That was partially true. Not everything made it to the Chesapeake. But I'm getting ahead of myself. Back to Frank.

By the time Frank came along, I had bought, in a neighborhood under renovation, a house with a great view of the Susquehanna. Everyone had assured me that the river would never rise high enough to overflow the new dikes, but Frank turned out to be a doozy. For four days running, I went in and out of my front door to watch the Susquehanna rising, foot by foot. I kept telling myself that lightning never struck twice in the same place. By the fourth day, I acknowledged that I was dealing with incessant rain, not lightning.

When I saw the electronics store down the street start to remove their inventory, I pulled out some suitcases and agonized over what to save: photographs, souvenirs of travels, important papers? All irreplaceable. Clothes, books, camera? All replaceable.

I made decisions, unmade them, packed, unpacked, all the while listening to the incessant pounding of rain on the roof of my newly purchased house. I berated myself. Why hadn't I opted for a view of a mountain instead of a river? Why hadn't I stayed in Washington, DC, and dealt with the high crime rate and increasingly bad traffic instead of coming to what I thought would be a peaceful town in which to live and grow old?

I was about to pack my mother's 1920s ivory comb, brush, and mirror set when the call came. It was my sister, Dorothy. She almost never called me, unless she had no one else to talk to.

I answered the phone with a nice high tone of hysteria. "I'm busy right now."

"What are you doing, Annie?"

"I'm signing up for swimming lessons," I said.

"Why are you doing that?"

I rolled my eyes. "That was a sick joke, Dot. Actually, I'm building an ark."

Silence.

Finally, Dot spoke. "Well, you'd better stop doing that and start sandbagging. They said so."

"Who's 'they?'"

"Don't you have the TV on?"

I realized that my sister had actually asked a reasonable question. "No, I don't. Who said something about sandbagging?"

"The mayor, silly. He said that trucks will be dropping off sandbags to houses along the river. Anyway, you're supposed to start sandbagging now. Pete said he's coming down to help you."

I was struck silent. I hadn't said more than five *hellos* to my brother-in-law, Pete, in as many years. We didn't see eye to eye on anything, including the changes he had paid some shady lawyer to make in my parents' will. It hadn't been worth fighting over, but I couldn't forget it. Nor could I forgive him for puncturing my tires when I complained about the garbage he kept sneaking into my cans at night because he was too cheap to pay for garbage collection.

"Pete?" I said. "Pete who?"

"Pete, my husband. He said he'd come down to help. I thought you'd be grateful."

I looked out the front window. The Susquehanna had risen another few inches. "Okay," I said. "Any port in a storm."

"I'd come myself, but I have to get to the hospital. If the river floods, the patients will have to be moved to higher floors or even to another hospital. So it's all hands on deck, including us nursing assistants. I was there all day yesterday. Had to help get patients ready. It's like Hurricane Agnes all over again."

"Okay," I said. "I understand." I did, too, this time. I knew the hospital sat smack in the flood zone and that its doctors had been worried since the river started rising. So my sister's excuse of having to work was legitimate. Usually her excuses weren't.

She rang off.

I heard thumps from outside. My God, I thought, it's the river, floating God knows what into my house. I ran outside into the pouring rain.

Thump. Thump. Thump. Three more sandbags joined the pile that was rising on my front lawn. "Get them 'round the house," the delivery truck driver yelled.

I looked at the pile of sandbags. Flour sacks, with numbers on them. I grabbed the edges of one of the bags and dragged it laboriously to the front of the house and shoved it against the foundation. Rain gushed out of the gutters and onto my head. I turned back to the sandbags, estimating that even if the river rose less than an inch over the next two weeks, I'd never have the sandbags in place.

I was dragging a sandbag to the base of the house when Pete arrived, roaring around the corner in his yellow truck with the flames painted on the side. He brought the truck to a screeching halt and hopped out. "I'll get that," he yelled. "Go inside and get together what you want to save just in case."

I dropped the sandbag, swiped wet hair off my face, and stared at Pete, amazed. Pete was even more of a genius than my sister at inventing excuses to get out of work. And in my case, he usually didn't even bother with an excuse. He just refused. I'd stopped asking years ago.

So what the hell was he doing here now? Suspicions flooded my mind faster than the water rising in front of me. Pete intended to put the sandbags in the wrong place and enjoy a good laugh when my house flooded. Pete was going to steal the sandbags and sell them to desperate house owners. Pete was...

Rain pelted down, dripping from my hair, nose, fingertips. I could hear the river gushing and gurgling. I quit thinking and starting dragging sandbags again.

"Go on in the house and get ready," Pete yelled. "If the river goes over the dike, I'm getting my ass and my truck out of here, with or without you."

That was more like Pete.

Thump. Thump. Thump. More sandbags dropped from the delivery truck onto my lawn.

I dashed into the house, ran upstairs, and began filling suitcases again. I'd already taken jewelry, photos, important papers, so now I just dumped in shoes, jackets, makeup.

I was about to head downstairs when I glanced out of my bedroom window, hoping to see the rain slow to a drizzle. I stopped and stared.

Pete was kneeling at the foundation of the dilapidated storage building next door that had once been Borski Jewelers. The Borskis had cleared out after Agnes. The deserted building had been slated for condemnation until a developer snapped it up with plans to turn it into condos. I had been delighted. I wouldn't have to stare at the graffiti anymore, including a big fat X someone had painted on a foundation block smack in front of my bedroom window.

So what the hell was Pete doing on his knees? Praying to the river god? I doubt that Pete had recited even one Hail Mary in the past thirty years.

I moved closer to the window. I could see Pete's elbows jerking back and forth as if he were scraping or yanking something. Or, was he digging? And if so, digging for what?

I raced downstairs and out onto my porch to check it out.

Before I could determine what Pete was up to, I was distracted by a young man who ran up, grabbed a sandbag, and plopped it next to those I'd piled at the base of my house. I could see other young people, probably college students from the nearby university, fanning out over the neighborhood to help. Bless them.

Then my neighbor Leona came bounding around the corner. I muttered a prayer of thanks. With Leona, I had hope. Leona had spent her childhood helping her father split logs and haul loads of lumber and coal to customers. She'd developed a fine set of muscles and had kept them in fighting order pulverizing punching bags at the local gym. She'd sandbag the house up to the top of the first-floor windows in ten minutes. I was about ready to fling myself into Leona's comforting arms.

"What the hell are you doing on the porch?" Leona yelled.

"I just came down. I was upstairs, packing some things."

"Well get your ass out here. We have to get more sandbags around your house. Mine's done." Leona ran to the edge of the lawn, grabbed two sandbags, hauled them as if they were pillows, and slammed them against the base of the house. She turned for more.

I was about to join her when all hell broke loose.

I felt kind of disembodied standing on the porch, watching what happened through the silver screen of rain, as if I were watching a movie, maybe *The Rains of Ranchipur* or *River of No Return*, ignoring the real danger of having my house flooded and my brother-in-law, my neighbor Leona, a student, and myself being swept away by the Susquehanna.

The first thing that happened was shouting. Had someone seen the river breach the dikes? Was a tsunami on its way?

Then the film ended and reality clicked in. I squinted, leaned over my porch banister, and peered through the sheet of rain. I could make out the foamy brown water of the Susquehanna. It was headed at full speed downstream toward Harrisburg, but it was still locked within the walls of the dikes.

I realized it was Pete shouting. I leaned over the other way to see what was going on. "Get the hell away from here," Pete yelled at the student who had approached him. "Keep sandbagging the house, you moron. I'll take care of this place." He rose and turned his six-foot bulk threateningly toward the student.

The student backed off.

Leona returned, dragging more sandbags, then went back for more.

I pounded down my porch steps into the rain that seemed to drill into my skin. I had to find out what the hell Pete was up to. No good, I suspected.

Again, all sorts of wild ideas ran through my mind. He was trying to dig a hole to the river to make sure I got flooded out. He was burying a packet of opium or cocaine or whatever his current drug of choice was. He was burying my sister's head, which he had chopped off in a fit of anger.

I raced around the corner of the house to where Leona and the student were now sandbagging and where Pete was doing only heaven, or hell, knew what.

At least, I tried to race. The grass was slick and slippery with rain and my right foot flew out from under me. I banged down on my ass, cursed, then pushed up on all fours, swiping at the rivulets of rain coursing through my hair and over my nose. I managed to haul my now soaking carcass upright and headed toward Pete.

"What the hell are you doing?" I shouted. "Don't waste sandbags and your time over there. That building is empty. Sandbag the house, you moron."

Pete, back on his knees, ignored me and went on digging.

I kept shouting.

Startled, the student looked from me to Pete, alarm written all over his face. No doubt he figured he had fallen in with a pack of maniacs.

Half sliding, half running, I managed to get to Pete. "What the hell are you up to?" I yelled.

Pete rose, turned, and pushed hard against my chest. I flew backward, splat down into a puddle. A fountain of rainwater sprayed furiously around me.

Pete took a step toward me. The student, his Batman instincts apparently aroused, leapt toward Pete and closed his arms round Pete's back and chest.

He was no match for Pete. Snapping his arms open, Pete broke the student's grip and swung around. He throttled the student and banged him against the wall of the old storage building. The student went limp. Pete let him slip to the ground.

I struggled up, screaming. "You maniac. Get the hell out of here." I stopped yelling and began backing up as Pete advanced, his eyes bugged out and crazed looking, focused on me. In his right hand he held a chisel, aimed at my face.

From the corner of my eye, I saw Leona arc around until she could bear down on Pete from behind.

Ridiculously, I thought of a line of Lord Byron's poetry, stamped into my mind from my English major days: "The Assyrian came down like the wolf on the fold." Only Leona resembled a grizzly bear more than a wolf.

The grizzly bear, muscles bulging, lifted a sandbag and slammed it down on the sheep's head.

The sheep slid down next to the student.

So there I stood in the pouring rain, with two unconscious men lying in front of me, a grizzly bear smiling, and a river raging twenty-five yards away.

Leona was shaking me. "Come out of it, Annie. We've got work to do.

When I snapped to attention, Leona was checking the student's pulse. "He's okay," she pronounced as he began to groan. She turned to Pete. "This one's still out," she said, looking up. "But he's got a pulse too."

I helped the student sit. "You hit Pete on his dense hard head," I told Leona, "so you couldn't have injured him much."

I ran inside and called the police. They advised me to stay inside the house and away from my attacker. They would send somebody out as soon as possible, but at the moment all the police were busy with rescue operations. "But we'll be pulling officers off rescue soon since the river has crested."

I sank into a chair. "Thank God."

I let my heartbeat slow down a little, then went back outside.

Leona was standing with one foot on Pete's chest, staring at something in her hands. "Annie," she called. "Look at this."

It was a green box, rusty and scratched on the sides and on the hinges. She had opened it and was staring at the inside, oblivious to the driving rain.

I leaned over and looked into the box. I stared, blinked, stared some more. "Holy Saint Hedwig," I said.

"More like holy Harry Winston."

The rain slowed but continued to drizzle into the box and all over Leona and me. That didn't matter to us. We were both soaked already. Nor did it matter to the contents of the box. Diamonds are diamonds. They don't melt.

"Where the hell did your brother-in-law get these and when and why the hell had he buried them here?"

"He did neither," I said. "At least, I doubt it. This place was once a jewelry store, a high-end one. The store was flooded out in Hurricane Agnes fifteen years ago, when the Susquehanna broke through the dikes. These diamonds must have been part of the store's inventory."

"What the hell were they doing buried in this box?"

"I have no idea. I remember rumors about diamonds floating out of the store on the muddy river water. Just rumor, of course. The store would surely have cleared out all the inventory when the threat of the river flooding became imminent."

"Well, these diamonds didn't float out. They were carried out and buried here, lodged firmly smack up against the foundation. That's why Pete was using a chisel. Look." Leona pointed to a hole in the building. "I spotted the box lodged in there. Pete had managed to loosen it from the surrounding concrete blocks before you came yelling your lungs out. And look there." She pointed to the concrete block lying about a foot away.

"It's marked," I said. "With an X."

"So that's how Pete knew which block to remove to get at the box!"

Pete groaned and stirred. Leona pressed down harder with her foot. Pete groaned again, but stayed still.

"But if Pete knew about the diamonds, why didn't he come years ago to retrieve them?" I asked.

The student groaned, trying to struggle to his feet.

A siren screamed. The police were on their way.

"Come on," Leona said. "Let's get this young man into the house and out of this rain. The cops will take care of your brother-in-law."

We helped the student inside, got him seated. Leona wiped the blood from his arm where it had scraped badly, probably against the concrete block. I rummaged in the first aid kit.

"Get him bandaged," Leona instructed. "I'm going back out. The police should have been here by now."

I had begun wrapping gauze around the student's arm when Leona returned, banging the door behind her. "That police car didn't stop here!" she fumed. "Now the bastard's gone. Judging by the muddy footprints, I think Pete staggered toward the river."

"Where are the diamonds?" I asked.

Leona yanked the box out of the big side pocket of her overalls. "Right here. We got them."

* * * *

Yeah, we had them, though not for long. Although the phrase "Finders Keepers" came to mind, we knew that almost no one, individual or company, including the Borskis, had been able to afford flood insurance back then. So Leona and I contacted the former owners and returned their jewelry. They gave us rewards: a gorgeous one-carat diamond for me and, for Leona, a delicate enamel hummingbird broach with a quarter-carat diamond for an eye. It looks great on her plaid flannel shirt.

Pete vanished. I don't know where he is and neither does my sister. Nor do either of us care. My sister, Dot, is beginning to develop her own personality again.

So how did Pete know where to look for the diamonds? And who had put them there?

Back to Agnes and my sister. During that first storm, when Agnes began to threaten the city, the owners and one of their clerks were packing up the jewelry for deposit in a private vault. Agnes dumped rain all over northeastern Pennsylvania, then moved off, heading for New York. We all breathed a sigh of relief. Sandbags were removed, windows were unboarded, and the jewelry began making its trip back to the store. Then Agnes changed her mind, stalled, and dumped more rain into the Susquehanna. Wellsboro was back in emergency mode, with everyone scrambling to remove valuables in a hurry. That's when the clerk, a faithful employee for fifteen years, saw an opportunity and took it. He squirreled away some of the jewelry and stashed it in the place where Pete had found it. He couldn't risk carrying the box around or putting it in his own house, which sat smack on the flood plain. If the dikes held, he could easily retrieve the box, return the jewelry to the store, and avoid suspicion. If the dikes didn't hold, everyone would assume the jewels had been washed away.

So how did Pete know about this? That's where my sister comes in. Shortly after Agnes passed through the area, the clerk took sick. He died in the hospital, but not before suffering fevered, piratical rantings about hidden diamonds, treasure hoards, biblical floods, and X marking the spot. His nurse and my sister dismissed the story as hallucinations caused by the medications.

But when my sister, whose memory was jogged by the second storm, Frank, told Pete the story yesterday, he decided to check it out... and spotted the X.

So I love that second storm. I have my sister back. I have a gorgeous one-carat diamond. And Pete is gone. Maybe he decided to take off for parts unknown. Maybe he got swept downriver to the Chesapeake Bay. No matter. The bay has worse pollution to deal with.

Marianne Wilski Strong holds an MA in British Literature from the University of Maryland. She is a published writer of numerous professional articles and of over forty mystery short stories. Her fiction credits include a series of mystery short stories set in Ancient Greece and a series set in the coal fields of northeastern Pennsylvania, all published in *Alfred Hitchcock Mystery Magazine*. She's currently publishing and working on a new series set in Cape May involving the gothic stories written by Louisa May Alcott. She has taught numerous courses, including the History of Detective Fiction, for Road Scholar and other venues.

THE HOUSE ON SHILOH STREET

by Adam Meyer

The house on Shiloh Street was smaller than I remembered, the front porch barely as big as the stained mattress in my motel room, the basement window—the one I'd crawled through to freedom years earlier—barely wider than I was. Everything about the place seemed made in miniature, like the dollhouse furniture that my mother wrapped in pink and yellow paper after she heard the police had rescued me.

I stared at the abandoned house a while longer, waiting for something new to come to mind. Anything, really. But all I had were the same stale memories I'd been nursing for years: the cool dank basement, its gray walls scarred with water stains, me tugging at the end of my chain like a dog left too long by its owner, straining to hear the sound of his master's voice. I still heard it in my dreams, though I could never quite remember what it sounded like when I woke up.

I closed my eyes, blinking away tears.

When I got to the far corner, the sidewalk was packed. Men in camel-hair coats, women in knee-length skirts and black tights. All poking at cell phones or talking to themselves, earpieces tucked discreetly in their ears. I stepped out of their way like a child on a busy escalator. In the old days, liquor stores had been where wine shops now stood, and the check-cashing joints I knew had given way to trendy bistros. I looked around in disbelief, the old images overlaid on the present, like a 3-D movie without the glasses.

When I set off again, the wind hissed at me, cutting through the hole in my hat, the thin seams of my coat. A hulking brownstone rose on my right, its darkened windows glittering with the gold letters of a law firm, and beneath it, three crooked steps washed in neon led the way down to a bar. Surely this place had been here thirteen years ago, yet somehow it had hung on. Like me.

Maybe that was why I went in. The warm dark wrapped itself around me. I found an empty place at the bar, which wasn't hard. The warm air scratched my throat and stung my eyes. I loosened my scarf so I could breathe again.

"What can I get you?"

The bartender had the kind of good looks everyone seemed to have: dark wavy hair a bit too long, liquid brown eyes that smiled even when his mouth didn't.

"Just a ginger ale, thanks." I'd never wanted a drink more than at that moment, but one would never do. Besides, even eight or ten couldn't erase the dread inside me.

"One ginger ale. By the way, I'm Josh. What brings you here?" He was wiping the spot in front of me with a rag. I stammered out something about driving up the coast to see an old friend, but the lie tripped me up, the details turning to mush. He didn't seem put off by my stumbling answer.

"Well, there's lots to see around here," he said. Maybe he was going to list all the second-rate tourist attractions my mother had never dragged me to as a kid. We'd only seen the free ones. "When are you heading back home?"

"Not for a little while," I said, forcing myself to smile.

"Good."

Josh drifted down the bar, but once the other customers had left, he settled in across from me. He was easy to talk to, or maybe just easy to listen to, since he did most of the talking. He told me about growing up with three older sisters in a Catholic family, dropping out of college, dropping out of life. He seemed convinced he wasn't going anywhere, but I could see him in five years, picking up a construction job from someone he met in the bar, marrying a girl who was heavy but pretty and who'd give him pudgy little babies.

When he asked me if I wanted to go back to his place, I started to stammer out some excuse but then he put a big soft hand on my chin, right at the spot where there was no scar, just smooth flesh. "Come on, Katie," he said, teasing out my name. "We'll have a drink."

"I don't drink."

He nodded at my empty glass. "Right. Then we'll just have ginger ale."

He lived in a five-story apartment building around the corner from the bar, in a cramped one bedroom on the top floor. There was a row of windows, three of them over an old hissing radiator, and I could see the city through the smudged glass. Streetlights glowing on top of wrought-iron posts. Cars slicked in icy sheaths. And down below, in clear view, the house on Shiloh Street.

It was set further back from the curb than its neighbors, its porch hidden like a mugger's face, its roof pockmarked with black cancer spots. It looked like something out of a dark fairy tale, asleep and forgotten. Light spilled across its overgrown yard from a neighboring house, casting an icy glow on the weathered wood.

"I'm out of ginger ale," he said from behind me. "Is that a deal breaker?"

I kept staring out the window. "That depends. What else have you got?"

We had warm cider, and he asked if I minded whether he poured a little rum into his.

I liked the taste of it on his tongue.

Soon we ended up in the bedroom. At least I didn't have to force myself not to look out the window anymore. He reached for a small lamp on the night table, but I pushed him back onto the bed.

"No lights," I said.

He smiled up at me, as if he liked a girl who knew what she wanted.

I wasn't that, not exactly. I just knew I didn't want him getting a good look at my scars.

* * * *

Josh and I had a late leisurely breakfast and he said he wanted to see me again before I left town. I didn't know if he was just being polite or not, but I told him I had some errands to run, which wasn't exactly a lie, and agreed to check in with him later that night.

The day was brisk, my boots clopping on the sidewalk of Shiloh Street. I approached the fence of the old abandoned house, which was rusting and crooked. A rusted padlock hung loosely on the gate, but I could've just climbed over if I wanted to. Instead I stood there on uneven concrete.

An image came to me back from when I'd been trapped in the basement here, something I hadn't thought of in years. An apple. Its red skin smooth as silk and brushed with green. My eyes had gone wide when I saw it. I'd never liked fruits or vegetables, but this was the first apple I'd seen in months, and my teeth were slick with saliva.

I sensed Hayley beside me, licking her dry cracked lips. She wanted that apple as badly as I did.

Scaggs held it out on his rough palm, so close I swore I could smell its juice. I strained at the end of my chain, reaching out, but I couldn't grasp it. Hayley just stood there, but then she hadn't been in that basement as long as I had. She didn't know that if you wanted anything down there, you had to grab it. I groped desperately at the apple, but he closed his hand around the fruit and held it out to Hayley. She reached out tentatively, as if he would snatch it away from her. He didn't. I heard the sound of someone whimpering then. It was me.

"Hush," he said, but he never took his eyes off her.

Hayley cupped the apple as gently as an egg and bit down, the crunch as loud as an avalanche. I curled my fists. That was my apple. I'd been there longer than she had. I deserved it. But she kept going, devouring the apple in less than a dozen bites. When she was done, there was nothing left but a brownish core and I was half surprised she didn't eat that too.

Even after everything Scaggs had done, I never knew true hatred until then. It started at the base of my spine and radiated out across my skinny shoulders. But it wasn't him I hated, it was her, the girl who'd taken the apple that should've been mine.

Now I put my hand against the gate post and took several deep breaths, trying to steady myself. I wasn't going in there again. Ever. I had promised myself that when I was eleven, and unlike most of the promises I'd made in life, I intended to keep this one. So what now? If I wanted to uncover more memories, staring at the house was only going to get me so far. I had to talk to someone who knew the past as well I did. Someone who'd been in that house, too.

* * * *

Detective Blauner was a big beefy guy, as solid as I remembered. Heavier maybe, grayer, but basically the same. I wanted to hug him hard, the way I did when I was eleven, but I looked blankly at his outstretched arms. After a moment he lowered them.

"It's good to see you, Katie."

The police station's bull pen looked like the back room of an insurance agency. The desks were made of fake wood and covered with laptop computers. Blauner's was a mess: old coffee cups, hastily stacked papers, a half-eaten muffin pocked with shriveled blueberries.

"I didn't expect to see you back again," he said. "Where you been living? Charleston?"

I'd left for Savannah six months before but didn't correct him. The truth would only get back to my mother.

"I thought you were going to retire," I said.

"So did I. But the city cut back on pensions, and my retirement fund's worth about as much as an old Pinto so I'll put in a couple more years before I call it quits."

I nodded as if I believed him. He was probably going to die on the job. Maybe even at this very desk, slumped over his food-stained keyboard.

"So what brings you here?" he asked.

"I'm trying to remember some things from Shiloh Street. Trying to put the story together."

He looked at me warily. "You know the story."

Mostly I did. I knew that I'd been kidnapped by a man in a blue van when I was out playing in front of my house one afternoon. His last name was Scaggs, though I only found that out later. He'd always told me to call him Lester, just Lester. Lester Scaggs chained me up in his basement and touched me in ways that no grown man should've and told me how my mother hated me, how she was glad that I was gone. Over time I came to believe his stories. You might even say I loved him.

Then he brought in Hayley and chained her to the other side of the basement, and from then on he left me alone a lot more. Maybe I should've been glad, but I wasn't. Hayley and I never bonded, really. We didn't even talk much, though we were alone down there for two whole months and we lived like that, side by side, until one day... what? All I could remember were bits and pieces.

"We've been over this," Blauner said now, leaning forward with a sigh.

"Why me?" I asked. It was the question that had hung over me for thirteen years. Why had Scaggs killed Hayley and left me unchained, allowing me to escape? It made no sense.

"You don't want to do this," Blauner said. "People like us can't understand what goes on in the mind of a maniac like him."

"Really?" I asked. "Because we've got it so together?"

He looked away. Blauner had his own regrets, I was sure, even though he'd been hailed as a hero. He'd stopped by the house on Shiloh Street to ask Lester Scaggs questions because of a neighbor who'd heard noises from the basement, but he didn't have cause for a search, so he left. Not long after that Scaggs—Lester, call me Lester—came downstairs. Closing my eyes, I could almost picture the knife he'd held, its steel blade glinting. The next image I could summon was Hayley on the concrete, her greasy blond hair streaked with blood.

After that, my memories were hazy again, but I'd read many times about what happened next: while Scaggs was back upstairs, I climbed out the basement window and flagged down Blauner, who'd been coming back to Shiloh House—that's what the media called it, Shiloh House—on a hunch. Blauner put me in his patrol car and called for backup and went inside, where he was ambushed by Scaggs. Scaggs had a knife and they wrestled, Blauner trying to get it away from him, when Blauner managed to reach his gun and fire the shot that killed him.

"I've been back to Shiloh Street," I said.

His look was a warning. "Why?"

"I wanted to see if someone had moved in. A nice family with a couple of little girls, maybe."

His eyes smoldered with anger, but he kept it in check. "Your mother said you were thinking about going back to college."

I shrugged. A lie I'd told to get five hundred bucks out of her at Christmas.

"There's some good schools down there in Charleston. I could send you a few links. What's your email?"

I shrugged again, as if I couldn't remember. I had so many accounts it would've been hard to choose. Random accounts set up and abandoned.

"It's good to see you," he said, holding out his card.

I didn't take it. "Don't tell my mother I was here."

But I knew he would.

"She worries about you, Katie. Me too. It wouldn't kill you to let me know you're okay now and then."

I nodded and took his card, but only because his hand had started shaking and I couldn't bear to watch.

* * * *

I left a message for Hayley's mother but she didn't call me back. A deliberate snub or was she just busy? Next I called Josh's cell just in case he really did want to see me again and he said he'd meet me at his place in twenty minutes. I had enough time to go back to Shiloh Street, but I didn't. I sat on the steps of his apartment building and waited. The eyes of women coming and going always lingered a second too long on my lanky hair, my out-of-date-clothes, my scuffed up boots, like I was some species they couldn't identify and didn't trust.

Finally Josh came up, kissing me lightly. I pulled my sleeves down to hide the scars at my wrists—the only ones on my body that Scaggs hadn't left—as we took the elevator to his apartment. He ducked into the bathroom to brush his teeth. Over the sound of water running, I stared out the window, looking down at Shiloh Street, that narrow two-story house wedged in between taller, sturdier buildings.

"What do you feel like eating?" he asked eagerly. "We could order Thai? Japanese? Middle Eastern?"

I shrugged. Back where I came from the choices were burgers, chicken, maybe steak.

"Whatever you want," I said.

"Hmmm." He nuzzled my neck, played with my hair. "I think I know what I want."

"Let's go to the bedroom," I said. He thought it was an invitation, and in some ways it was. But really, I wanted to stop looking out the window at Shiloh Street.

* * * *

My mother had moved us out of the city less than two months after I returned home. Maybe it was all the bad memories she had, or maybe it was to get away from all those reporters. Or maybe it was just what she said, that she wanted to go out in the middle of winter without wearing three layers of clothing. But Hayley's family had stayed. They stayed in the house she was abducted from, on the street where she used to play. They stayed long after the missing posters had been pulled down and the candlelight vigils were over. They stayed there, waiting for their little girl to come home, and all they ever got was me.

House number 1428 was spotless. The lawn perfect, the paint job fresh, the ten-year-old car in the driveway waxed so often there were swirlmarks in the paint. I pressed the doorbell, stepping back to avoid the shade of a huge birch tree. The sun was surprisingly warm, the air moist and heavy, as if it might snow, but I couldn't remember what snow felt like on the skin. I hadn't been this far north in thirteen years.

An old woman with reading glasses perched on her nose came to the door. Hayley's grandmother? But no, not the way the eyes moved over me, lingering.

"Can I help you?" Hayley's mother asked. Her hair was all white and permed in a cloud around her face, her makeup not thick enough to disguise the bags under her eyes.

She must've known who I was, but she was playing dumb. Fair enough.

"It's Katie Sullivan. I called you…"

Her eyes didn't change, just grew narrower, so that she was staring at me through slits like ports on a battleship. "Oh yes, I got your message. I'm sorry I didn't have a chance to return it but…" She turned up her hands. Apparently I wasn't even worth making up excuses for.

"I wanted to talk to you about Hayley," I said.

"Hayley?" Her eyes widened as if that was a surprise. But it wasn't like we had anything else to talk about, really. "I can't see what I'd have to say."

"Please."

She had flecks of pink on her teeth, like a predator who's been chewing raw meat. "Come in."

The couch was covered in flowers, the yellow padding visible beneath the threadbare pattern. She probably hadn't replaced it since

Hayley was taken, but then everything in the room was old and sun-faded: the seascape on the wall, the plastic flowers on the credenza. Framed photographs of a little blond girl stood bunched up on a table beside the TV, crammed in like headstones at an old cemetery.

I expected a few polite questions about what I'd been doing. Most people asked even if they didn't care about the answers, just for appearance's sake, but not her. She'd probably given up caring about appearances years ago.

"I don't see what I can tell you," she said.

"Tell me about Hayley."

Her mother seemed taken aback. "Tell you what?"

"Tell me what she liked."

"I can't see why this matters."

"It doesn't, exactly. I just…"

I was surprised at the strain in my voice and started to turn away, but then I heard Hayley's mother speak.

"She loved to draw. She'd draw pictures all the time, especially horses. We took her to a farm once, and we couldn't drag her out of the barn. She begged us to get her a horse. We told her it was impossible, here in the city, so I said…" She stopped talking, choking on her own words. "I said maybe someday when she was old enough to buy one for herself."

Hayley had never talked about horses in the basement. She'd told me once that her mother was strict and always tried to tell her what to do. My mother worked so much I hardly ever saw her except when it was time to go to sleep or wake up. I didn't tell that to Hayley. I made up stories so she wouldn't know how lonely I'd been even before I got to the basement.

"She was an only child," I said, hoping to prompt her again.

"Yes, we tried but… yes. She loved other children, though. She had lots of friends here in the neighborhood."

Hayley had been the kind of girl who would have lots of friends. Blond, pretty, a big smile. Little Hayley Kerr, the blue-eyed princess of Shiloh Street. The two of us the poster children for what had happened there, one living and one dead. She was from a solid middle-class home, so just a few days after my escape, naturally the headlines had shifted to her. Or maybe it was easier to make an angel out of a dead girl instead of a living one.

I stood to go. Hayley's mother stared at me, her eyes boring in like drills.

"Tell me something. Why you and not my Hayley? Why did he let you live?"

I gave her the party line, the one I'd repeated to myself like a prayer. "It was just luck. He probably would've killed me, too, if he'd had the time."

I blotted my sweaty palms on my jeans.

"He must've liked you better than her."

"I'm not... I didn't..."

"You must've done things for him that she wouldn't. You must've given him things he wanted, the kind of things my Hayley..." She shook her head. "She was a good girl."

"No," I said, and then the words almost slipped out after it: the apple, she stole my apple. But what did it matter after all these years, a stupid apple? Why did any of this matter? "I'm sorry, coming here was a..."

Mistake. The word was on my lips, but I couldn't spit it out, just shut my mouth and stumbled out into the cold.

* * * *

I walked all the way back to Shiloh House, an epic journey that took me through good areas and bad. When I got to the edges of the gentrified neighborhood that had swallowed Shiloh Street, I had an idea. All this time I'd tried to avoid the inevitable, but it was pointless. I wanted to finally answer the question Hayley's mother had asked, the one I'd been asking myself, and to do that I had to go back there.

First, I needed something.

I found the army-navy store in between a pawn shop and an Ethiopian restaurant. I poked through racks of camouflage pants and oversized tents and found a glass case with all kinds of survival weapons. Sharp, jagged blades with steel or bone handles. I looked around as if considering the options, but I knew what I wanted. There, in the back corner of the case. Steel blade almost as long as my arm. Simple black handle. Nothing flashy. Just like him—efficient, ruthless, dangerous.

I put the money down on the counter. Cash.

"Will that be all?" the clerk asked, a baby-faced guy with eyes as round as the canteens hanging over his shoulder.

"Oh yeah," I said. "That's all I need."

* * * *

Brown paper bag in hand, I braced myself against the cold, feeling the dampness and electricity gather in the air around me. A storm was coming, I could feel it. Maybe it would be the kind of old-fashioned blizzard I hadn't seen since I was a kid. I could watch the heavy flakes fall from Josh's window, a white curtain filtering the image of Shiloh House. For once I wished he lived in some other part of the city, or even some other city altogether. Maybe out west, Arizona or New Mexico, places I'd never been, but which always had a kind of scrubbed timeless beauty in the pictures I'd seen. Places where there were horses.

Josh buzzed me into the apartment, and I headed upstairs. The shades were drawn, and welcome relief shuddered through me. I wouldn't have to look over at the house. But then I saw Josh working at the computer, and when I saw the screen, my relief quickly curdled into anger.

"What the hell?" I asked, my fingernails biting into my palms. "What are you doing?"

"I just... I wanted to know what was going on with you, that's all. Why you were here."

The words on the screen were too far away to read, but I knew that black-and-white photo of the preteen girl with her downcast eyes and the policeman's big beefy arm reaching out to block the camera. It was taken just after I got out of the basement.

"Is this really you?" he asked, half studying the screen, half watching me.

"Good-bye. Thanks for everything."

I zipped my coat, started for the door. He blocked the way.

"Not yet. Sit down."

I sat.

He offered me a drink. Wine. I swallowed it in one gulp and crossed the room, peeling back the blinds so I had a glimpse of Shiloh House: the rickety porch, the window on the side, level with the driveway. Yes, I'd climbed out that window, but I had never escaped, not really. My soul was still trapped down in the basement.

"How'd you know?" I asked after Josh had refilled my wine.

"The scars..." he said, hesitating. "I couldn't figure out why you had so many."

I shook my head, unsure why I was defending Lester Scaggs after so many years. "A lot of them are from me, not him."

"But how?..."

"I cut myself. It's something I do."

He looked at me sadly. I stood, holding the knife in its brown paper bag close to me.

"Why?" he asked.

Which why? Why had I inflicted more wounds on myself than Scaggs had? Why had I come back to the place where my worst memories had been forged? Why had I gotten involved with Josh when I knew it was going to end like this? Whatever the question, the answer was the same.

"I can't help myself."

Josh put his hand on my arm. I flinched. The bile of fear coated the insides of my belly, sloshing around like battery acid.

"I want you to stay. Please."

Either he wanted me to stay out of pity or he was just being polite, but it didn't matter. I couldn't stay there, not anymore.

* * * *

The house on Shiloh Street loomed in the icy, damp dark. Lester Scaggs's house, my house. The only one with its windows dark, its shades drawn. I climbed over the rusted gate and crossed through the weed-ridden lawn. The walls looked crooked, the cracks in the paint like chiseled rock. I couldn't turn away. The floorboards of the porch groaned beneath me. The front door, warped in the frame, had been secured with a padlock. The knob turned slightly but wouldn't open.

I went around to the side, looking up at the thick gray underbellies of clouds, which choked off even the promise of moonlight. The tiny window where I had crawled out was still there, covered in plywood. A couple of jabs with my elbow and the wood collapsed into the darkness. There was no glass behind it anymore.

I slid my legs through the frame, the concrete cold against my jeans. As I slid inside, my breath caught, and then I threw the bag with the knife down, listening to it land with a soft thump. Now it was my turn. The window frame pinched against my hips, my legs dangling in darkness. What if I landed on something and broke my neck? Well, there would be no one to call for help. I'd die in that basement. Maybe that was fitting.

I pushed myself through and hit the floor with a thud, a cloud of dust and stagnant air rising around me. I coughed it out, struggling to see. The darkness was so pure, just the way I remembered, although the silence surprised me: years ago, even when I was alone, there'd always been the clank of pipes or the squeak of footsteps.

Reaching through the gloom, I half expected to feel the chains that had once bound me. Instead, I found the paper bag. As I brought out the knife, my eyes began to adjust. The basement was smaller than I remembered, just like everything else here. Smaller and uglier. I couldn't make out much in the way of details—the water-stained wall where my chains had once hung, the old work sink where he'd filled the bucket for my sponge baths, the stairs that led up to the rest of the house.

Why had I come here? What was I after? There was nothing but ghosts. Scaggs was gone, Hayley was gone. I was all that remained.

I headed back for the window. Looking up, I wondered how I'd hauled myself up there. I could barely even get high enough to reach it now, and I'd surely been too short at eleven. Oh, right. I'd stood on a milk crate, the one he used to sit on sometimes. He'd sat on it that last day, talking to us gravely. What had he said?

A cop stopped by this morning. A detective.

I'd felt a sense of fear and excitement. Maybe the detective would save me. But no, Scaggs said the cop was dumb, he had no idea we were even down there. Still, Scaggs thought we should get out of town for a while, and Hayley and I were going with him. At least one of us was, but we'd have to decide which one. At first I thought he meant someone was going with him and the other would get to go home. I felt sure he'd take Hayley.

Then he brought out the knife.

He went over to Hayley and unlocked her chains. A moment later he did the same for me. The cuffs hadn't been off my wrists in weeks. The blood in my arms was still sluggish. He set the knife on the concrete between us and said that we would decide who got to come with him.

Hayley started to beg and plead. "Please don't hurt me!" She still didn't get it. But I did.

He explained that one of us had to die, and if we didn't handle it ourselves, then he would act for us, and he might just decide to kill us both. Hayley and I looked at each other. She shook her head at me. *Don't believe him. He's bluffing.* But she'd only been there two months. I knew better. Besides, if he handled it himself, I knew just who he'd choose.

Hayley shook her head, as if she couldn't believe what she was seeing. *No,* she mouthed, or maybe she was screaming, but no words seemed to come out of her lips. *No no no!* I picked up the knife and moved in close and grabbed her by the hair and my hand just flew, even though I told it not to. Heat splashed against my wrists and arms and cheeks.

Blood. Hayley's blood, red as the apple she'd eaten here once.

He stood over me when I was done, smiling, nodding, proud as any parent whose kid just brought home a great report card. You did it, he said, and I nodded, sobbing. You did it.

There was a thump from upstairs. Scaggs looked scared, and that threw me. A moment later the heavy tread of footsteps on the stairs. Scaggs reached for the knife, but I swung it at him, slicing a cut into one of his palms. He stared at me in disbelief. There was a shadow on the stairs. Scaggs turned.

A gunshot.

Moments later, the policeman stood over me. He looked at the blood on my hands and the knife at my feet, and he seemed to understand what had happened, or at least enough. He said, *I was here earlier, and I knew something was wrong. I came back on instinct. I'm glad I did.* He looked down at Hayley and shook his head. *I just wish I could've saved both of you.*

I nodded, waiting.

Scaggs killed her, he said, but in his eyes I saw that he knew the truth. *He killed her and you got on the milk crate and climbed out that window.* He pointed to one of the small windows, painted black so that no one could see in. *I was driving by, and you flagged me down, and you told me what was going on. When I got in here he'd already done that to her.*

I tried to say okay but couldn't. He told me the story a few more times, made me repeat it back, and then he set the milk crate by the window, but I still wasn't tall enough. He gave me a lift, helped me climb out. He wanted everything to be as close to the story we were telling as possible, I understood that now.

I looked down at the blood, and it was so real, as if I was back with Scaggs again. My whole body shook. But no, I was here, I was now, and the blood was mine, a thick black pool dripping from my wrists, blood I'd drawn with the tip of the knife. I saw it now: Scaggs hadn't killed Hayley. I had.

Someone was coming toward me, a ghost. Scaggs. I brought the knife up, splashing my cheek with some of my own blood, but no, this was no phantom. It was Detective Blauner. Rescuing me again. No, not again. Even though he'd helped me get out, he hadn't saved me. Not quite.

"How'd you find me?" I asked through chattering teeth.

"Shh. Don't talk."

"How?"

"Your friend the bartender called the precinct, seems he was kind of worried. Dispatcher mentioned it to me as a courtesy."

"You lied for me," I said as he pressed his hands against my bloody wrist.

"What was I going to do? Tell people that one little girl had killed another, let the media make you out to be some kind of monster?" He shook his head. "You were a victim, same as her."

I opened my mouth. Wanting to explain it all. But no words would come.

"You were here for months. The things he did to you, the things you saw… I don't care if it was your hand on the knife or not. He killed her, not you, and that's the truth."

Faintly, I heard the sound of a siren. More police officers, coming for me? Blauner had lied, I was going to be arrested, and punished at last. I stumbled on the first step out of the basement, my feet too big and clumsy in those old boots.

"I've got to tell the truth. I've got to pay."

He shook his head. "You've already paid. More than enough."

I looked down at the blood on my hands and wondered. I'd certainly paid. We all had. But was it enough? Blauner put his arm around me but the stairway was too narrow for us to go up side by side, so I led the way, up and out of the darkness. Minutes later, I stood on the porch, where snow had started to fall. It felt like an icy kiss on my skin, there and then gone.

Adam Meyer is a fiction writer and screenwriter. He's the author of the novel *The Last Domino*, an ALA Quick Pick for Reluctant YA Readers, and many short stories, which have appeared in the Mystery Writers of America anthology *Vengeance* and on the website popcornfiction.com, among other venues. He's also written several TV movies, including *My Life as a Dead Girl* and *The Other Wife*, and recently finished a screenplay based on a novel by Lawrence Block. His other work for the screen includes series for the Discovery, National Geographic, and History channels.

STEPMONSTER

by Barb Goffman

Lightning flashed, and my handgun's silver barrel shone bright as a full moon. Then, just as quickly, the gloom settled in again, and I could barely see a thing. The night's blackness invaded the porch where I hid and enveloped the acres surrounding the old farm house. It slithered between the pine trees at the far end of the property, the same way it had crept into my heart and planted roots five years earlier.

Thunder rumbled. The autumn storm clawed closer, each clap louder than the last. This one had rattled the windows. I smirked.

Did you hear that, Jan? Are you trembling in your nice warm bed? Trying to convince yourself that you're safe? That there's nothing to be afraid of?

I chuckled, thinking of the wrinkled hag cowering upstairs, chiding herself for being so afraid of thunderstorms, especially at her age. My dad used to try everything to get her through such bad nights. He read to her by flashlight. Told her jokes and funny stories. Once he even sang to her. "I figured she'd either laugh or cry," he'd told me on the phone the next day. "Either way, she'd be distracted." She loved to be distracted when she was scared. But Dad's not around to do those things anymore.

You made sure of that. Didn't you, Jan?

With a whoosh the wind picked up, sending crackling leaves adrift, flying over the railing onto the wooden porch. A few settled at my feet. They brushed against the size-six shoes I'd stuffed my toes into a half hour before, right before I trekked from my nondescript rental car safely parked a half mile away on the other side of the woods. I knew my feet would hurt from wearing shoes two sizes too small, but the pain would be worth it. Any tell-tale footprints would send the investigators in the wrong direction. Not that they'd even consider me. Not after all this time.

Thunder boomed again, and a bolt of lightning split the sky. Then came the rain. Fat drops slammed into the farmhouse's roof, slid down its eaves, and dripped onto the porch railing. Steadily it poured, pounding like a fetal heartbeat, rapid and relentless. Upstairs, Jan likely had pulled the covers over her head, chanting that there's nothing to be afraid of.

But you don't really believe that, do you, Jan? You know that demons hide in the night, waiting, waiting for their chance. Waiting for enough time to pass that no one would suspect them when the next horrible crime occurs.

I skulked to the front door, key in my pocket, warm against my thigh. I hadn't lived here for more than a decade, but I'd kept the key all these years. Not that I'd probably need it now. Folks around here typically didn't lock their doors, but I wasn't going to take any chances. Not tonight. I leaned on the door, my gloved hand resting on the knob. The door eased open with a squeak.

Dad never would have stood for that. He'd have oiled the hinges straight away. But my stepmonster was always too busy going to church or Bible study classes and chattering on the phone with her friends to do anything as mundane as keep up the family homestead. I hoped she heard the squeak now. I hoped it scared her to death.

I've waited five long years, I thought as I approached the staircase. I've been patient. I've planned.

And now, Jan, I've come for you.

Another clap of thunder shook the house as I climbed the stairs. The nearest neighbor—Old Man Adams, a couple of miles away—had probably flown to his bedroom window to check if his barn was still standing, before flipping on his porch lights and heading outside for a better view.

But you can't turn on your lights, can you, Jan? Oh, no. 'Cause I cut the phone and power lines when I approached the house, just in case you found the courage to peek out from under your covers.

Are you hiding under the same blanket now, Jan—the blanket Dad lay on as he was dying? Are you reassuring yourself that everything's fine, the way you did when Dad was writhing on that very bed, eyes clenched shut, powerless against the pain racking his body?

I reached the top of the stairs and began creeping toward their bedroom, remembering. The night before the funeral, when Jan and I were alone at the house, she told me what really happened the night Dad died. He hadn't died in his sleep, even though that's what she'd told everyone else. She'd actually found Dad about ten o'clock the night before, obviously having a heart attack. She'd offered—so magnanimous of her—*offered* to call an ambulance. But Dad had refused. "No no no no no no no," were his last words. She couldn't bear to see him like that, so she went downstairs, picked up her knitting, and turned on the TV for distraction.

"Don't look at me like that," she'd said as my mouth dropped open. "Your father was a very stubborn man. You would have done the same thing."

I'd thought of him lying cold and still in his casket at the funeral home. My hands shook with rage. It took every ounce of self-control I could muster to keep from reaching out and strangling her, squeezing every last breath from her useless body. "No," I said at last. "I would have called an ambulance."

He'd been dying, and instead of calling for help, she'd turned on the TV. And then she had the nerve to unburden herself to me so she'd feel better. Remembering now, my hands trembled so violently I nearly dropped the gun. Outside the bedroom door I paused and leaned against the wall, forcing myself to breathe deeply. My head banged against a frame hanging on the wall. We'd never had anything hanging in the hall-ways, I thought, putting things together. The bitch had redecorated. I'd been mourning my dad all these years, and she'd been using his money to redecorate the house.

My face grew hotter as my anger boiled. I stepped over the threshold, into the bedroom, raising the gun. The floor creaked, as if announcing my arrival.

Jan... I'm here.

She lay like a lump under the blanket, snoring, larger than I remembered.

I edged closer, until I was a foot away. Then I planted my legs so I stood like a teepee, and aimed the gun at her mid-section. I wanted to make sure she didn't die right away; she had to suffer first, as Dad had. I waited for the right moment. Five seconds passed. Ten. Then lightning lit the room, thunder roared from the sky, and I fired.

My mouth spread into a grin as the screaming began. *I did it, Dad. I've avenged you.* But then my eyes widened. That didn't sound like Jan.

With bile rising in my throat, I yanked the blanket back. *Jesus Christ. Who the heck was that?* A man. A man I didn't know. Not Jan. *Not Jan!* He was grabbing his chest. I'd aimed too high. Lightning flashed again, and I could see blood pouring out of the wound as he moaned in agony.

"Oh my God," I cried. "Who are you?"

"Lester," he croaked out. "Why... why did you shoot me? Help..."

I dropped the gun, grabbed the blanket, and pressed it hard against his chest, trying to stop the bleeding. He moaned in pain.

"Ambulance," he said.

I shook my head, trying to get a hold of myself. I couldn't call for help. Not now. Not when I was so close.

"Where's Jan?" I screamed.

"Who?"

Thunder rumbled again, and the whole world seemed to shake.

"Jan Vieta. Where is she?"

"She sold me the house a few years ago." Lester's breathing was shallow. "She moved… away."

"Where?"

No answer.

"Where did she go?" I yelled, shaking his arm.

"She moved," he rasped, "to…"

And he took a deep breath, and exhaled, and a stillness overtook the room. No more moaning. No more answers. Just the revolting smell of his bowels evacuating as he died.

I fell back against the wall, gasping for air. I'd never get my revenge now. I couldn't find Jan without putting myself at risk of being discovered. And I'd killed a man, an innocent man. I was going to go to hell for nothing.

I'd hated Jan all these years because she hadn't called an ambulance for Dad, and now this man had begged me to call for help, and I'd refused. Who was worse?

Tears began pouring down my cheeks, but then I started laughing, roaring like the thunder outside.

Yes, I'd eventually go to hell. But I'd see Jan there.

* * * *

I finished reading my story aloud, sat back in my chair, and glanced around the dining room table. This was a new critique group, an hour's drive from my house. I hoped they'd be helpful.

"So," I said. "What do you think?"

"It's powerful," Cheryl said. "I like your use of the weather to keep the tension up."

"The writing was clear," Lori added. "And I *loved* the twist at the end. Although, if your protagonist really wants to kill Jan, shouldn't she—or he, I guess—be willing to do whatever it takes to find her, even if it means risking getting caught?"

"That's a good point," I said. "And my protagonist could be a *she* or *he*, whatever works for the reader. But did you believe everything my main character did to try to get away with it from the beginning? Do you see any flaws in how I set up the story?"

"The rental car could be a problem," Dina said. "Sure, she—I'm going with *she* because of the small shoes—hasn't been home in five years, but the police will always look at family first. If they find evidence that she flew home and rented a car, her goose will be cooked. So if your goal is for her to get away with it, you might want to change that part of the story."

"That would only be true if she actually killed *Jan*," Lori said. "She doesn't know this Lester guy. The police probably will look at *his* family for suspects."

Cheryl nodded. "Unless she's spotted before she gets away. Her clothes likely will have blood on them."

"She could bring a change of clothes with her," Lori said. "And then burn the clothes she wore during the killing."

A change of clothes. Another good idea.

"Not that all of that should be on the page," Dina said, "but it's good that you're thinking things through. You need to be sure you're making the story realistic for your readers."

Over the next ten minutes, they offered more helpful suggestions, and then it came time to move onto Cheryl's work. I excused myself to the bathroom.

They seem like a good group, I thought as I shut the door. Too bad I'd have to drop out. I couldn't let them get to know me too well. I examined my dye job in the mirror. It had been a good idea, as had been using fake names. For me and Maureen—Maureen, whom I'd kept tabs on. Who I knew had never moved.

I plopped my purse on the countertop. It was heavy from the all the cash inside, including several rolls of quarters for the tolls. Flying in and renting a car at the airport could indeed be a problem. That was why I'd planned to drive halfway, rent a car where no one knew me, and then drive the rental the rest of the way. I had to remember to remove my EZ-Pass from my dashboard so there'd be no evidence my car was anywhere out of the area.

I reached inside my bag, found my phone, and punched the weather app. Thunderstorms were still expected later in the week back home. Terrible storms. A nor'easter. The storm of the century, perhaps. I smiled.

Can you hear them, Maureen? They're coming for you.

As am I.

Barb Goffman is the author of *Don't Get Mad, Get Even* (Wildside Press), which won the Silver Falchion Award for best short story collection of 2013. Barb also won the 2013 Macavity Award for best short story, and she's been nominated fifteen times for national crime-writing awards, including the Agatha (eight times—the most ever in the short story category) and the Anthony and Macavity awards (three times each). Barb's an editor of the *Chesapeake Crimes* series and runs a freelance editing and proofreading service, www.goffmanediting.com, focusing on crime and general fiction. Learn more about her writing at www.barbgoffman.com.

THE GARDENER
by Kim Kash

Enormous dust storms called shamals *periodically sweep across the Arabian Peninsula. The palm trees shush and rasp. The dusty wind moans around corners and seeps through cracks in window casings. The sky turns brown and glows with an eerie light. Even after the wind stops blowing, the air remains thick with dust for hours, like a malevolent fog.*

* * * *

He showed up as the moving van pulled into their driveway, hustling across the street in faded coveralls, the dark skin of his face framed by a light-colored cloth draped loosely around his head. Tricia had already seen several workers on the oil company's housing compound in Saudi Arabia with this type of head covering, doing double duty as hat and sunglasses.

"Sir, madam, you need gardener." It was not a question.

Glen and Tricia were standing in the yard, and the movers were piling out of the truck cab. The grass was thin and dry.

They looked at each other, squinting in the Arabian Desert sun. The temperature was about ninety-four on that April morning. Tricia's floral sundress was tight and sticky with perspiration.

"I'm not really sure—" she said.

"How much?" Glen said.

The man put his hands up in a practiced indication of protest. "If you like, you pay," he said, shaking his head to ward off the unseemly topic of money.

"If I like, I pay?" One of Glen's eyebrows arched above his aviator frames. The sun was so bright that his striped golf shirt seemed to shimmer.

The gardener waggled his head, not yes, not no, but a kind of side-to-side wiggle. "Yes sir, no problem." He offered a small smile and cast his eyes down.

"Huh," Glen said.

The moving truck's rear doors opened with a screech.

"I come tomorrow."

"Well now, I don't know—" Tricia began to protest.

The gardener turned and hustled away. Glen strode across the lawn to the moving truck.

That's how they came to have a gardener, though Tricia preferred to do her own gardening.

* * * *

The gardener showed up the next morning, as he had promised. Wearing silk pajamas and a flowery, quilted robe, Tricia was drinking her second cup of tea. She knew he had arrived because she heard the heavy patter of the hose turned on high, drumming insistently on the back patio, the sliding glass doors, and the patio furniture. The patio furniture!

"Hey!" She yanked open the curtains and rolled the sliding glass door all the way open with a heavy thud.

The gardener was now flooding the empty flowerbeds with water from the hose: raw water, they called it here. It was so full of minerals and salt that it wasn't drinkable. Tricia was told it would pit the metal patio furniture and kill delicate plants.

The gardener turned and looked at Tricia in surprise, the water blasting full force from the hose. He dropped his gaze in embarrassment. She looked down and pulled her robe more tightly closed.

"What do you think you're doing?" She gestured toward the furniture, tea sloshing over the rim of the cup. "Don't use that water on my patio furniture. Don't water those flowerbeds with raw water, either. There's nothing planted yet anyway. What are you thinking?"

"No problem, madam," he said, giving her that little head waggle and turning away. He continued to shower the barren ground with briny water.

Tricia was too shocked to do anything but retreat back inside. She jerked the curtains closed, then peeked through a gap, watching the gardener soak the whole yard with raw water. Then he aimed the hose at the birdbath, whose placement she had carefully supervised during yesterday's move. After he finished soaking everything, he unscrewed the hose—*her* hose, a heavy-duty, reinforced rubber model with brass fittings, packed and shipped from Maryland—and walked away with it. The back gate clicked shut, and he was gone.

Tricia rushed outside, across the flagstone patio and the squishy lawn to the birdbath. It was too heavy to tip, so she dumped the dregs of her Earl Grey and used the cup to scoop water out of the wide, shallow bowl. Then she soaked up the remaining water and wiped out the birdbath's mosaic interior with a corner of her robe. She returned to the house, so distracted that she tracked mud across the carpet, and filled a soup pot from the "sweet water" tap at the kitchen sink. She hauled this water outside and filled the birdbath.

Tricia called Glen at work, livid, but he didn't understand. "I've got a meeting with the department head in five," he said. "Just handle it, honey, okay?"

Tricia slammed the phone down.

* * * *

Shamals often blow northwest over Saudi Arabia, Iraq, and Kuwait. They can happen at any time of the year, ruffling the palms playfully at first, giving just a hint of warning before the heavy beige fog rolls in.

With the right vantage point on a high desert bluff, it is possible to witness an approaching shamal, to watch it rush in like a brown tidal wave.

* * * *

Within the first week of their arrival, Tricia had a state-of-the-art sprinkler system installed with automatic, multi-zoned timing and remote, wireless tracking. Glen found a black-market plumber willing to tap into the house's sweet water line for the sprinklers. It was strictly forbidden on the housing compound to use drinking water for gardening. Tricia understood the importance of water conservation in the desert—but not in her yard.

With the sprinklers in place, Tricia dug a generous mix of fresh topsoil and peat moss into the flowerbeds, and planted 750 new plants. Most were seedlings, but she splurged on a few mature specimens, including several olive trees and a lovely fig. She mulched everything heavily with additional peat moss, enjoying the rich, damp fragrance. The smell reminded her of a humid summer day in Maryland.

Her garden at their home near Annapolis had been the star of every annual neighborhood garden tour, but this! This walled back garden was going to be Tricia's greatest achievement. She had never had a private, walled garden before—she was used to every square inch of her yard being in the public eye. But traditional Middle Eastern yards are screened off to give women who cover themselves for religious reasons some freedom to enjoy the outdoors, away from prying eyes. Though not Muslim, Tricia was starting to enjoy the feeling of freedom and seclusion in her garden.

She had hoped that the gardener had pilfered her hose and simply disappeared. No such luck. The day after she finished her initial round of planting, Tricia was watering a few delicate seedlings by hand. The gate latch clicked and in came the gardener, with Tricia's hose looped over his shoulder.

She stood up and crossed her arms, watching him amble into the yard and screw the hose into the bib by the corner of the house.

"Hey!" she called.

"Hello, madam," he said briskly, turning on the spigot full blast and hosing off the patio.

"Listen, we need to get some things straight, mister," Tricia said, planting herself in front of the gardener. "Turn off the water."

"Yes, madam," he said with a deferential smile and a head waggle. He continued to water the concrete patio, and then took aim at the glass-topped table.

"Stop it!" she cried, turning off the water.

The gardener looked at the dribbling hose nozzle in his hand and then at Tricia, hurt and puzzled.

"No raw water on the furniture, or anywhere in the garden. In fact, really, we don't need a gardener. No gardener."

"I am gardener," he said, gently touching his chest.

Exasperated, she said, "Okay, okay, but no hose in the back garden. You can hose off the front walk only. Only front. Okay?"

"Yes, madam," he said. He unscrewed the hose, coiling it around his shoulder and under his left arm, and let himself out the gate.

* * * *

The next day, Tricia drank her first cup of morning tea in the garden, taking pleasure in the slow hiss of the sprinklers. They started promptly at 5:30 a.m. and went silent with a gentle gurgle at 5:45. That was her cue to go inside and put breakfast together. By 6:40, Glen was backing out of the driveway, well fed and ready for his day at the administration building.

Shortly after Glen left, the gardener arrived. Tricia watched out the front window as he carefully hosed off the front walk and the driveway. Then, much to her relief, he disconnected the hose (which she recognized was no longer hers), rolled it up, and walked down the street.

This pattern continued for several weeks, though Tricia never could figure out how often the gardener would show up, or at what hour. He'd just arrive with the hose, wet down the walk to keep the desert dust under control, and leave.

Glen was settling in well at the new job, and the wives of his colleagues were starting to invite Tricia to their luncheons and card games. However, socializing was not her thing. She didn't enjoy coffee or scrapbooking or gossip; besides, her plate was full with projects in the yard. Tricia knew it would help her husband's career if she made a bit of an effort, but honestly, there was no time for all that plus the garden. On the oil company housing compound, that was very odd. All the other wives left the gardening to the gardeners.

Maybe she should look for a really knowledgeable gardener, one she could trust, Tricia thought one morning as she sat on the patio with a second cup of tea after Glen left for work. She doubted if such a gardener existed. Besides, she didn't want to give control of her garden to someone else. Tricia liked to know exactly what was transpiring on her little plot of ground over the course of the day. Is the sprinkler head over by the palm tree sticking slightly as the head pops up? Does the mint need a little trim? Are the canna lilies going to open today? How could she keep track of all these things if a gardener—even a good one—were doing the work?

It was probably a moot point. Tricia had observed that the gardeners on the compound didn't have much of a track record for keeping plants alive under the blistering sun. They were almost all from the Indian subcontinent, where growing conditions are much different. Of course, Tricia had had no experience gardening in this extreme climate when she arrived, either. However, she'd done extensive research before leaving the United States.

She couldn't blame the gardeners for trying. They were working to rake in the riyals just like everyone else, sending good money home to their wives and children in India or Bangladesh. When they were done with their day jobs as laborers, they came to the American houses, and they labored some more—usually under better conditions and for more pay than they got from their official employers. Americans paid premium rates for this garden labor, but still much less than they'd be shelling out for basic lawn service back home. So it was a win-win situation. But not for Tricia.

* * * *

Shamals can bring in all kinds of weather anomalies. In the summer, temperatures can reach 120 degrees or more on the Arabian Peninsula, and a shamal does not necessarily bring relief—it still feels like the inside of an oven, only now the air is infused with grit. Other times, the temperature drops twenty-five degrees or more. Occasionally there is hail, big enough to dent the hood of a car. Sometimes a shamal will collide with a freak rainstorm, causing mud showers.

* * * *

On Tuesday, June 3rd—she would never forget the day—Tricia spent hours in the back garden, repotting some experimental cacti. She wasn't a fan of desert plants, but it seemed absurd to ignore them altogether while tending a garden in the Middle East. She forgot about lunch, working through until four o'clock, when it was time to get dinner started.

Glen called to Tricia from the door when he arrived home at 5:20. "Hey, hon, are you, uh, trying some sort of new look out front?"

Tricia carefully wiped the Japanese filleting knife with which she'd been preparing that evening's fish entrée, and grabbed the glass of iced tea she'd been drinking. She joined Glen on the step and looked out across the front lawn.

Her scream shattered the quiet afternoon. The drink slipped from her hand, bouncing off one suede ballet flat, splattering Glen's suit pants, and littering their front walkway with glass shards.

Centered on her formerly pristine front lawn—and taking up nearly a third of it—was a brand new bed of bright white gravel, framed with bricks. The bricks were half buried so as to form a sawtooth pattern, and painted orange and chartreuse, one color alternating with the other. An enormous cement birdbath sat in the gravel circle, painted turquoise.

Glen guffawed. "I didn't think this was quite your style."

Tricia gaped, speechless.

"Dunu?"

Her horror turned to confusion. "What?"

"Gotta be Dunu, right?"

"What the hell are you talking about?" Her voice shook with fury.

Glen waved his hands defensively in front of his chest. "The gardener! The gardener must have done this, right?"

"Obviously. What in God's name is a dunu?"

"Dunu is the gardener," Glen said, clearly exasperated. "You don't know his name?"

Tricia felt her face flush.

"Oh."

"How can you not know his name? Don't you see him all the time?"

Tricia clamped her jaw shut and felt her back fillings gnash as she glared at her husband. Glen winced.

"How *could* he?" She jabbed a finger at the blinding white gravel, the sloppy cast-cement birdbath. "Why?"

"Aw, honey, I'm sure he was just trying to be nice. He probably did it because he knows you like birdbaths," Glen said. "He's a sweet guy, once you talk to him a little."

Tricia shook her head, incredulous. "I have no reason to speak to him. I do my own gardening."

Glen sighed patiently, put his arms around Tricia, and squeezed her in a hug. He smoothed the russet curls away from her forehead. Tricia's jaw finally relaxed and her arms went around Glen's waist.

"I'll talk to Dunu," Glen said. "I'll get him to put the lawn back the way it was, okay?"

She nodded her head and sniffled into his shoulder.

* * * *

A few days later, the birdbath and the gravel were gone. Glen bribed someone at the company's housing-maintenance department (he didn't say how much that cost, and Tricia didn't ask), and a swarm of workers completely cleared the whole front yard and rolled out a new carpet of fresh green sod.

The gardener must have noticed that his creation was removed, but neither he nor Tricia mentioned it the next time he arrived. Tricia felt slightly awkward about her brusque behavior toward the gardener, and she avoided him for a couple of weeks, until one morning she saw him washing off the driveway with careful, unrushed sweeps of the hose. Back and forth across the width of the drive, he shuffled in his shapeless coveralls and his too-big shoes. He wore them like many of the other laborers, with the heels squashed down under his own heels to make them easy to slip on and off.

"Dunu," she called, stepping out the front door in linen shorts and a silk tee.

The gardener turned, startled, the spray swooping in a wide arc across the lawn. He nodded, dropped his eyes.

"I, uh, I just…" she stammered. This is ridiculous, she thought. She felt like an idiot. "You're doing a nice job with the driveway. Thank you."

He squinted at her for a moment, confused. Then his face broke into a wide, unrestrained smile. He nodded at Tricia vigorously. She stepped back into the house and closed the door.

* * * *

July came and Tricia left the plants—and Glen—to fend for themselves for the summer. Like most of the other wives, she flew back home to the States. Back in Maryland it was hot, but not so hot that you could fry an egg on the sidewalk, as could actually happen in the Arabian Peninsula.

Before leaving, she stocked the freezer with meal-sized packages so Glen wouldn't subsist on pizza for two months. She heavily mulched the garden and set the sprinklers to water three times every twenty-four hours: at one a.m., five a.m. and eight thirty p.m. Watering during the day wouldn't do a thing: every drop would evaporate before it could soak into the soil. She left strict instructions that the gardener was not to touch anything in the garden.

When she returned in September, Tricia found Glen no worse for the wear. However, many of her tender garden plants had died. It nearly broke her heart.

After a few days of recovery from jetlag, Tricia managed to wake up with Glen one morning and see him off to work. She stepped out the front door with her cup of tea and waved as Glen backed down the driveway.

The gardener arrived just then, carrying the hose. He smiled and nodded when he saw Tricia. She offered a small wave.

"Hello, madam," he said. "You are home."

"Good morning. Yes, I'm back."

He smiled, dropped his eyes, then looked back up at her quickly. "You like?" he asked, pointing to the yard across the street.

The neighbors' front garden was what Tricia would call low rent. There should be a trailer over there, she often thought, and not a four-bedroom, single-family home with a red-clay tile roof and a generously shaded front entry. The neighbors' house was identical to Glen and Tricia's—but not the yard. The neighbors were heavily into plastic planters and lawn ornaments.

Several palm trees towered over the yard, and the trunk of each one sported a fresh coat of white paint up to about four feet from the ground.

Tricia mustered a vague smile. "Very nice," she said. He beamed.

"I did," he said proudly. "I am gardener. This is how we do in my country. You like?" he asked again, more insistent.

"Yes," she said wryly. "Good work." She turned and walked back into the house.

* * * *

Shamals extend several thousand feet into the air. The suspended grit and sand can halt air and sea travel for three to five days. Roads become impassable. Winds can reach up to fifty miles per hour, and the suspended sand can take the paint off a car.

* * * *

That day on BBC World Service radio from Bahrain, Tricia heard a weather report. A heavy storm was sweeping down from Kuwait, and was expected to hit the rest of the Arabian Peninsula tomorrow. Visibility in Kuwait was nil, and several multi-car pileups were being reported along the main highway into Kuwait City.

Glen had told Tricia about a couple of shamals that had hit while she'd been back summering in Maryland. But Tricia had never seen one herself. She felt nervous about the damage the storm might do to the garden, already fragile from a season of neglect. She was also curious about it—the way someone from the Middle East might feel about seeing a snowstorm for the first time.

The next morning dawned clear. Tricia stepped into her backyard early, wearing her sturdy L.L.Bean overalls and garden clogs. Glen had gone into the office for a meeting, and she was planning to make a new bed by the back wall and transplant several fruit trees. She grabbed her heaviest shovel from the storage shed just outside the door and turned to the yard.

Her gaze rested on the garden.

She blinked once, twice. Her jaw dropped.

She was too distraught to scream.

Every tree and every woody vine sported a fresh coat of bright white paint, from ground level to a point about four feet up, like some kind of trailer park wainscoting.

There, in the far corner of the yard next to a pile of newly delivered topsoil, was the gardener. He was putting the finishing brush strokes on Tricia's prized fig tree.

She leaned heavily on the shovel handle, breathless. Her eyes burned with tears. Then suddenly the whisper of despair whipped into an inferno of rage. Tricia hoisted the shovel like a baseball bat and stalked across the yard. The gardener was carefully dabbing the tree trunk, his brush dripping with house paint.

He turned around just in time to catch the brunt of the shovel square in his face. He dropped like a stone. Two, three, four, five more solid whacks and he stopped twitching.

Tricia bent forward at the waist, gasping for air. After a moment she caught her breath, leaning on the shovel. The freshening wind cooled the sweat on her brow. Tricia stared at the gardener and realized she should feel some remorse, but she didn't. He'd desecrated her beautiful plants, and she'd done what had to be done. She ran a hand through her tousled hair and considered corpse-disposal options. It took hardly a minute to come to the perfect, elegant solution.

A raised bed.

Quickly, decisively, she rolled the gardener's body over and over until it rested against the back wall. This was no problem: he couldn't have weighed more than ninety pounds. It was distressing to look at his face, so Tricia used the first few shovels full of topsoil to cover it. She continued working at an efficient clip until the gardener's body was completely covered. Then she relaxed a little, but not too much, because the wind continued to pick up and the sky began to glow with an odd, diffuse light.

By noon the mountain of topsoil had been shoveled into a neat, oblong bed across the length of the back garden. But it was blowing all over the place. The sky was beige, the trees were straining sideways in the wind, and Tricia was having trouble breathing. Her eyes watered furiously.

Desperate to anchor the bed—and the gardener—in place, she scooped up the hose (*her* hose) from the ground near where the gardener had fallen, and screwed it into the hose bib. She sprayed down the new bed. It was distressing to pollute the garden with raw water, but there was no other way to keep all that topsoil from flying away. She promised herself that she would work in an extra layer of organic fertilizer as soon as the storm cleared to try and make up for it.

Finally the bed was firmly in place, with the gardener at the bottom of it. But her work wasn't finished, not by a long shot. She ran inside for a bandanna and a pair of sunglasses. Tying the bandanna bank-robber style over her nose and mouth, she stepped back out into the shamal.

Tricia dragged all the furniture off the patio and onto the grass. Then, using a spade and sheer brute force, she pried up the flagstones. One by one, the stones released from the hard-packed earth.

The wind howled. Tricia could feel dirt collecting in her ears, on her scalp. It stuck to her skin, which was damp with sweat. The muscles of her arms and back screamed, but she kept working, ramming the spade into the ground and levering up stone after stone.

Finally the last piece was loose. A rectangle of raw beige earth remained where the patio had been—not that Tricia could see much of this. She stumbled, almost blind, back and forth across the yard, hauling the flagstones one by one to the new flowerbed. She lined them up neatly in front of the raised bed. They formed a row all the way down the length of the bed, then turned the corner on each end to create a rectangular terrace against the back wall. She pushed on through hacking coughs.

Once the foundational layer had been placed, Tricia began stacking the flagstones: a second level, a third level, a fourth. At one point a palm frond flew through the air and slashed Tricia's exposed forearm. A line of dirt settled into the open wound. The air was so thick she couldn't see the house, which was less than thirty feet away.

Finally the dry-stacked terrace wall was tall enough to contain the raised bed. Tricia stepped into the soft topsoil bed, fell to her knees, and coughed until her ribs ached. She yanked her bandanna down and vomited. Her throat felt like she had swallowed scouring powder.

She curled into a ball, taking tiny, painful breaths.

A moment later, Tricia pushed herself back up to her knees, slid the bandanna over her face again, and got on with it. She smoothed the topsoil into the corners, creating a smooth, level surface. She felt a moment's revulsion to be crawling around on top of the gardener's body. Then she smiled at the thought that he would be of more service to the garden now than he'd ever been before.

* * * *

By the time Glen arrived home, Tricia was showered, dressed in a mauve velour tracksuit, and curled on the couch with a box of tissues. "Honey, I'm really sorry, but you're going to have to fix yourself a tuna sandwich for dinner," she said, her voice hoarse. "I'm just not feeling well. I did some gardening today, and I guess I stayed out in the storm for too long." She sniffled gently.

Glen gave Tricia a gentle kiss on the forehead. "Oh, sweetie, that's a good way to get a sinus infection. I'm sorry you're not feeling well. How about I make you a sandwich too?"

Tricia smiled gratefully. "Thanks, Glen."

* * * *

A week later, Glen and Tricia sat out on their new herringbone-patterned brick patio and enjoyed a glass of iced tea before dinner. The yard was lush and green, and the raised bed looked spectacular. It had a selection of citrus trees, a vivid red hibiscus, and night-blooming jasmine that tumbled over the rear wall.

"The flowerbed in the back looks great, honey. You did a really good job," Glen said.

Tricia beamed. "The secret, really, is nutrient-rich soil," she said. "It's surprising how much can grow in this sandy ground, with the right nutrients added."

"Well, whatever you're doing, it's working great. You know, I have to say I was surprised you pulled up the flagstone patio, but I like the brick even better."

She blushed and smiled modestly.

He fidgeted in his chair. "So, uh, I hate to bring it up, but what's with the whitewashed tree trunks?"

Tricia rolled her eyes. "Dunu did it."

"Why?"

"I looked it up on the Internet," she said. "Painting tree trunks is an old-fashioned method of protecting the bark from insect damage. It's still common in India, Mexico, you know, places like that."

"Really?"

"Apparently so. But there's no reason for it here. We don't have those insects in the desert."

"Oh," he said.

"More like uh-oh. It looks terrible. That was the last straw. I had to get rid of him."

"Well, it's probably for the best."

"I think so. You know I prefer to do my own gardening."

Kim Kash is a graduate of the College of Creative Studies at the University of California Santa Barbara. She is the author of two Jamie August mystery novels: *Ocean City Cover-up* (2015, Capri House) and *Ocean City Lowdown* (2014, Capri House), and the best-selling travel guide *Ocean City: A Guide to Maryland's Seaside Resort*. She divides her time between Maryland and the Middle East, which can be weird.

PARALLEL PLAY
by Art Taylor

The Teeter Toddlers class was finally drawing to a close—and none too soon, Maggie thought, keeping an eye on the windows and the dark clouds crowding the sky.

Ms. Amy, the instructor, had spread the parachute across the foam mats and gathered everyone on top of it. The children had jumped to catch and pop the soap bubbles she'd blown into the air. They'd sat cross-legged on the parachute and sung umpteen verses of "Wheels on the Bus" and two rounds of "Itsy Bitsy Spider." The routine never varied, the children's delight never waned—at least until the time came to raise that parachute with its spiral of colors into the air.

"Everybody off and let's go under," Ms. Amy said in a sing-songy voice. The children scrambled clear. The adults pulled the edges of the fabric tight. The parachute rose. All the kids raced beneath.

Or nearly all of them. Maggie's son, Daniel, grabbed her leg with his chubby fingers and held on tight.

"Don't you want to join your friends?" Maggie urged, same as she did each week. Daniel shook his head.

"No like," he mumbled into her thigh.

Despite what he said, Maggie knew he *did* like the parachute—or at least watching it, how it rose and fell, how it floated at the top for a moment and then drifted downward as the children giggled and tussled beneath. He seemed enchanted by it really—and Maggie saw some comfort there too, the parachute like a blanket slowly coming to rest, encircle, and enfold. But much as Daniel liked to watch, he refused to join the other kids underneath it, and generally he kept a distance from them, preferring to play on his own. Ms. Amy always asked one of the parents to crawl beneath as well, to keep the rowdiness under control, but the one time Maggie had volunteered, beckoning her son to join her, Daniel had stood at the edges and wept, almost frantically, until another parent—Walter, the only dad in the class—had graciously swapped places with her.

Walter was actually looking her way now too. He smiled, Maggie shrugged. What could you do?

"Maybe next time," Maggie said to Daniel, as Ms. Amy began to sing.

Come under my umbrella, umbrella, umbrella,
Come under my umbrella, it's starting to storm.
There'll be thunder and lightning, and wind and rain.
Come under my umbrella, it's starting to storm.

Maggie could hear the steady patter of rain overhead now. Through the windows, the sky was nearly black.

As she'd told Amy when they got to class late, her husband, Ben, was away on yet another business trip, and with all her hustling to get Daniel dressed and ready for class, she'd felt lucky to have gotten them out the door at all. Now she kicked herself for forgetting to check the weather earlier—and for forgetting an umbrella.

"Almost done," she whispered, more to herself than to Daniel. But as she ran her fingers through his wispy blond hair, she could feel his tension easing up a bit.

* * * *

By the time they'd gotten shoes tied, hands washed, and made their way out the lobby door, the skies had indeed broken open—a hard, driving rain. Short gusts of wind pushed a cold spray under the awning, splattering it against Maggie's bare calves. First the forgotten umbrella, and now this. She kicked herself a second time for wearing such a short skirt today. She could feel that spray even when she stepped to the back of the sidewalk as other moms rushed past her to their cars, each of them hoisting a child in one arm and holding an umbrella up with the other.

All those *good* mothers, Maggie thought, the ones on top of everything.

Perched in her arm, Daniel leaned against her shoulder. She held up a hand to shield his face.

"If my wife hadn't reminded me this morning, I'd have forgotten mine, too." A man's voice, beside her. When she turned, Walter smiled and hefted a big golf umbrella, closed tight. "If you're game, mine's big enough for two. Or four, I mean." He nodded to Daniel. His own little boy—Jordan, a redhead wearing a dour look—stood beside him.

Wife, Maggie thought. At least that cleared up some things.

Another woman in the class (Kristen? Katrina?) had wondered whether Walter was a single dad or maybe a widower. Or maybe his wife worked and he stayed home? No one had asked him directly. Maggie wondered if there hadn't been some interest on Kristen/Katrina's part. Walter wore thick-rimmed glasses, was graying at the temples, but he wasn't unhandsome really, and Maggie had even caught herself admiring the way he handled his son. Unlike the occasional father who tagged along with his wife or filled in for a single class—checking his smartphone every few minutes, awkward, distracted—Walter seemed eager and attentive, always making sure Jordan didn't cut in line for any of the activities, always encouraging a "please" or a "thank you." Once, several of the mothers had gone across the street for frozen yogurt after class, and Walter had tagged along too, giving his son the bites with the most sprinkles and finally all of the cone.

"Chivalry lives?" Maggie asked.

"Common courtesy," Walter said. He shrugged. "It's up to you. But it doesn't seem like it's going to let up anytime soon."

As if on cue, a ripple of thunder rushed toward them. Heavier rain now, puddling and splashing. She turned to Daniel, who met her look with a hopeful one of his own.

"Jordan," he said, pointing down at the little boy—surprising Maggie.

Jordan stared forlornly into the parking lot, seemingly impervious to the rain, but Walter smiled again.

"If you're sure you don't mind," Maggie said. "We had to park three rows that way and then halfway up. We'd be drenched before we got there."

Walter picked up Jordan. With a flick of his hand, he opened the umbrella wide and tilted it slightly her way. Each of them tried awkwardly to match the other's pace as she led them toward her car.

"I think we're going to get soaked anyway," Walter said, raising his voice over the sound of the rain. "Here." He huddled closer to her, almost stepping on Maggie's toes—close enough she could smell his cologne, some blend of mint and leather.

"I'm fine," she started to say, or "No worries"—something like that, but then Daniel started wiggling, and it was all she could do to keep him and herself balanced.

As she opened the back door and wrestled Daniel into his seat, Walter maneuvered the umbrella over her, leaving himself almost completely in the rain. She struggled to fasten the buckles quickly, fumbled too much, then Walter walked her to the driver's side and spread the umbrella across the open door.

"Knight in shining armor," she said. "I mean it." Another gust misted the inside of the car.

Walter's face was dripping now. His glasses wore a thick sheen of water. Something twitched at one corner of his lips—maybe trying to muster a smile. "Tougher dragons to slay, I'm sure."

As she started the car, she saw in the side mirror that he'd knelt down by the rear tire. The spokes of his umbrella scraped lightly against the glass. How he kept his hold on Jordan, she wasn't sure.

He stood back up and knocked on her window.

"Your tire," he said when she rolled it down. "Looks like it may be going flat."

She nodded. "Thanks. I'll get it checked."

"Seriously," he said. "I'd be worried, if I were you."

* * * *

Most of the traffic on the highway crawled through the mess, while other cars sped and weaved around the slower ones, swerving sharply to avoid the puddles rimming the road. Sometimes they missed, and water sprayed across Maggie's windshield, blinding her. A Toyota in front of her hydroplaned briefly, then righted itself. The brake lights magnified and blurred in the downpour. Her wipers could barely keep up.

By halfway home, Maggie could hear a dull rumble from the back corner, something indeed wrong with the tire, and the problem quickly got worse. Even when she turned onto the two-lane toward Clifton and was able to slow down more, she felt the whole car shimmying a little, pulling to the left. In the back, Daniel had begun to whimper.

Nowhere to stop at this point, and too many rollercoaster hills and turns still ahead. Sometimes cars barreled down right on top of you along these turns, impatient, impulsive, but the road was mostly clear today. She'd met one truck in the oncoming lane and glimpsed only a single pair of headlights far behind her, apparently as cautious as she was.

Her cell phone sat in the cup holder. She reached toward it, pressed the talk button. "Call Ben," she said and then was surprised when he picked up.

"How's my best buddy doing?" he asked, his voice tinny, distant over the speaker. Other voices in the background.

"He's fine, but I'm struggling." She explained about the tire, about the weather.

"Call Triple-A when you get home. They should be able to swap it out for the spare, at least for now." She could hear him turning away, saying something to someone else on his end.

"Wish you were here," she said.

"I know, I know. You hate to call the repairman."

But that wasn't what she'd meant.

Another bit of conversation on the other end. Then: "Sorry, hon. Between meetings, but duty's calling. Tell Danny I love him." And he was gone.

"Daddy says hello," she repeated, even though Daniel had surely heard. "He loves you."

After the call ended, the phone chirped a battery warning. Apparently she'd forgotten to charge it.

Lucky to have gotten out of the house at all that morning, just like she'd told Ms. Amy.

* * * *

She breathed a little more easily when she finally turned onto the last road home, the trees overhead blocking some of the rain, the Kinseys' house and the Millers' and Frank Hadley's small field, the familiar run of mailboxes, the UPS truck parked at the top of Mrs. Beatley's drive. What an awful day for that job, she thought, rushing in and out of the weather with packages in hand—then felt a brief twinge of guilt, trying to remember if she was expecting one herself.

And then they were home, the car limping down the long, steep drive toward the house. She slowed as the water sluiced down the pavement, kept the car steady, eased them the final few feet.

More than anything, her husband had wanted a house with lots of land. No neighbors on top of you, room for Daniel to have a big yard, the kind of place Ben never had as a boy himself. Maggie understood how nice it was, especially in a dense area like northern Virginia. A refuge, a haven, Ben had said more than once, and she could see it too. But sometimes, especially with him traveling so much, and especially on a day like today, the space felt isolated, lonely even.

"Let's go, little man," she said, hoisting Daniel out of the car. They had a carport instead of a full garage, and here too the rain was sweeping underneath, but she stopped for a minute to check the tire. It was completely flat, and the edges of the wheel had been ground up a little where she'd driven on it. Ben would love that.

She went inside, took off Daniel's shoes, and was heading to call Triple-A when the doorbell rang. Daniel rushed to it immediately, darting around her, already pushing past her as she reached for the knob. He loved when the mailman came by and the UPS driver too. Poor man, she thought, readying her apology.

But it wasn't UPS at the door.

* * * *

Walter's glasses were still covered by rain, the drops so thick she couldn't see his eyes, and somehow that troubled her nearly as much as having him show up on the doorstep. Jordan stood beside him, and there was something unreal about that too, as if the two of them had materialized there, same as they'd been standing back at Teeter Toddlers. Except he wasn't the same, was he? No, he wasn't holding an umbrella now and...

"The tire," he said. "I didn't think you'd make it all the way home, figured I'd have to play knight in shining armor again. But here you are."

Too stunned to answer, Maggie tried to snatch Daniel back and shut the door, but her son pulled away from her like it was a game, poked his head around one knee, then the other, and then into the doorway again.

"Hey, Daniel," Walter said, stooping down, leaning forward, releasing his own son's hand to take Daniel's instead. "It's Jordan, your friend."

"Jordan," Daniel repeated, and Maggie could hear a mix of pleasure and surprise in his voice, like when he got a new Matchbox car.

Walter stared up through those smeared glasses. "I hate to barge in for a play date unannounced, but given the circumstances..."

Maggie shook her head, tried to hold back the tears suddenly welling up behind her eyes, finally found her voice. "It's really not a good time right now. My husband—"

"Away on a business trip." Walter nodded. "I heard you talking to Amy, that's what got me thinking about this, making sure you got home in one piece." He looked at Daniel again, smiled. "Surely you could spare a few minutes for the boys to play."

She nodded—unconsciously, reflex really. "A few minutes," she said. "A few, of course."

Her words sounded unreal to her, more than his own now, and even as she said them, she knew it was the wrong decision—everything, in fact, the opposite of what she'd always thought she'd do in a case like this. But really what choice did she have, the way Walter had inserted his foot into the doorway and held so tightly to Daniel's hand?

And then there was the box cutter jittering slightly in Walter's other hand, raindrops glistening along the razor's edge, the truth behind that flat tire suddenly becoming clear.

* * * *

"They call it parallel play," Walter said a few minutes later. They'd settled into the couch in the living room. The scent of his cologne seemed suddenly oppressive. Maggie was self-conscious again about having worn such a short skirt, different reasons now. The boys played on the floor a few feet away—out of Maggie's reach, but at least out of Walter's as well. Jordan still hadn't smiled, but he pushed a couple of Daniel's cars across the top of the coffee table, something Maggie didn't allow Daniel to do, since Ben worried it would scratch the wood. As Daniel pushed his own cars on the floor, he stole glances at each of them in turn—smiling broadly, as if he couldn't quite believe all this was really happening.

Maggie tried desperately to work past her own disbelief, to fight that feeling of everything crumbling and crashing, to figure out a way through this. She'd heard about the bank teller who talked the robber into releasing all his hostages, the receptionist who convinced the school shooter to lay down his guns. Such things had happened, they had.

"I don't know what you mean," she lied. "Tell me more."

"Parallel play," Walter said again. "Kids this age, they don't really play together, they just play side by side—sharing the space but not really connecting, not yet." Walter's hand rested loosely on the box cutter between them, and Maggie was vaguely grateful it was at least closer to her than to her son. "It's like us, really."

"Like us?"

"Don't you agree? Think about it, how our lives have run along these parallel paths. Both of us becoming parents about the same time, both of us having little boys, both of us struggling to teach and correct and nurture those little boys. And then us coming together at Teeter Toddlers once a week—crossing paths, chatting here and there, chasing after our kids, turning away, coming back together again." He tapped the couch with his index finger, the rest of his hand not leaving the blade. "Sometimes, between our meetings each week, I think about you."

Maggie looked around the room, at all the things she sometimes took for granted. Wedding photographs and honeymoon pictures, Ben hoisting her up in his arms on the beach in Cancun, those carefree early days. The Champagne glasses from their wedding stood on a bar in the corner, the ones they took down each New Year's for a toast to renewal and recommitment. And then the photographs of Daniel as a newborn, the framed birth announcement, even the little hat he'd worn in the hospital, folded up in a small box frame—the first exciting taste of parenthood. On a higher shelf, an antique clock from her parents whirred and ticked in a glass case. She'd recently moved it out of Daniel's reach, since it was so very fragile.

Everything seemed fragile to her now, fragile and fleeting, seeing it like this.

She saw the room too with another set of fresh eyes. Those heavy candlesticks Ben's mother had given them, the marble paperweight on the desk across the room and Ben's brass letter opener beside it, the fire tools—everything she might use against Walter, all of it too far away. The phone was the closest thing to her, mere inches from the couch. But how quickly could she get to it and dial 9-1-1? And how long would it take anyone to respond—especially out here, especially today?

"I can only imagine how it's been for you," Walter went on, "but for my wife and me... Well, hardly feels like we're husband and wife anymore, some days hardly even friends. You think of being parents as being part of a team, bringing you closer, unifying you, but at best we're like a tag team, a couple of caretakers. One or the other of us takes the late shift, one or the other gets up for early morning, each of us taking note of who did what and for how long—bean-counting, pettiness. What have you done for the baby lately, huh? And with her working full time, eight to five, and my job—"

The lights flickered, browned briefly, like the whole world skipping a heartbeat. The boys perked up their heads. Daniel turned a worried eye toward his mother. The rain held a steady patter against the roof and windows. The power caught again.

"It's going to be okay," she said, to the boys, to herself. She'd been clenching the fringe of the seat cushion. Slowly she released her grip. "I think it's normal, the nature of parenting," she said to Walter then, the kind of thing she'd read in advice columns. "My husband and I are very happy."

Walter turned her way. "Are you?" He squinted a little, crow's feet at the corners. "Because the way you've looked at me sometimes in class, and then this morning, flirting a little with me—"

On the floor, Jordan grabbed at something in Daniel's hand—a little blue convertible, his favorite car.

"Stop," Daniel cried. "Mine." His face was suddenly anguished.

Jordan seemed neither angry nor concerned—simply kept his grip on the car and stared at Daniel, unremitting.

"Children, children," Walter said. "Remember to share." His voice was calm and patient, and the way he wagged his hand at them would've seemed innocent except for that box cutter. Maggie wasn't sure which of the boys he was reprimanding.

She didn't realize she was holding her breath until Walter put his hand back on the couch—the blade closer again to her instead of pointed at the boys.

* * * *

Before Daniel was born and even afterward, during all those breast-feeding sessions, all that rocking him to sleep, Maggie couldn't get her fill of books and articles and blog posts about parenting a newborn: not just why to breast-feed but how, swaddling techniques and sleeping routines, advice on balancing the baby's needs with her own, tips for managing the changing relationship with her husband. Ben had joked about her addiction, but she'd found so much of it educational.

She remembered now getting caught up in a discussion board right after Daniel was born—one headlined with a single, simple question: "Would you die for your child?" There had already been pages of comments in reply, almost unanimously "yes," but Maggie had felt compelled to add her own comment.

"In a heartbeat," she'd written, with a surge of love and pride, and when she'd told Ben about it later, he'd agreed.

"What parent wouldn't do the same if it came to it?" he'd said. "What good parent?"

It had seemed so easy at the time, the world in balance somehow.

Now everything seemed in disarray, verging on chaos.

Outside, the rain had intensified again. Lightning flashed. Fresh bursts of thunder sounded in the distance. Wasn't that usually before the storm—the warning signs of trouble ahead?

"Mama," Daniel said. "Juice?"

"Of course, honey," Maggie said, then caught herself. She turned to Walter. "Is it okay for me to get him something to drink?"

Walter crinkled his forehead. "Of course. Why wouldn't it be?"

When she stood, Walter rose and followed her. The living room and kitchen were an open floor plan, only a few steps away, but he'd probably considered, as she had, the knives in there, the kitchen mallet, the meat cleaver.

At least he'd be farther away from Daniel, she thought, but having him behind her, out of sight for even those few seconds walking to the kitchen, unnerved her in a different way. Step after step, she waited for him to attack. Silly, really, to have worried right then. He could've done it at any time.

He stood close to her as she poured the juice. She made a sippy cup for Jordan as well, for which Walter thanked her. As she watched the boys playing with their cars, vrooming here and there on the floor, she gauged the distance to the knives in the block. Then Walter stepped in between, gesturing at something else on the counter.

"You have a tea set," he said. "Actual silver?"

"Stainless," she said.

"Some tea would be nice, don't you think? On a day like this?"

The unreality of it all struck her again, his casual, conversational tone. Keep him happy, Maggie reminded herself, keep him satisfied. "Would you like me to make some?"

"Only if you'd like a cup yourself." He smiled. "I'd hate to impose."

* * * *

"Delicious," Walter said, taking a sip with his left hand, keeping the other one between them as before. "And such a beautiful set."

She'd brought out the complete tray: a full pot, cups and saucers, a sugar and creamer, a pair of ornate spoons. A small plate of crackers too, which the boys were enjoying with their sippy cups. "Here's your favorite," she'd said to Daniel, touching his hair—some small comfort in the midst of all this uneasiness before Walter had patted the couch for her to join him again.

"You know," Walter said. "This is what I'd imagined really, when I pictured being a parent. Kids playing on the floor, my wife and I sitting on the couch—doing the crossword or reading a book or having tea like this." He held up the cup in his left hand, a little awkwardly. "But my wife these days, she'll make a cup of coffee for herself and never even think I might want one, never even think." He laughed, ugliness behind it. "Do you and your husband ever do things like this?"

She shook her head. "It's tough to find time."

"You have to *make* time." A sudden sharp edge underscored his words.

Maggie sipped her tea. She'd loaded it with sugar, but it tasted bitter.

"And isn't time what it's all about?" Walter said. "I'd thought we were lucky, my wife and me, with our situation. My schedule had always been pretty flexible—project management over at MicroCom—and since most of us telecommuted anyway, I figured I'd stay home with Jordan, work at nap time and then nights after my wife got home. Keep him from having to go into day care immediately, you know? But it was so much harder than I'd expected, especially since Jordan has never been a good sleeper. Sometimes, you know, I wanted to shake him. Don't you know I've got emails to answer? Don't you know there's a deadline looming, and the boss is waiting? Why can't you go to sleep?"

He smiled at Jordan, who had glanced up at his name. "Isn't that right, little fella?" he said, but his son just stared back at him with another dull expression.

"And then my wife, the way she'd come home sometimes too tired to take over like we'd agreed. Too tired for him, for me, for anything, it seemed like, and all of a sudden it's falling back on Mr. Mom again, right? Me pushing back those emails and those deadlines, her pushing me away." His fingers drummed against the cushion, his palm against the box cutter, the blade catching and cutting lightly into the cushion. "Sometimes I wanted to shake her too, shake all of us up, shake everything loose. I've been so tired."

"I know." Maggie forced a small laugh. "I feel like I haven't gotten a full night's sleep since Daniel was born."

"That's not what I mean," Walter said. "It's more of an… existential tired." He shook his head. "I feel like I'm disappearing bit by bit."

The children had moved onto wooden blocks now. Daniel had built a small tower of them, and as he put a red triangle on top, Jordan calmly and deliberately pushed a pickup truck into it, toppling the pieces.

"Play nicely, boys," Maggie said, unsettled by Jordan but trying not to seem like she was reprimanding him alone. Walter didn't seem to notice, and neither of the boys responded to her, but Jordan did pick up the blocks and begin to help Daniel rebuild.

Daniel smiled. Maggie felt relieved. If it weren't for the circumstances, she'd have felt grateful her son had found a friend.

"I got laid off last week," Walter said. "And if I felt like there was nothing left of me before…" He was staring off into a corner of the room now, or maybe somewhere inside of himself, the box cutter still fraying the fabric of the cushion. "I don't know if you know how that makes a man feel. How useless, how… how impotent. And since my wife and I—" He shifted, turned toward Maggie. His grip on the cutter tightened again. "Do you know how long it's been since…"

Maggie tried to keep eye contact as he struggled to find the words. Whatever she'd been trying to do here, talking him down, whatever, she was losing faith it would work. At some point, he would force himself on her, and she could take that, she thought, she could survive it, as long as he didn't kill her. But she worried more about Daniel. Whatever Walter was going to do with her, would he do it in front of the boys? Would he take her away to the bedroom and leave the children alone out here? And what if something happened to one of them while they were—

"What is it you want?" Maggie asked finally, barely getting the words out herself. "From this, I mean."

"The way we talked this morning, I thought we might be…" He seemed to be searching for the word. "Friendly. I need a friend."

"And this is the way you try to find that?" She glanced toward the box cutter. She tried to sound firm.

"Sometimes friendliness needs a little encouragement." He smiled, satisfied. It was a terrible thing to see.

The lights flickered and browned again. Something in the distance buzzed and hummed, sizzled, burned. Then the power went out for good.

"Don't worry. It's going to be fine," Walter said, and he put his hand with the box cutter on Maggie's thigh. He seemed to intend it as a gesture of reassurance, but his hand was colder than the blade.

His talk about impotence, the comment about being existentially tired, about disappearing. His calmness. His coldness. Everything came together, and she could picture how easily, there at the end, they all might die.

* * * *

In the instant after the power went out, the instant after he touched her bare leg with that cold hand, Maggie lunged forward and grabbed the teapot. She swung it toward his head. She felt the blade nick her skin, ducked from his hand as it swung upward. She pulled the top off the pot too and splashed the hot tea toward his eyes. Then she hit him again.

The room wasn't dark, only shadowed. The boys had surely seen at least dimly what she'd done. Already startled by the power outage, they hustled back on the rug, away from whatever was happening, and then jumped again when Maggie leapt past the coffee table toward them.

"It was an accident," she said. "Everything's going to be okay." She could hear Walter moaning and writhing behind her as she reached for Daniel. He squirmed and pushed against her as she started toward the door. Almost by reflex, she grabbed Jordan too.

Then she ran.

Out the door, into the rain, anywhere but in the house.

Wind and water lashed against her. The boys tucked their heads into her neck, held tight now, trying to shield themselves. At least that worked in her favor.

Daniel had grown so much heavier in recent months she'd struggled sometimes to carry him for long, and now Jordan added extra weight. Would Walter have hurt his own child if she'd left him behind? She couldn't even consider that phrase: *left behind*. Instinct, maternal instinct maybe. Either way, she would do this, she would.

But where to now?

As she ran, everything lurking at the back of her mind rushed to the forefront, and everything she saw struck her with an awful clarity. With the power out, the phone had been dead. Her own cell had been dying, useless she was sure. It didn't matter whether her tire was flat, because Walter's car was parked behind hers, angled slightly across the driveway, maybe to make sure she couldn't steer around it. As for the drive itself, the water coursing down made it impossible for her to get to the road, a steep climb even without two children.

She could've stayed in the house, she knew. Those candlesticks, the letter opener, the knives in the kitchen. But could she have used any of those things on him while the boys watched? She shuddered at the thought.

What neighbor would be home? The Millers next door wouldn't be back from work for hours. Hadn't the Kinseys gone on vacation?

Frank Hadley, who lived across the fallow field, had retired. That's all she knew about him really. Kept to himself, never much more than a wave in passing. Still her best bet, and she made for it.

Her hair matted against her, clung to her face, blocked one eye. Her arms ached. Her legs too, especially against the uneven dirt of the field. Her thigh was warm. Blood, she knew.

Daniel was crying now, soft sobs into her shoulder. Behind her, she thought she heard her name being shouted from back at her own house. Another shout, this one indistinct. A flash of lightning above.

"We're playing tag," she said. "We're playing hide and seek." She wasn't sure if either of the boys heard her, if Jordan even knew what hide and seek was, but she kept on. "It's a game, it's all a game."

She ran harder.

* * * *

No car at Hadley's. The power out there as well. Maggie's ankle had turned somewhere in the field, the same leg that had been cut, and she was limping now. All of them were soaked.

"We have to hide," she said. "We've got to win the game, okay? I need you boys to help."

Daniel looked bewildered, Jordan looked dazed. She couldn't imagine what she looked like to them.

Then she heard a banging and saw a workshed behind the house, the door hanging loose where the wind had caught it. She glanced back across the field. Walter was on the far side, making his way toward them. She rushed toward the shed, hoping Jordan hadn't seen him.

The shed was the size of a small garage, the inside mostly shadowed, but light filtered through a couple of dirty windows. She could make out a small workbench with a few tools on a rack above, and more hanging on the wall. A concrete floor, covered here and there with dirt or sawdust. A small lawnmower had been pushed into one corner. A couple of sawhorses stood nearby, a faded tarp draped across them.

She put the children down, her arms nearly numb now. Water dripped from her hair, from every inch of her. "Over here, boys. Come on." She lifted the tarp. Neither of them moved. Jordan stared at her with apprehension. Daniel shook his head. They were soaked too.

"Everybody up and let's go under," she said, trying to mimic Ms. Amy's singing. Jordan seemed curious now, even if the drab tarp was a poor substitute for the colorful parachute. He moved tentatively toward her, but Daniel seemed even more fearful.

"I need you boys to do this," she said, and she felt herself beginning to crumble again—fought to keep things light. She reached out and touched her son, smoothing his wet hair behind his ear, trying to comfort. "Daniel, you've got to be my little man, okay?"

Daniel shook his head more firmly, determined. "No like," he said. Behind him the door banged, startling them all. Jordan jumped toward her, and she hugged him, easing him behind her. It wasn't Walter yet, just the wind again, but he was coming, he'd be there soon.

She began to sing, her voice trembling and cracking. "Come under my umbrella, umbrella, umbrella. Come under my umbrella, it's starting to—" She wanted to go back to the morning, to the comfort of the class, the parachute there. She wanted to erase having accepted Walter's umbrella, to undo everything that had happened since then.

"Car," came a voice beside her. Jordan. He held up a tiny hand, one of the Matchbox cars clutched in it. She hadn't even seen. "Here," he said. He opened his hand toward Daniel.

Slowly, too slowly, Daniel moved past her, took the car, and the two of them sat down together beneath the tarp.

Maggie smiled, felt the tears finally come. She wanted to crawl under there with them, snuggle close, hide from everything. But instead she forced herself to pull down the edges of the tarp and shelter them inside. She couldn't let them see—not her tears, not any of it.

Would you die for your child?

Yes, yes. In a heartbeat.

Would you kill for him?

She lifted the pitchfork she'd seen hanging on the wall, took a quick breath, and headed toward the door.

* * * *

Maggie kept Daniel and Jordan under the tarp in the shed, each of the boys sitting on one side of her, until Hadley came home. They sang "Wheels on the Bus" and "Itsy Bitsy Spider" and "Twinkle, Twinkle Little Star." Each time one of the boys tried to move away, she sang "Come Under My Umbrella" again and hugged him tighter. Daniel touched occasionally at the wound on her thigh. "Band-aid soon," she said, glad neither of the boys had noticed the blood elsewhere on her.

When she heard Hadley's car on the drive, heard the car door slam, she lifted the tarp and shouted, "We're in here." Hadley wouldn't know who *we* were. Just someone. Someone needing help, she hoped. She didn't take the boys back into the yard, didn't dare, and the minutes crept slowly before Hadley himself opened the shed door. Grizzled, stoic, he was carrying a shotgun when he came in, poised and ready. Even after he relaxed his grip on it and asked Maggie if she and the boys were all right, he kept staring at her with some mix of concern and curiosity and fear.

She knew what he'd seen, could imagine why he'd been cautious about coming into the shed. "I've called the police," he told her. A comfort? A caution? She wasn't sure, but she'd already figured he would call for help.

She heard the sirens a few minutes later, and the boys echoed the sound. When they left the shed, a police cruiser blocked their view of the body—strategically so, she thought. The rain seemed, finally, to have stopped.

Soon the whole yard buzzed with action and investigation, questions and more questions, lights circling, people moving. Social services were called for Jordan—maybe his mother too, Maggie wasn't sure.

Even as the paramedics cleaned and bandaged her thigh, she kept repeating "We're all right" and "He didn't hurt the boys" and "He didn't hurt us."

"But he would've," Ben said, when she called him from Hadley's phone. "That's what you need to remember, what you need to tell them."

Self-defense, he said more than once, and *preservation instinct* and then *maternal instinct*. She wasn't sure if he was reassuring her or building a defense—trying to be with her in the moment or already planning for the future—and when he told her how brave she was, when he called her a hero, she didn't correct him.

Maggie would tell him later about the worst images that had run through her head and about what she'd convinced herself she'd have been willing to do. And she'd tell the court too, if it came to that: what Walter had said, the way the box cutter felt on her leg, her fear for herself and her child—and for *his* son too. That was important.

But there were other things she'd never tell anyone, not even Ben. How Walter was right with so much of what he said. How lonely it had felt reading all those childcare books and articles on her own, and how lonely it still felt being nearly the sole caregiver to Daniel, with Ben's job demanding more, keeping him on the road for days, weeks at a time. How lonely it felt when Ben did come home and rushed right past her, barely a quick kiss, to give his best buddy a hug, then turn away from them both the moment his cell phone rang. And how many times had Ben simply given up on trying to rock Daniel to sleep and shrugged it off on Maggie? Even two nights ago, before this latest trip, he'd done that again, and when she'd finally fallen into their own bed, he'd nudged her into making love—exhausted, hurried, far from energetic. But after all, Ben would be leaving for several days, and it was important to connect.

It had been a pleasant surprise at Teeter Toddlers to have a handsome man offer up his umbrella, chivalry not dead and all. He had smelled nice, and she'd enjoyed for a moment that little spark of flirtation between them—innocent, of course, playful at best, but flattering. And Walter had always seemed so good with his son too, attentive in ways Ben had never been.

Those were the things she didn't want to admit, even to herself—those other thoughts that had been pushing her forward when she emerged from the shed, pitchfork in hand, and Walter rushed toward her with his arms outstretched. It wasn't bravery, and it wasn't just fear. She'd felt ashamed, she'd felt betrayed. She'd felt more alone than ever. And she'd felt sure she could drive all that away, stab after stab, as the winds whipped and the rain battered against them and the pitchfork plunged into Walter again and again and again and again.

Art Taylor is the author of *On the Road with Del & Louise: A Novel in Stories*. He has won two Agatha awards, an Anthony Award, a Macavity Award, and three consecutive Derringer awards for his short fiction. He teaches at George Mason University and writes frequently on crime fiction for both the *Washington Post* and *Mystery Scene*. www.arttaylorwriter.com.

ABOUT THE EDITORIAL PANEL
AND COORDINATING EDITORS

David Dean's short stories have appeared regularly in *Ellery Queen Mystery Magazine,* as well as a number of anthologies, since 1990. His stories have been nominated for the Shamus, Barry, and Derringer awards, and "Ibrahim's Eyes" won the *EQMM* Readers Award for 2007. His story "Tomorrow's Dead" was a finalist for the Edgar for best short story of 2011. He is a retired chief of police in New Jersey and once served as a paratrooper with the Eighty-second Airborne Division. His Caribbean thriller, *Starvation Cay,* is available on Amazon Kindle.

Sujata Massey is an Agatha and Macavity award-winning author of eleven mysteries and one historical novel. The first book in her Rei Shimura series is *The Salaryman's Wife,* and the most recent novel is *The Kizuna Coast.* She lives in Baltimore, Maryland, with her family.

B.K. (Bonnie) Stevens writes both novels and short stories. Her novel *Interpretation of Murder,* published by Black Opal Books, is a traditional whodunit that offers readers insights into deaf culture and sign-language interpreting. *Fighting Chance,* set in Virginia, is a martial arts mystery for teens that was published by the Poisoned Pencil/Poisoned Pen Press. B.K. has also had over fifty short stories published, most in *Alfred Hitchcock Mystery Magazine.* One story won a Derringer Award, one was nominated for the Agatha and Macavity awards, and another won a suspense-writing contest judged by Mary Higgins Clark.

Marcia Talley is the author of *Daughter of Ashes* and thirteen previous novels featuring Maryland sleuth Hannah Ives. A winner of the Malice Domestic Grant and an Agatha Award nominee for Best First Novel, Marcia won an Agatha and an Anthony award for her short story "Too Many Cooks" and an Agatha Award for her short story "Driven to Distraction." She is editor of two mystery collaborations, and her short stories have appeared in more than a dozen anthologies. She divides her time between Annapolis, Maryland, and a quaint Loyalist-style cottage in Hope Town, Bahamas.

Bios for **Donna Andrews** and **Barb Goffman** appear with their stories.